Taylor –
Please enjoy!
[illegible]

LABRELOTTE BAY

LABRELOTTE BAY

Mark Williams

ISBN-13: 978-1523647149
ISBN-10: 1523647140

Special thanks to the advisory team
Nancy McCurry, All About Books, NancyMcCurry.com,
Nancy.McCurry@gmail.com

Cover Design by Bob Ryan Writing & Creative Direction,
Phoenix, Arizona

Back cover photo: Lori Wooldridge Studios Ltd.,
Phoenix, Arizona; London, England; Ouray, Colorado

Marilyn Limb Ltd.

Thanks to John Lynch for his encouragement, guidance, participation, and influence and for your partnership in this adventure.

Special thanks to the people of St. Lucia for their love, compassion, and sweet friendship for without it, this book would never have been inspired.

This book is for you.

Dedication

To those with soft and kind hearts,
loving smiles, and a welcome drink for
the tired and the weary—

Thank you.

You know

Author's Foreword

Every book I write, I try to say something that strikes at the heart. It isn't always clear and sometimes, if you skip a page, you miss it, but I always try to talk to or about the human heart. *Labrelotte Bay,* is another one of those books. It is the first book after the *Emancipation Series* and for much of the novel, its fun.

But I have a problem.

I still wanted to write about that *heart thing*. I wanted to write about you, and I, and our friends, and the people we work with, the simple guy on the street and how we struggle and gnaw at our bindings as they have stayed on for so long, they become a part of us. Life with them is easier than life without them, at least we think so. We know better—in our heart.

But then we come to a place where, with time and love, they fall off—literary, fall away and we are, somehow—someway—free. Maybe it happens in a place like Labrelotte Bay in St. Lucia, a real place that generated such a hope I, to this day, cannot explain. Maybe it's in our backyard with a bottle of Malbec and good friends, or over dinner, I don't know. What I do know is it can happen, I've seen it. And when peace is in your heart, you fear no war.

I hope, in these pages, you laugh, really laugh, and maybe a tear. It is a happy book with a happy ending. I hope you finish it, lay your hand on its cover—

—and smile. Maybe then you too, will have a heart of hope.

Mark J. Williams
Author

"...sing like never before,
Oh my soul...."

The storm had stopped three hours before, leaving the streets with a sheen of drying rain water. The smell of wet asphalt and wet dirt, carried by humid, hot air filled the Phoenix night the night Ted, June's husband, died in a gun fight.

It had been a lightning storm as well and there was the smell of ozone, the smell that made rain smell so good. It was late July and Arizona was in the middle of its monsoon season. Ted and June always thought it was a funny term for rains in Arizona—*monsoon.* Ted always said to his wife it made it sound so tropical and lush. "Like there's going to be some little Asian looking kid standing on the stern of a dug out canoe polling his way down the mile wide Salt River," he would joke.

It always made June laugh. Ted could do that, make her laugh. July and August, were always the time when the storms came. It got hotter and humid and people moved from their air-conditioned house to their air-conditioned car, to their air-conditioned office. If a person was really unlucky, you landed a job as a roofer or worked on a road crew, laying some of the same asphalt the rain was landing on that night he died. It laid out smoother when it was applied in the summer. The heat helped the tar melt in to the cracks and small parts of the streets. Lucky for the crews. If they paved a grocery store parking lot, it would get so hot and stay hot for so long, shopping carts left outside would melt some of their rubberized wheels, giving them the telltale wobble in the store, the wheel taking on the shape of a flat pancake on the one side that was in contact with the ground.

Ted and June had been married five years. They had a three year old daughter named Maggie. The two were Phoenix police officers, meeting in the academy and marrying as soon as they graduated. They loved their job. They loved it so much they occasionally worked part time gigs as police security to earn a little extra, for those special things they wanted.

The large retail store they typically worked, had their own security personnel. The police were just for show and any needed help the store people might need. They had both taken turns working the job at the store at the end of Christown Mall. The extra job was close to their home and easy work. Cops were just a police presence. It quashed almost all the ideas anyone had about pulling a robbery or theft from the store. No one wanted to mess with cops.

Unless they had no fear of cops.

The first police units arriving at the store that night when they heard the 'triple nine' come out over their car radios—an officer was involved in a shooting, came with lights and sirens. This was the ultimate call for police, the ultimate response, a fellow officer was in a gunfight for their life. The responding offices knew, by the time they got there, the fight would be over. The average police gunfight was less than ten seconds and no more than three feet away. So close explosive powder and body parts would spray on everyone involved and anyone nearby. This event at the store that night was no different, seconds long and close, but the responding units drove as fast as they could.

It 'rained blue' as those in the trade liked to call it. Police units came, seeming from the heavens.

It was too late. Ted was dead.

The couple just wanted to take a trip to San Francisco, one of those *specials buys* they would work the off-duty for. It was June's idea. The two of them and Maggie wanted to go back to where they went on their honeymoon.

June was watching the news, drying her short-cropped hair and getting ready to head for bed when she heard about the shooting as a breaking news story. A police involved shooting at the store they worked. There was only one police officer at that store, Ted. No one had called her, not yet. The officer's name had not been released pending notification of next of kin.

She had just been notified.

She quickly called her neighbor, who had watched Maggie before, and asked her if she could come over, telling the neighbor what she knew. By the time Sweenie, a sixtyish Filipino widow woman who lived next door with her two Pomeranians, had walked over, June was dressed in a pair of jeans, a pull-over shirt, and strapped in with her belt-badge and holster. She still had the presence of mind to realize she would need some ID when she pulled up to the scene at the store where Ted was working.

The news on the TV said there was a police related shooting at the store, nothing else. She figured it was Ted. All the way there, just about two miles, she fought to keep from speeding. Her mind was racing and running the spectrum of thoughts. She struggled with just operating the car and getting there quickly, not killing anyone in the process. She practiced her breathing, like she used on hot calls when she worked the street. It didn't help, he would want her around. She ran the thoughts of what he might be doing while she was driving to the store. He wouldn't be telling anyone too much, they allow for that in the department, time to de-escalate before the shooting team started to ask the details of what happened. But she knew his first thoughts would be of her, so she wanted to be there for him.

The parking lot was taped off from Fifteenth Avenue. She pulled up and ID'd herself to the officer at the perimeter. He radioed others and was told to allow her to enter and where to park to meet the detectives. She did as she was told and as she pulled up, she saw a man signal her with a flash light. It was a detective she didn't recognize. He walked up to her side of the car, carrying a clip board in one hand and the flash light in the other.

"My husband, Ted Hersher, was working off duty here tonight," she said as she got out of the car. "Is he all right?"

"Mrs. Hersher, I'm Det. Hannratty, part of Phoenix's shooting response unit. Do you know your husband's shield nu—"

"—8970. That's Ted's number. Is he okay?" Her voice was rising. She was starting to feel panicky. Since the announcement on the television, she never thought he would be hurt. Ted and June had talked about being shot, getting hurt before, many times, it was part of life. They talked about funerals, insurance, who would re-marry and who wouldn't, but the true thought of death never crossed her mind, at least not to any detail.

"Mrs. Hersher, I think it is your husband."

"What do you mean 'you think'? I want to talk to him."

"Mrs. Hersher, I am sorry to inform you, your husband was —"

"Nope, uh, no," she said and shook her head, both hands gripping her own body tightly. "No, he was just working a few hours. You don't get killed working this shit. It was just a little off-duty work. I want to see him."

The detective was calm but firm with his response while another detective came up behind him. "Not yet, Mrs. Hersher. We need to take care of him first. We don't want you to see him just yet, okay?"

"What do you mean? I want to see him." She tried to walk by the two detectives who gently stopped her. "Mrs. Hersher, please. Allow us to prepare him for you. Please—you don't want to see him now, not like this."

She stopped and looked at the officers. "Why did you need his shield number?"

The two looked at each other. The other detective spoke. "Mrs. Hersher, there was a serious gunfight. We don't know all of what happened yet, but it appeared to have been a robbery your husband interceded in. From what we can tell, he engaged three suspects, killing all three. One was the driver who seemed to have expired in the suspect vehicle across the lot after trying to leave. But they killed Ted." It was delivered cold and business like. The way cops are trained to do. Deliver the information needed, and hope you never have to hear it yourself.

She stood with her hand over her mouth. She closed her eyes for a moment. *This can't be happening. This has to be a dream.* "Why don't you want me to see him?"

"Ma'am, he took, what we think, were three rounds from the driver to the head and chest, right where his name tag was. The manager didn't know the name of the officer working tonight. We couldn't identify him except for his shield number. We are so sorry for your loss."

June Hersher sat back down on the front seat of her car with the door open. She sat there for two hours and never moved. They just wanted to go to San Francisco.

It would be months before she stopped walking in to each room of their house, in the middle of the night, and simply standing there, waiting to hear the noise of life her husband brought. Most nights, after she put her daughter to bed, she carried one of his shirts from the hamper, holding it up to her face and breathing him in, then crying—again.

The first two months were simply pain, grieving, sobbing pain. Then, one day, there were several hours of no crying, just an ache. The body began to adjust after that. She couldn't tell where she was, except maybe abandoned. She couldn't feel anything, like the lines of the palm or the secureness of the protective fingers of the unseen hand, holding her nearly crushed body. All she thought was she was alone, just her and her daughter. She couldn't— she wasn't supposed to, see the love that wrapped itself around her. It was going to be a long run. Every night, however, she fell asleep—every night, in the soft crease of the love lines. She didn't know it and it would be years before she would.

They say blood is thicker than water. Maybe that's why we battle our own with more energy and gusto than we would ever expend on strangers.
—David Assael

Eighteen years later

June was in the kitchen, her arms crossed. "What do you mean I'm hard to live with?" June said to her mother. On many weekends, June and Maggie would go spend the night at June's parents' house in Carefree for an early morning trail ride on the family horses.

Emma Morgan, June's mother, was washing a batch of strawberries sitting in a colander in the large farmer's sink anchoring the polished concrete counter in front of the kitchen window, a window looking out over the mountains to the north of their home and horses in the stables. She was in her sixties, looking like she was in her fifties, wearing her jeans and boots and a red and white plaid shirt in preparation for the morning ride, but she wanted to wash the berries first, maybe have some for breakfast. "I didn't say that, dear. I just said you can be a little *tense* sometimes, especially to those around you."

"Same thing," June said, finding herself irritated easily by the topic that had come up numerous times in the last few months.

Emma looked over her shoulder at her daughter. It had been eighteen years since Ted's death. June stayed with Phoenix and was now one of two women homicide detectives. She had been doing it for the last five years.

Maggie was sitting at the table across the kitchen from her grandmother. "Mom, Grandma didn't say that," Maggie said. "Although sometimes—"

"'Sometimes' what?"

"See?" Both Emma and Maggie replied in unison.

"'See' what?" June said. "I'm being accused of something, of not being a good parent or daughter or something. Can't I ask why?"

Maggie and her grandmother just looked at each other and shook their heads. "June, honey, could you be having the menopause?" her mother asked.

"Yeah, or maybe your PMS's are just much much closer together," Maggie added.

Heavy footsteps came down the hall. "Morning Junebug," Henry Morgan, June's father, said walking into the kitchen and kissing his daughter and Maggie on the head and patting his wife's bottom and smiling at her. Henry was a little under six feet tall, in his mid-sixties, with silver, close-cropped hair and mustache, wearing a pair of well-worn jeans, a green Carhart long-sleeve shirt, and a matching pair of well-worn Durango boots. He put his patina-stained Resistol hat on the side table as he came in the room. He asked in June's direction but to no one in particular. "We eating before our ride or after?"

"I don't know," June started. "According to Mom and my daughter, whom I have worked so hard to put through college and give her a wonderful life, I am crappy to live with." She took a sip of her coffee and then put it down and crossed her arms again. Emma and Maggie just looked at each other again and then back to Henry.

Father looked at his wife. "You didn't ask her about her cycle did you? Tell me you didn't do that," he said.

Emma just kept washing the fruit. "Well, it very well could be an issue. Your sister—"

"Sussy?" Henry asked.

"Yes, Sussy," Emma said.

"What about Sussy?" Maggie asked.

"Oh don't ask," Henry said. "Never ask your mother—"

"Well, she had that same issue your mother appears to have. The mood, first it's in the sky, then it's in the basement. Remember how she would swear at the newspaper guy when he missed the driveway?"

"She didn't really swear," Henry shook his head.

"Well, it sounded like swearing. She would yell 'hey, dumb ass, hit the drive way once in a while'."

"Aunt Sussy said that?" Maggie said with a short laugh.

"Come to find out it was some kind of endometriosis issue. They thought it was a cyst but once they cleaned her out—"

"Jeezus, Mary and Joseph," Henry said looking in to his as yet empty cup of coffee.

"She was fine as a button. Maybe you got the endometriosis like Sussy."

"Don't forget the PMS stuff," Maggie reminded them.

June's father walked over near June with his cup and poured himself some coffee. "You think you're sweet and kind and a joy to be around all the time, Junebug?"

"Well—," she hesitated, analyzing her father's tone. "I have some moments in which I can be."

He nodded. "You do. But you think you don't have any tension issues, no stress, and none of that affects your disposition? How about that menapausy thing your mom mentioned?" He continued talking as he finished fixing his coffee and turned back to her, leaning against the counter.

"Well, Dad, I do have a pretty difficult career field and I haven't been to the doctor about the other two, but I don't—"

"And you're sitting in that chair with your arms crossed right now—because? And you didn't wake this morning with a frowny face? When you and Maggie spend the night out here, and believe me when I say your mother and I truly love it, you always wake up with a frowny face, like the one you have right now. I hate to tell you this, Junebug, but your frowny face has been there for a while. I think the menza and the PMS stuff is just adding high octane to a long running forest fire." He finished the sentence as he turned around to put some more cream in his coffee. "Didn't you always tell us non-verbal communication makes up about two-thirds of what we say? What are you telling us right now, baby?"

She quickly unwrapped her arms.

The side door to the house, just down the hall from the kitchen, could be heard opening with gusto. "Good morning everyone," Aunt Eleanor said as she blew in to the room. She was June's aunt, Emma's sister. As a real estate agent in neighboring Cave Creek, and a successful one at that, she had finally convinced Emma and Henry, just before the bottom dropped out of the housing market, to sell their home and attached horse stables in Gilbert, which sold on the same day they listed it for ten thousand more than they were asking. She wanted them to move to either Cave Creek or Carefree on the north side of Phoenix, but as the market was tanking, Emma and Henry decided to wait and see after first closing the sale of their Gilbert home and leasing the stable space for the animals back from the buyer. A move Eleanor didn't agree with but after three years and the market continuing to fall, they still had their funds and now they bought property almost three times the size and about one-third the original price, making Eleanor a very happy real estate agent.

June grew up on the horse ranch in Gilbert and helped her mom and dad train horses. Emma and Henry operated a working shelter for maverick horses from the Bureau of Land Management before it was cool to be a rescue center. Later, when her parents "retired" from their Gilbert home and operation and moved to their place in Carefree, they still had horses they trained, mostly to get ready for saddle and rider. The benefits of waiting to buy land and then buying more than they ever owned before, offset the benefits of retirement. The two were not made to sit and watch the world go by.

Henry did much of what he did in Gilbert, help break some of the BLM horses' people in town bought or adopted. June's mom helped him while working at Joe's Tack and Feed, on Cave Creek Road, three mornings a week. The other times, she worked around the house and painted, desert landscapes mostly.

Aunt Eleanor was the gregarious one between herself and Emma. She had been married three times, having just gotten rid of number three, a Cuban 'iron artist' she met while on a trip in Austria. After a while with him, she discovered his 'art' consisted mostly of old hubcaps, old tricycle frames, and old barbed wire soldered to both and then welded to pieces of rusted iron. It had to be rusted, according to Number Three. That was part of the 'art.' People, mostly from New Hampshire and Vermont, bought his work on line. The same people who bought 'authentic' Kachina dolls and Navajo blankets, not knowing they were from a warehouse in Benghazi.

Eleanor liked the good life. Things not soiled by dirt and horse hair. She liked leather and chrome, dark woods and things that shined in the sunlight. She wore tailored clothes and when she could, she liked to wear designer items people could tell were designer items from ten feet away. But almost every week, she liked to go to Emma's house and sit and drink coffee while they rode. Her jeans and boots were worth almost as much as the horse, but only she knew that.

The sisters complimented each other, one of the earth and the other from some other solar system. Eleanor also spoke what she thought, even if no one asked or didn't want to know. "You guys going riding this morning?"

June moved over to the table and found a seat next to her daughter. "Aunt Eleanor." June wouldn't let it go.

"Oh honey, don't start with Aunt Eleanor too?" Henry said.

"Do you think I'm a bitch to live—"

"Screaming," Aunt Eleanor said, interrupting June's beginning rant as she walked over to the coffee pot.

Henry simply shook his head a few times and moved over so Eleanor could pour herself a cup. "I told you not to start with her."

June was stopped in her verbal tracks. "Wha—what?"

Eleanor went to the refrigerator and pulled out a container of peppermint mocha creamer and splashed some in her coffee. "Oh, honey, you don't mean to be, but yeah, you are sometimes." Another of her former lovers taught her to love this combination of coffee and creamer. He was a chef in Barcelona. His specialty was chocolate filled croissants and Angolan egg nog around the holidays. Eleanor dumped him after she could not get over his back hair.

"I told you mom," Maggie said as she sat next to her mother.

"No you didn't. You just said I was a little hard to—"

"Junebug, sometimes—"

"Geez, Dad." The kitchen filled with conversations, all happening at once.

Eleanor symptomatically clutched her chest in false embarrassment. "Did I say something—again, I shouldn't have? Honey, they have pills for people like us. It helps with the hormones, makes us, well, nicer. The doctor put me on it about six months ago. People around me really, appreciated it," Aunt Eleanor said, taking another sip of coffee. "One of the side effects is I emit some kind of pheromone which attracts the younger stallions, if you get my—"

Mother sighed. "Yes, sister, maybe a little bit."

There was a quick pause. Then June spoke. "Mom—I think I am kind—"

"Sure," Mother said.

"and loving—"

"Always," Maggie nodded.

"and caring—"

"Absolutely, Junebug," Henry said having to turn his back to the conversation.

"And sweet."

"Ha!" Aunt Eleanor snorted as she almost spilled her coffee. She quickly recovered. "No, sorry, I just—the coffee was a little hot."

"Liar," June said crossing her arms again next to her daughter.

"Honey, we just think you are wound a little, well—tight," Emma said as she reached across the table and touched her daughter's arm.

"Yeah, like Grover Cleveland's bowels," Aunt Eleanor said stirring her colored coffee.

"What? Who?" June asked with a frown.

"Grover Cleveland, *President* Grover Cleveland? Everyone knew he had colitis—it's a bowel issue," Eleanor said punctuated with a sip.

"Ellie, you're not helping," Henry said. "As a matter of fact, this train might have made it around the bend had you not come by for coffee—again."

Eleanor didn't stop. "You're like a Slinky, ready to *explode* down the stair case, careening end over end until you crash at the bottom of the long flight of stairs!" Aunt Eleanor said as she took another sip and reached for some more creamer in the refrigerator, ignoring her brother-in-law. "Let me ask you, how's the man issue?" Eleanor asked June. "Dating anyone?"

"You really aren't helping," Henry said again, leaning against the sink his wife was just working at.

"Oh, how about women?"

"Sister," Emma tried to intervene.

Maggie leaned back in her chair. "Mom, we love you. We just think you could use a vacation, you know, get away for a while." Maggie looked a lot like her aunt when Eleanor was Maggie's age. Cute, with chocolate brown eyes, her hair a little lighter in color, lying on her shoulders and under her eyes was just a dusting of freckles.

Eleanor added. "Yeah, like spend a year in the Congo's rainforest, darting monkeys, making soup out of their paws, and eating roots."

"Sister!"

"What? I'm just trying to help. Spending some time alone might be good for the girl. I've seen those rain forest trips. Breath-taking! And she gets to kills things, a positive tension reliever for a homicide detective if you ask me, as long as she eats what she kills, that's the rule there. Oh, or make some form of clothing out of its hide. Some of those animals are poisonous and you don't want to eat them, but they would make a pleasant scarf, or a hat. Maybe even a belt."

Henry said—again. "You're really not helping,"

"I'm not?" She said with overly large doe eyes. The collective shook their heads.

June said "I can't leave even if I wanted to, leaning against the back of one of the kitchen table chairs.

"Why the hell not?" Aunt Eleanor asked.

June paused for a moment, thinking of what to say. "Who's going to take care of Maggie?"

"Mom, I'm almost twenty-two. I think I can manage for a week or—ten." She mumbled the last word to herself.

"Wait," Mother had a light bulb look of an idea. "Eleanor, you have your time share still don't you?"

"Oh, now you want my help," Eleanor said.

"Don't you?"

"Which one?"

"The pretty one. The one down in the Caribbean."

"Windsong?" Eleanor answered with a questioning look.

"Sure," Emma said along with a shoulder shrug. "I don't know the name of it, but if that's the one, yeah, the one you went to last year. Could you let your niece use it?"

"That's my favorite," Aunt Eleanor said with a frown. "I might want to go again."

Emma sat back in her own chair, still holding her coffee. "You told me you can't go back there, at least not for a while. You said something happened the last time with a couple of local men you were dancing with."

Eleanor frowned. "I told you about that?" Her frown grew deeper. "I need to learn not to tell the whole story." She stopped for a moment and the look on her face indicated she was pondering something. "Did I say we were—*dancing*?"

Emma nodded. "You came over with a bottle of Malbec and a red solo cup and you and I sat on the couch and you told me about two men. Along about the second glass, you began to share a little too much and I stopped you, but there was a story you were trying to share—about two men and the police," she said trying to pry the memory from her sister.

"Well they were not both from there. Gosh, that was good wine," Eleanor said with a look of memory on her face. She took her finger and rolled it around the brim of the coffee mug as if she was wiping it off. "One man was from the island, the other was from England—Cheshire, I think. He thought he was defending my honor from the other or maybe it was vice-versa. It was all a big mistake, a misunderstanding. Something just got lost in the translation.

"The police were called?" Maggie piped in.

"But then they went away," Eleanor said, bushing the air and the story away with the back of her hand.

Maggie smiled. "Aunt Eleanor, is that the trip and story you told me about you doing your white Tina Turner impression *on* the bar?"

"Yes, dear. You remembered." Eleanor said with a sense of pride.

"How many do you have?" June's mother asked.

"What? Stories? Many I'm afraid. There were only those two men. There was a third but he was a no—"

"No! Time shares, focus with me, sister. We're talking about getting June to a timeshare and unwind so she isn't, how did you put it, 'like Grover Cleveland's bowels'."

"Well that trip would have done it for her," Eleanor said while looking at Maggie and they both laughed.

"Again. Focus dear," Emma said directly. Eleanor had a tendency to wander off topic.

Aunt Eleanor thought then looked down at her cup. "You mean total?"

"You just answered the question," Dad said.

June spoke up "Does anyone want to ask me if I want to go? Going to some god-forsaken island is not necessarily my idea of relaxation. There's probably bugs and snakes and stuff. What do you have in Paris?" I might have something to say about this."

Eleanor said with a touch of sarcasm. "Windsong is special. That's my favorite place. See? She doesn't want to go there. She wants to go to Paris," "Everyone wants to go see Paris. Frankly, I don't have anything in Paris. But the Caribbean, that's different. There are snakes and bugs. Actually, there's boas and the third most poisonous snake on the planet. She wouldn't like it," Eleanor said trying to dissuade the audience.

"See?" June said. "I don't want to go where there are boas. I don't want to Glock a boa."

"It's for June, your niece, whom you love. She needs to get away," Dad said as he ignored Eleanor and June's responses.

"We *need* her to get away," Maggie said.

"What if she doesn't want to go?" Aunt Eleanor asked.

"We can convince her," Henry said.

"Hello! I'm still in the room!"

"That's nice dear. Now, just hold on another minute while we work out the details with your aunt here."

"Geez."

After another couple minutes of discussion in the kitchen and no clear decision about breakfast before or after the ride had been made, Aunt Eleanor took a deep breath and shook her head in loss. She didn't want to give up her week on the island. She didn't tell them she owned two weeks there, so giving up one still left her the other. There was something about the place she didn't want to share, out of the four she owned around the world, Castries, St. Lucia; Edinburg, Scotland; Whistler, Canada; and her real favorite in Cabo San Lucas, she didn't want to allow anyone else in on what she knew. But after some convincing by all parties, with the exception of June, she relented and turned to her very large designer purse to find her cell phone and call the time share company.

She found an open week available in three weeks at the Windsong Resort, which sat on Labrelotte Bay on the island of Saint Lucia. It would be the middle of June, their off season, just before the beginning of the hurricane season and warm, not a lot of clients there so Aunt Eleanor was able to arrange the booking on the phone while they all finished their morning coffee.

"Junebug, why don't you try calling your sergeant and see if you can get it off while your aunt works this call," her father said. June, with a heavy labored sigh, "I don't think he will clear it on such short notice," she said as she dialed her own cell phone and waited while it rang.

Everyone in the room could hear the sergeant answer his phone. They could also hear how he responded when she asked him for the time. "Are you kidding me, Hersher? Christ, Christmas just came early—Genius of an idea! Tell me you're not teasing me!" the sergeant said, his voice bleeding out into the room. The only one who couldn't hear was Eleanor, still on the phone with the timeshare company.

June looked around to see if anyone was listening in and heard the sergeant's response. Emma and Henry made good use of themselves and turned as if they were distracted. Aunt Eleanor hung up her phone and was now fully focused getting up to pour some more coffee, oblivious to the workings of others in the room.

June tried to turn a bit in her seat so she wasn't fully exposed to everyone hearing. "Well, I was just wanting to know if—"

The sergeant could be clearly heard. "Yes, yes! When—three weeks from now? How about next week? God there's hope!" The faceless, happy voice said with a little giddy laugh as if he just got an early parole for a crime he had actually committed.

Emma and Henry averted their eyes when June looked around again quickly to see if they could hear. If they were standing outside the kitchen window, they could have heard her sergeant's response.

June turned to Maggie who was watching her. "Well, that's good—good. I'm glad you are going to try to clear some time for me," she said into the phone, trying to deflect the voice coming through the small speaker.

The sergeant spoke again. "Clear some time? Hersher, you on vacation means the suicide watch will drop on most of us around here. Do you need some time to pack? I can cut you some time off to pack. How about a ride to the airport? I think there is a motor unit you pissed off somewhere who would gladly escort you to the gate. We can bypass TSA if it will help. Dear Baby Jesus! There is sunlight again!"

She looked around again at her family. She saw her mother lean over to Eleanor and whisper "What did he say?"

Aunt Eleanor just mumbled out of the side of her mouth half stuffed with berries that were still sitting in the colander in the sink, "I'll tell you later."

June thanked the sergeant and then hung up. When she did, Maggie just gave her mother a tender smile.

Eleanor asked after she took another sip "All set on my end. How about you?" Still looking at her niece and giving her a smile as June hung up her phone. "So, is your sergeant single?"

MARK WILLIAMS

Man is so made that he can only find relaxation from one kind of labor by taking up another.
—Anatole France

When June would come up and see her parents on weekends and go riding, her father would borrow Mitch, a seven year old gelding, from Jan and Paul, the neighbors next door. Mitch was tame and mellow. Even though June's parents had horses, they still had wild in them. Jan and Paul lived across a dried wash about a quarter mile away, a sizable wash would bleed down from the Continental Mountains in their backyard. When it would rain, the wash filled with water, about sixty feet wide. June would come out on the cooler weekends, sometimes with Maggie, from their townhouse in central Phoenix and ride a couple times a month up into the foothills behind the house and around the town. Sometimes, the group would ride with Beryl, the veterinarian Emma and Henry used for their stock. He was about June's age and widowed, his wife dying of cancer five years prior.

He was a chiseled man on a six foot frame. His cheeks were thin and led down into a squared jaw and soft lips, the top one hidden by a neatly trimmed mustache and making the turn on the corners. His hands were soft, June remembered when she would shake his hand and unusual she thought, for a man who had a job that required working with animals to have such soft hands.

Two years prior, Beryl had asked June out for coffee when Beryl, June, and her parents were on a ride together.

He wanted to go for coffee. She thought he wanted to date. She didn't handle the question well with a poorly worded turn-down. Both her parents looked over their shoulders at her like she had just insulted their friend. Beryl was an easy going man and simply nodded his head to June and said he understood. He even gave her a slight smile, which she nervously tried to imitate back to him.

To Beryl, it was a bit of a relief. At least now he could say to his friends who had been pushing him to get out more with women, he had tried.

Beryl got his veterinarian's doctorate after an undergrad degree in forestry and a brief stint working for the United States Forest service in Flagstaff for five years. He then went to Auburn University where he met his wife, Jolie. After they graduated, she moved with him back to Arizona. He loved her, and she him, but cancer was extensive in her family and it got to her when she was thirty seven. She was dead at forty-one. There were no children so he threw himself into his work with animals, specializing in horses. The prior work with the U. S. Government gave him an in with the BLM and their wild horse program. He had been the vet for June's parents while they were in Gilbert and he lived in Cave Creek. When Emma and Henry moved closer, the relationship developed in to a full scale friendship.

This weekend at June's parents' house was no different. They met Beryl at a dirt trail that led near to his small ranch. "So Beryl," Henry always started with Beryl once they got out on the trail. "What's new with you this week?" That's how each ride started. Beryl would ride alongside June's dad and June and her mother would follow. Maggie would, when she went, ride with either group or gallop ahead on her own. Aunt Eleanor rarely went. "Because," she would start, "I smell like horse for the rest of the day plus, riding on a saddle makes my butt bigger."

When the group went riding, leaving Eleanor behind to read the paper and drink coffee, the conversations on the trail were always light and non-descript. What the open conversations were between the sisters, was almost opposite between June and her mother.

"So," Emma would start at her and June walked their horses side by side. "How are things? Did you have a good week?"

"Fine," June said.

Emma would ask June how she was and June always gave the 'fine' answer. Being a homicide detective tended to cause a person to stay away from downer conversations. Not too many people wanted to know about gunshot stippling or blood splatter patterns. Emma may have wanted to know, truly, how June was doing, but June didn't want to tell her. That little fact also kept June's mother from sharing anything remotely heavy with June about her own life. She didn't want to burden her daughter. Not here, not now.

Emma followed with a change in topic. "I'm glad you're taking your aunt's offer for her timeshare."

"I'm not quite sure there was an offer," June said, looking sideways at her mother riding next to her. Maggie was on the other side of her grandmother, pretending not to listen.

Emma smiled. "Oh, she sounded like she was protesting but she wasn't really. You need to relax. You haven't relaxed since, well, since—"

June spoke as if throwing the words away, not at her mother. "Since before Ted's death? Yeah, your spouse getting murdered has a way of setting a person back on their pockets."

"Honey, you know we love you, we just want what's best for you and Maggie, that's all." She glanced over at her granddaughter.

June nodded towards Beryl with her head. "So, is that what's best for me?"

"No, your father and I aren't saying that. You know he rides with us all the time. You, riding with us, is the odd event. You still dwelling on him asking you out a couple of years ago?"

June shook her head. "No, but it did make things a little odd and please, Mom, keep your voice down."

Emma looked towards the men then back at June she said in a hushed tone so neither of the men in front of them could hear. "He just wanted coffee, probably a little company with something that didn't have four legs. We both think you miss-read that." The men didn't appear to have heard anything. They were too swallowed up in a conversation on the California water crisis.

"I think so too, Mom. I think he just wanted some company," Maggie said from the other side.

June's mother continued. "We are worried," "I think almost two decades is enough time to process. It doesn't have to be the doctor, but it might be nice to have someone, someone other than the people you work with."

"You don't need to worry about me. I'm fine. I'll be fine."

"You've been saying the same thing for years. June, stop. Think. You're life since Ted's death has been work and Maggie, and if you were to ask Maggie, probably not a whole lot of her." Emma looked over at her granddaughter who was pretending to look at the cactus they were walking by.

June looked across her mother towards her daughter, then back to her conversation with Emma. "Did you talk to her?"

"No, and she wouldn't say anything bad about her mother anyway, she loves you. You know that. But, what happens when Maggie leaves and starts her life and eventually you are too old and weak to hold a gun any more. You don't see too many seventy-five year old cops anywhere." June was looking at her mother when she spoke and glanced over at Maggie who was looking back at her and nodded in agreement. June's Mom and Dad had a way of simplifying the visions in June' life.

"You think a man is it?"

"No, we think *life* is the answer. It might mean a companion, maybe a man, but maybe not. You aren't living life. You are existing. You are surviving. You aren't living. You haven't for years, except for Maggie. What joy, other than Maggie and maybe a thrilling, challenging homicide, do you get out of life?" She waited for a couple of heart beats for an answer. When none came, she spoke again. "That's my point. You need to look around and see the beauty around you. Life, *does* go on. A man isn't an answer for you, but it might be something which adds to your life, a life you might want to share. A partner to do life with—a hobby, something to get up for in the morning other than work involving dead bodies and daily drudgery. Tell me, when was your last vacation?"

"Gee, I ah," June hesitated.

"I know when it was, when we all went to San Diego for Maggie's eighteenth birthday. You took the Friday off and we drove over for a long weekend. It was like pulling teeth to get you to do that. You have about a thousand days in leave built up. What are you saving it for?" Emma asked.

"Yep, I remember that trip," Maggie started. "You were on the phone for most of it, then you made us come back in the early afternoon on Sunday. You said you had work to do and when we got back, you said it had been taken care of. We just sat around at home. Like you just had to touch it and be here instead of over there." She shook her head. "We were gone for hours—just hours before we turned around and came back."

June looked at her daughter then back to her mother. "Well, when I retire I will get paid for—"

"Really? You're saving your vacation days for pay when you retire? Really?" Her mother again had a way of focusing on the simple.

"It's a good investment."

"Invest in what? Look, take the trip. Maggie will be fine. You will go and relax, kill some snakes. Go and buy a swim suit and lay on the beach for a week."

"Mom, I really don't want to go. There will be couples and any men will just want to try to pick me up."

"Honey, you are giving yourself credit in an area I am not sure you can take credit for."

"Mother!"

Maggie spoke up. "Mom, Grandma's right. We need to get you a swim suit, a good one. Maybe a couple. You've been out of the game for a while. Maybe things-well, you know, closed up." With a telltale smirk, she put heels to her horse and took off down the trail out front of everyone, not wanting to hear her mother's response.

The two men in front turned around and looked over their shoulders towards the sound of the voices as Maggie galloped passed them, then they got right back to their conversation.

Emma said with her own smile "June, they might only want coffee. Let them buy you coffee."

Just short of three weeks, the night before the trip, Maggie was in June's room, with her mother's bed and floor covered in clothes to take on the trip and suitcase choices to take them in. "Okay, let's go over the list again," Maggie said. She was reading from an actual list her mother had put together for the trip. She could tell her mother was nervous about leaving the next morning. June had told Maggie she was working on the list at work while typing up a report on a dead body found in a trash can. "It had been folded in half so it would fit," she said a matter-of-factly. Detectives always had to rule out suicide. "It was folded backwards, which was a good indicator it was not a suicide."

Maggie just frowned. Stories from her mother's work were customary.

"Okay, yeah, good. Let's do that," June said. She had never been to a tropical island and had everything from swimsuits to jeans laid out.

"Swimsuits?" Maggie called out.

"Swimsuits-check." June found the item and put it in the suitcase.

"It says swimsuits, like its plural. Do you have more than one swimsuit to take?" Maggie asked.

"Three," June said counting them as she put them in. Maggie made a note.

"Sun block?"

"Check."

"Underwear?"

"Check—eleven pair."

"You're only going for seven days? If I were you, I wouldn't even take underwear."

"Keep reading."

"Shorts?"

"Check?"

"Passport?"

"Check."

"Sandals?"

"Which pair?"

June held up three pair.

Maggie looked at them before she answered. "All three."

June looked in her bag, found a corner and stuffed them in.

"BCD?"

"What?"

"Birth control device?"

"Maggie!"

"You always told me to wait until I was married. Well, you were married and so I think you just need to—"

"No, no BCD."

"Why not? What if something or someone gets interesting? You're a good looking woman, Mom. There are men, lots of men, and a few women—"

"Maggie."

"You're going to buy one down there? The FDA doesn't have an inspection station down there. At least I don't think so. There could be a confidence risk."

"Can we change the subject?"

"Should I take it off the list?" Maggie was smiling. June was not.

"There was nothing on the list which addressed this topic? I know, I wrote the list."

"I added it," Maggie said with a grin.

"Want to go over the list I have for you while I'm gone?" June asked, flatly.

"It's off the list," Maggie said while she checked off the item from the paper she was reading.

June arrived at the Sky Harbor Airport early the next morning. She didn't mind waiting, getting her cup of coffee and nesting at the gate two hours before her plane was even scheduled to leave. The flight left for Miami at 7:45. She arrived at Miami International in the afternoon and took a cab to her hotel.

The plan was June would spend the night at the Intercontinental Hotel downtown then the following day, she would leave for St. Lucia on the southern tip of a string of islands heading south towards South America. When she told the counter agent in Phoenix where she was going as she was getting her boarding pass for the first leg to Miami, the woman looked at her with a smile. "Oh, that's nice. I heard they have the third most poisonous snake there—and boa constrictors. Have a nice trip."

LABRELOTTE BAY

A man travels the world over in search of what he needs and returns home to find it.
—George Moore

She checked in to the Intercontinental in the heart of Miami. She wore a pair of slacks and a nice blue blouse along with a light sweater on the plane because every time she ever flew, it was always cold on the aircraft and this flight was no different. Along with the slacks, she wore comfortable shoes. Comfortable shoes meant no heels and good arch support. Something advertised on orthopedic shoe commercials, or worn by an eighty year old grandmother. In addition to all of that, she wore her hair short. From certain angles, she looked like a short, middle-aged man. Since she started in detectives, she cut her hair short. Stuff had a tendency to go from the crime scene and stick to her body, eventually, to her hair. The straw that caused the grooming trend was when she had come home and was showering after a not so unusual day with the dead. She was shampooing and felt something in her hair. She worked for a moment to dig it out of the tangle it was in. It was a human fingernail. She was sure it wasn't hers, since she never wore fingernail polish; however, it did match the pink fingernail polish on the corpse they had two days prior in a dumpster behind a pawn shop. She tried to remember how long it had been since she had the dead woman's hands in plastic bags at the crime scene and then how long it had been since she had washed her own hair. That day, she guessed, since she tried to wash her hair every day, because dead peoples stuff has a tendency to do just this, come off and land on her and in this case, in her hair.

June, wearing her hair short, would cause her to sometimes be mistaken for a man As she was collecting her bags, a man came up from behind and simply said 'excuse me sir' as he was trying to get to the conveyor belt to recover his own. He was looking at her from one of those certain angles. Seeing his mistake and staring into the scowl of the detective, he excused himself and went in another direction—away from her. She couldn't have everything to look just right, she thought, but maybe she could look a little more feminine. "Why?" she asked herself. She had grown comfortable with the way she dressed and the way she looked, her orthopedic shoes and her man pants and short hair. At least she wasn't finding dead people's body parts hidden in places on her body. Slacks kept her from having to shave her legs for days. Flat shoes were comfortable, especially since she got the shoes with the *'arch-o-matic infusion gels*—she remembered the jingle.

June didn't have time or was just too tired to paint her nails on any regular basis, and latex gloves had a way of rubbing the polish off of them anyway. Even though she was good looking, in shape, and watched her diet, she was still a middle-aged woman who had not had a relationship since her husband died, unless counting the relationship she appeared to still be having with her dead husband.

When she got to the hotel and walked through the huge gapping lobby, she was wondering why she just couldn't stay here for the whole week. She toyed with the idea of fake-calling home and pretending to be on another part of the planet but she knew the family would eventually find out. Maggie made her take her iPad so she could skype and send pictures of the resort so evidence would be demanded and she would have to produce it.

That night, she ordered a pizza and had it delivered to her room. She walked down to the small snack shop in the lobby and purchased a soda to have with her pizza and a candy bar for later. She never had either at least not all to herself, but she was on *vacation*. She figured she would throw caution to the wind. She laid on top of her bed in her pajamas, which consisted of an old T-shirt and a pair of old soccer shorts, and watched television, lingering on the Cuban/Latin network, as she continuously scrolled through the channels.

The next morning, she repacked the few items she had removed from her bag and caught a taxi back to the airport, snagging a free bagel and coffee on her way out the door. It was a three and a half hour flight to St. Lucia from Miami. She decided, after the luggage incident and the man thinking she was a he, while she packed and snacked on her left over pizza that morning, to at least wear shorts, which meant she needed to shave her legs. A task she was having trouble remembering the last time she had performed. "Crap," she said as she then remembered she didn't pack her razor. After reassembling her bag, she again went back down to the store in the lobby and bought a disposable. So far, she was thinking, the travel was a lot of labor, making her do things she really didn't want to do, not sleeping in her own bed, and having to walk and take elevators to get a drink and equipment just so people didn't think she was a he.

Starting her second leg of the trip, she found herself on the aisle and unable to see too much of the island when the plane was on final approach for landing, but as the aircraft banked, June looked across the aisle and out the side window as the plane started its decent into Hewanorra International Airport on the southern tip of St. Lucia island. She saw the twin Piton Peaks, left over from old volcanos and the tropical jungle surrounding them. She was wondering what Jurassic movie she was landing in. It was a stark contrast with the Valley of the Sun. All she could think about was her hair, even though short, was going to be a mess all week from the humidity, making her boyish look even worse. This, as well as the island being the home of the third most poisonous snake in the world. Oh, and boas, she couldn't forget about the boa constrictors.

The passengers de-planed out of the front and rear doors, down the stairs and onto the tarmac. It was a tiny airport compared to Phoenix and the terminal, although modern, was dwarfed by the four large 757's and 767's parked side by side, almost touching their wing tips. The air was tropically-humid, with a slight breeze the smell of ocean was noticeable from someone coming from the desert.

"Is this your bag?" the customs officer asked June as she placed the bag in front of him. He was impeccably uniformed with a blue short-sleeved shirt, trimmed in the gold unit emblems associated with his rank and unique to British Commonwealth units. His skin was a deep black and his teeth were a contrasting white. He was professional, but polite.

"Yes, it is."

He looked at her passport, then to her, then to her bag before he handed it back to her with a smile and "Have a wonderful stay in St. Lucia."

She was disappointed she wasn't searched. Didn't fit the profile *whatever that looks like*, she thought. *A single woman with short hair, shorts, and freshly shaved legs must be okay in these parts.*

She walked out of the customs area and into the main open air lobby where passengers were both arriving and departing in an area about the size and shape of a football end zone. Even this time of the morning, she was getting warm, actually, she was starting a full on sweat. Every pore in her body was open and leaking bodily fluids. She could feel the sweat begin to roll down her spine when she saw her name on a sign held by a man about the age of her daughter, and wearing a dark blue tropical shirt.

He didn't appear to be sweating.

June approached him. "Hi, I'm June Hersher," She took a swipe of her forehead with the palm of her hand and pushed the sweat away from her eyebrows. Her palm was now wet as if she had stuck it under a faucet of water. Her swiping also pasted down pasting the front of her hair to her forehead.

The large man's face moved gently into a smile to match his size and a voice so soft she could barely hear him. "Hello, welcome to St. Lucia. I am Garlen, your driver to Windsong Resort. Please, let me take your bag." Before she could answer, he reached down, with a hand the size of a baseball mitt, and took June's suitcase and picked it up like it was air. She started to tell him it had wheels and he didn't need to carry it, but the two moved off as he led the way to the car. The curbs were steep, with sunken concrete gutter pans forming a small trough channeling an apparent large amount of storm water away from where ever it landed.

Garlen opened the trunk of the Lexus sedan and put the bag in. Before he shut the trunk, he reached into an ice chest and pulled out a cold bottle of water. "Would you like a refreshing beverage?" His accent was of French creole, with a hint of formal English. The word choice seemed to be from an ad he had seen. She liked it.

"Oh, thank you," June said. She had tried to dry off her hand after wiping her forehead as she walked to the car, but it was still clearly damp when she reached for the bottle. Her sweat now running down her back had passed her waist and was working its way down between the cheeks of her bottom. She noticed Garlen didn't have a drop on him. She opened and took a healthy swig from the bottle as Garlen opened the back door to the car for her to get in.

They traveled for a little under an hour from the airport on the southern tip of the island, to Windsong on the northwest coast. June could have landed at the airport in Castries, only five minutes away, but she would have had to spend a night in Puerto Rico and she preferred Miami instead. Castries being the capital, only had room for a smaller airport and smaller island hoppers, allowing only the turbo props to land. Hawthorne International Airport, on the south end of the island, could park six of the largest jets side by side along its single runway. Plus, she got to see most of the island she found out later she probably never would have seen unless she scheduled a personal tour to do so.

Two minutes out of the airport, along a single lane, asphalted road, they passed a huge stadium, complete with the Olympic rings hanging five stories tall to the outside of the professional sized arena. Directly across from it a small boy tended three goats mowing the grass along the road. The boy was moving them to the next section for the goats to eat. The grass in the area they were just grazing actually looked like it had been mowed.

Before she spoke, she quickly tried to think of any Olympic games anywhere in the Caribbean or neighboring countries. She couldn't think of any, but she wasn't much of a sports enthusiast so she could have been wrong and missed one even though they come every four years. "You guys had the Olympics here?" June asked Garlen as she pointed to the stadium.

He looked over and snickered. "No, we have never had a team." He started. His voice so soft, it was hard for June to hear him from the back seat. "We might have had athletes on a Caribbean team but never one of our own. We are a poor nation and just can't afford that."

June frowned. She looked back over her shoulder at the fading image of a stadium many pro teams in the United States would love to have. She was trying to make the equation make sense. "Then what about—"

"The stadium and Olympic rings were a gift from the Chinese."

"The Chinese? Why did they give you a stadium?"

Garlen shrugged. "I don't know. I don't think anyone really knows."

"So, why the rings?"

Garlen smiled. "Fashion style. There was a big empty space on the wall and they decided to fill it with the rings."

June smiled back. "Fashion style?" She looked again. "Those rings must be six stories tall."

"They are closer to five. If you were going to decorate a stadium given to you as a gift, you might as well make it look like something," Garlen said.

June thought about what Garlen said. She determined it would be hard to argue the point he just made and the logic behind it.

She was sitting in the back seat on the left side and driving on the left side. She had never traveled English style. It felt weird to her, driving on the *wrong* side of the road but St. Lucia was a English territory and she found herself pushing on the imaginary brake pedal on her side as she looked around and asked questions as they drove. No road shoulders to speak of, unless there was an open driveway or the area in front of some building or shop. In many places, especially along the coast, the cliffs were within inches of the side of the road. June found out from Garlen a hurricane several years prior caused much of the erosion they were seeing. Erosion the island still, five years later, hadn't mended. They drove up the rocky east coast then crossed the center of the island through the rain forest.

When they entered the forest, the roads narrowed even more. They drove along roads not much wider than two small American parking spaces at the mall and no place along the road for a car to pull off. No place to escape in case they needed to get over, except for the occasional side trail with the Rainbow Eucalyptus towering along the roads, climbing at least two hundred feet, chased half that distance by bamboo, huge pipes of bamboo, marked the road. As a matter of fact, June noticed, the only sidewalks or driveways she'd seen were at the airport curb Garlen had hoisted her suitcase over. They drove through communities which would be construed in the States as below impoverished. More goats were seen on the drive tethered along the road in front of brightly painted homes as a way of keeping the grass in check. Dogs, lay lazily in the street or paths, roosters ran wild. Banana trees grew like weeds along the way, as well as large mango trees whose fruit had dropped and was rotting on the ground, minus those being eaten by the goats. Garlen narrated the trip, pointing out spots of cliffs and beaches, hurricane wreckage from years before, plantations, the names of small villages they drove through, and answering all questions coming from June. After a while, she quit asking and just looked, watching the new world drive by while she sipped her 'refreshing beverage' of water.

The rainforest was oval in shape, in the center of the island. They drove from the southern tip, up the east coast and then at a diagonal through the heart of the rainforest, and into the capital of Castries on the Northwestern coast. It clung to the sides of the green hills and down to the small sheltered harbor. There, they passed the island's other airport, in the center of town by the docks where the large tourist ships pulled in. Up the green lush hill, around one then around two smaller hills covered in forest and vines, Garlen turned down a small, neighborhood street. There was no sign about the resort at the turn. Nothing to indicate a world class beach resort tucked back behind the old and sometimes broken homes and of course, at the turnoff, two more tethered goats and behind them, in a fenced pasture waist high in long green grass, were two cocoa brown horses, enjoying the day.

About a mile off the main road was a sign with *Windsong* written on it. At the turn, the world changed. Garlen turned down the long, flower-bordered drive way and came to a stop at a guard gate. There were three guards, all of whom appeared to recognize him, logged his license plate and raised the gate arm for the car to enter. The car proceeded down a floral wonderland on both sides of the sloping driveway to the main, two-story, finished white stucco portico June noticed a man standing in a crisp white shirt, power-red tie, and dark slacks. He had one hand behind his back and the other holding a silver tray June was greeted by Morgan, the assistant resort director, carrying a formal silver tray with a cool towel scented with lemon and a heavy square glass of pink rum punch.

"Good day Mrs. Hersher. Welcome to Windsong," he said. It was as if he had known her for years. June figured he knew Garlen and knew who he was picking up or the guard at the gate called ahead, still very impressive. He was a medium size man if all the men measured were ancient Mayans, with his shirt creased so sharp it could cut butter. His red tie was knotted just so and the tassels on his shoes had one lying towards the right and one towards the left on top of each shoe. He used a pair of silver tongs to lift the towel from the tray and then presented the tray with the drink on it, all done while Garlen opened the trunk and pulled out her luggage. All June had to do was get out of the car with her purse and receive the towel and drink.

Her suitcase was taken by the bell captain and with gentle direction by Morgan, she went over to a table and a cluster of chairs where she sat in a large overstuffed chair to register while wiping her face and the back of her neck with the cool towel, the lemon scent transferring from the towel to her skin, *or was it lime*? The entire main floor was open on three sides by large, arched Spanish-style breezeways. She took a sip of the rum punch-*much more rum than punch*, she thought, so she stirred the drink and sipped through the little pink straw again. *Ah, much better.* The air was warm but the ceiling fans kept a breeze moving through the large, open-terraced room and over her, cooling her body. There were no windows and minimum walls. Large eaves would protect the interior, to a degree, from most tropical rains but if it came down hard enough and with a breeze, June could see the interior getting wet. The concierge was at a desk open to the lobby and to the pool deck outside.

She took another sip. She missed the sidebar conversation the Bell Captain had with Morgan after she was seated and the Captain returned to where Morgan was standing.

"It's true, its back," the Bell Captain whispered into Morgan's ear.

Morgan rolled his eyes and whispered. "Are you sure? How do you know?"

"The gardener. They found its skin hanging in one of the coconut trees."

"Where?"

"Terrace Three."

"How long this time?"

"Almost two meters the gardener said. It was hard to judge because the skin had dried. It's their best guess."

Morgan nodded. So, it could be longer?"

The Bell Captain shrugged. "Most definitely."

June was comfortable in her chair, finished registering, filling out the registration form presented to her on a clipboard while she sat in the chair, just as Morgan came back with her room pass. His face offered no expression of concern. Morgan, if nothing else, was a professional at his work as a resort executive after a brief, but lively turn in island politics.

He had worked for the resort for approximately three years when he got the political bug. He had a brief career as a politician but lost his one election when he ran for alderman of his district.

He lost, badly.

When they asked some of the voters why, they unanimously said they voted against him because he never smiled and always wore a tie.

On St. Lucia, people are smiling much of the time and apparently they never wear a tie unless they are suspect of some shenanigans or with the local Christ Church of the Beatitudes. Those men always wore ties, as well as some of the women.

Morgan was a man of work. Work, to him, meant focus and determination to be the best assistant director the resort or any resort had ever seen. He was dedicated to the task of perfection of the vacations people would have and the pursuit of the act of relaxation. It was a science to Morgan, a science deserving of study and thought. The bar towel and drink on a silver platter was his idea. The perfect atmosphere, the perfect beach chair, the perfect experience, was his goal in life. He didn't marry—the resort was his mistress. It was he who ran the day to day operations, not the managers and not the resort director, three in all while he was there. He did not question why he was never promoted. He knew his time would come. He was not ready, it was not yet his time. Morgan, in his starched white shirt, his tasseled shoes, and perfectly knotted tie, was a man of plan.

The Bell Captain transferred June's suitcase to one of the small van shuttles taking guests up and down the hill. June looked up the hill and figured the walk up would be an issue, with one hand holding her drink and the warm towel and the other hand clutching her purse, she eased herself into the bench seat and took the shuttle to her 'villa' as Morgan called it, not knowing what a 'villa' here would look like. She just knew it was up a very steep hill.

The shuttle drive reminded June of a ride at Disneyland, with sharp hairpin turns, manually shifting to lower gears quickly before the vehicle started to slide back down the hill it was trying to climb, and a road grade she was sure was too steep for American construction codes. She gripped the overhead handle above the door and wrapped her arm in the straps of the purse while propping her feet in to the corners of the floorboard where the front seats were bolted in just in front of her, but still holding the drink and managing a sip on one of the straight sections of the small road. Between the sharp turns and the jarring remains of the van lunging forward and backward between gear shifting, not to mention the never ending cliffs and shear drop offs next to the road, she was sure many of her kind had met their end at this resort and were buried somewhere under the bread fruit trees.

When she got to the sidewalk of her villa, she felt she had to pry her fingers from around the overhead handle. June had a noticeable death grip on it. The van leaned away from the sidewalk she still needed to climb, but as she came around the back of the van to meet her driver and her bag, she looked up at an unrestricted view of the Caribbean. It stunned her. She got out of the van and the driver collected her bag from the back of the van, asked for her room key opened the door and place the bag in the room. She followed him, climbing a short flight up stairs through a lush lawn bracketed by hydrangeas, dwarf palms, and iris flowers, she stopped again on the front porch of the polished white stucco villa and looked around. It was striking in looks and somewhere around her, she could smell jasmine. She truly was in a breathtakingly beautiful place. From every room, she had a view of the Caribbean on three sides and the forest jungle surrounding her unit to the hills behind her. The three room suite had a wall which could slide back and opened the patio to the living room. A bouquet of yellow roses sat on the coffee table. June pulled the envelope and opened it. It was from her parents.

'Enjoy and try to relax, love Mom and Dad.'

She smiled and walked out to the patio and the short stucco white wall around it. The sun was starting to paint that side of the hill and the breeze was warm. It didn't keep her from thinking about the office and things she was missing. It didn't keep her from thinking about her daughter. And she was determined not to think about the years gone by.

"Miss," the voice called from behind her.

She pulled up her head and snapped too, turning back to her shuttle driver. "Yes?"

"I put your bag in your room. Would you like me to unpack your things?"

She smiled. "No, no, thank you." She was given a quick tour of the three rooms, if the bathroom was counted. It was the size of her bedroom back home. He told her about the restaurants, showed her how to use the air-conditioning remote, told her about the beach, and if she needed anything to just pick up the phone and dial '0'.

"Is there anything else I can do for you? Would you like me to make a dinner reservation for you? Maybe a spa appointment?"

June thought for a moment; her eyebrows rising.

He smiled. "Ah, I see. A spa day," He went over to the phone and keyed in four numbers "Hello, Bernice. I would like to make an appointment for Mrs. Hersher." He covered the phone and looked at her. "When would you like? This afternoon? Tomorrow afternoon?"

"Late today would be fine." She almost said 'no' but remembered why she was there.

The valet finished his call for scheduling the appointment then hung up. "You are all set, today at four this afternoon with Bernice. Is there anything else?" There was a paper and pen lying next to the phone and after the valet hung up, he wrote down the information June would need. He stood with a smile on his face June translated into sincerity. She thanked him and gave him a five dollar tip, which caused his smile to transform into a huge and friendly grin giving a slight bow before he left, shutting the door behind him. His body language told June he was not expecting a tip.

She began to unpack her suitcase, working through the pieces and placing them in their respective drawers. It was then she heard the sounds of loud voices coming from up the hill, in one of the larger units behind her own. She couldn't make out what was being said and couldn't tell if it was in anger or someone playing. It was clear they were voices, but not much beyond that. She couldn't even tell if they were male or female. By the time she got to the front door and stepped out on to the small patio to look up the hill in the direction of the noise, the sound had stopped, the late morning sun starting to leak over the edge of the hill behind wherever the voices were coming from.

She went back in and finished unpacking. June walked the perimeter of each of the rooms, looking in the spaces, gazing out at the sea, moving from room to room before she found herself flopping backwards and laying under the mosquito netting in the bedroom. She laid there for two or three minutes before she started to cry, softly at first, with just a tear running down the corner of her left eye, then both eyes. Then, she rolled over and sobbed.

It was the first time since the loss of her husband she had cried, really cried. It had been almost two decades and she had no idea where this emotion came from, but it was consuming her on the bed. It was like a wave, surprising her where she was laying. Ten minutes before she was fine. The whole trip was because she hadn't processed any of life since his death.

After about thirty minutes of tears, and snot, and tired abdominal muscles, June lay in on her side, curled up around one of the pillows, closing her eyes and feeling the weight of the years driving her into the glorious comfort of the bed. Her limbs and head were like lead weights. It was a conflict of senses-the miserable pain of heartache, and the pleasure of the cool bed.

It was three hours before she woke.

LABRELOTTE BAY

It is better to sleep on things beforehand than lie awake about them afterward.

—Baltasar Gracian

The sun was low in the west the first afternoon and when she awakened June felt like she had been beat up in a losing bar fight. Maybe it was the trip, maybe it was the sadness, she just knew she needed to go for a walk, get out of the villa, and keep moving. *That's what kept me going for the last years* she told herself.

She changed her clothes, putting on some tennis shoes, changed to another pair of shorts and a light shirt and started down the hill, working her way to the lobby. She passed two porters who were talking in hushed tones and didn't see her approach. She only picked up part of the conversation and their accent kept her from capturing and understanding all of what they were saying and gave it no real thought.

"What kind was it?" one man said to the other.

"Same one as before."

"The same one?" the other said. "I thought we were able to capture it last year."

"Think so. They said it was about two meters long. It would make it the same one."

One of the porters saw June approach and smiled at her with his big beautiful white tooth smile followed by "Hello, Miss."

June smiled and nodded. It was hard for her not to smile back. Everyone seemed content and showed it with their smiles. She felt guilty about the crying. She had no idea where it came from, but knew she had enough of it. No more, not for her.

"Good afternoon, Mrs. Hersher. Have you found the accommodations to your liking?" It was her valet that had joined the two porters.

"Yes, very much, thank you," she said passing the three.

June walked under the portico and turned toward the lobby desk as she heard her name being called as she entered the lobby. Behind the chest high counter was Eldin Cornwall, the resort director. He was also the senior vice-president for the holding company which ran Windsong, a position he was offered within the last month. He had been the resort director for the last ten years and was a native of Grenada. He had moved to St. Lucia thirty years prior when he was in his twenties to get out of the destitute poverty that was Grenada and work on the wharfs where the cruise ships docked, letting their passengers out to tour and spend their money on the island and in downtown Castries.

When he arrived from Grenada, he lived in a small apartment on the hillside up from the downtown open market with three other men who also found work on the docks. It seemed almost everyone, at one time or another, started work or spent time working the Castries harbor. He worked his way up then transferred to a groundskeeper job at another local resort catering to the young newlyweds who frequented the island, working during the day and attending local college classes at night. The move from the docks was a gamble. The docks were good solid work, the resorts were dependent on the market, but there was much more room to grow. So, he turned in his hard hat for a pair of pruning loppers.

He, like the others working at Windsong, after he made a leap between resorts, was dark brown with beautiful white teeth. Even though he was in his mid-fifties, Eldin still cut a striking figure with his six foot three, freakishly tall and lean frame for a Grenadian. He symbolized expectation, always part of the air left over from the European colonialism on the island, he was always in a starched white shirt. June noticed the shirts, even the woman wore, and the pure white of the garment. She could never remember anyone in the states having it look better or more professional than here. Maybe it was the whiteness of the shirt against the dark skin—the contrast. June didn't know why it struck her as such a noticeable picture. From the school children she saw in the towns on the drive in, to the head of the resort, the people of the island were impeccably dressed, even the villages Garlen drove her through, it was clear they were poor, but none appeared anything less than proud. But the island and its people had their secrets as well.

Eldin Cornwall, professional resort director, corporate executive, respected man of his staff and neighbors, a man who climbed a ladder out of the poverty of his early life, had an issue with gambling, specifically betting on the ponies at Santa Anita via the internet.

He had a system, a system that only seemed to work when the other horse was destined to win. It wasn't scientific, nothing on the island including Cornwall's plan was reliant on science, although he could justify it, but only to his closest friends, friends who had the same betting and gambling issues along with similar failed systems. It consisted of betting on any brown mare with white stockings in the third. Never mind the odds, Eldin hit one that way once, won fifteen hundred dollars and never looked back. He had a PayPal account and a new iPhone. There were times staff could see him speaking on the phone, keying numbers on the phone, nothing surprising for a man of his level of resort management. He seemed to always be on the phone, negotiating contracts, talking to corporate, at least that's what the employees thought. They didn't know he was giving account numbers to the animated computer voice recognition and transferring funds for the day's runs, applying scientific analysis and discernment to the day's races—except for the browns with white stockings in the third. That was a given.

He was quick with an answer and sure on his selection, never betting more than five dollars on any race, but on a day with ten races, fifty dollars added up quickly, especially if he lost all of them, which he did—often.

The gambling was an issue and sometimes Eldin would blame himself because of his own breaking of protocol. Like most, Eldin had a dash of superstition. He never tied his right shoe before his left shoe, he was always opposite with the buttons on his shirt cuffs, and he never bet on the ponies without wearing his silver sequined thong. He would have to change later, after placing the bet, in to a pair of Fruit of the Looms, but he would tolerate the chaffing issues associated with sequins around the groinal regions for the few moments to place the bet or as he would sometimes tell his small community of secret betting friends, his 'Happy Playground."

Eldin's release to the dark side started with a cruise, three years prior as the assistant manager, he was tasked with going on to better understand the tourist industry for the corporation. He didn't want to go, leaving his resort was not his choice, but like a good soldier, he went—and then almost didn't come back.

There were no rumors that survived his return. No one on the boat who knew him or where or who he was representing; only one of the many discussions by the crew and staff of another passenger on another cruise. The crew had hundreds of such stories. Eldin's just fell in the box with the rest. This one was about the tall man who would dance each night until he was a sweaty lather, his shirt unbuttoned to the naval, swinging a napkin over his head to the raucous beat of *Carlos, and the Heart Throbs,* a rescued street show band who played remakes of tunes from the 70's, 80's, and occasionally some modern stuff to the cocktail lounge group in the *Feng Shui* Show Lounge, just below the Promenade Deck. There was a small dance floor surrounded by dark cushioned furniture with small round tables holding a single battery lit candle in a small glass case in its center of each table.

Carlos, would whip the middle-aged crowd into a frenzy with his renditions of Michael Jackson, Tony Orlando, or anything from the Bee Gees. During the last part of the act, Carlos would reach in to his very tight pants and act like he is pulling off something, coming out with his underwear. It was the same every night and he would sling the colored Hanes boxers into the audience, aiming at the cute and very drunk ladies, having targeted the older ones with no rings on their wedding fingers and appearing to be traveling in packs, which usually resulted in Carlos and the rest of the Heart Throbs to get a few napkins with room numbers written on them.

Eldin, intoxicated on the freedom away from his growing persona at the resort and aided by Saki bombers, made it his mission to catch as many soiled boxers as he could, standing like a center for the LA Lakers, his arms waving and shuffling side to side. As Carlos tossed the slightly used garment, Eldin moved like a linebacker, following the thrown object like ground based radar and terrifying any woman who dared to look up and see the huge sweaty tree of a man come barreling down on them, his size thirteen wingtips falling on their size eight and a half open-toed pumps.

He picked up the loose dainties and swirled them over his head before he wiped his brow with them then tossing them to the crowd, dancing on one foot while he turned to his left before he reversed direction, switching feet, his shirt open, sweat running, his arms over his head like he's reaching for the cereal box on the top shelf, his hips undulating in his high-waisted Haggar slacks made of stretchy Dacron polyester and their patented *'Expand-o-Matic'* waistband, coming in very useful on this trip, all the while wailing "Carlos, weeeeeloooooooovvvveeeeeyyyoooouu!!!!"

Carlos was actually Jack Laswick, an out of work insurance agent from Tulsa, let go during the down turn but landed this gig on the cruise line because he could sing, looked nice, and frankly, they needed a lounge singer since their last one was arrested three ports back for trafficking pharmaceuticals by taping them in small pouches to the inside of his thigh.

Eldin's selection of winners was better left to the resort and its operations, depending heavily on his assistant managers like Morgan. He was a much better director of a resort than a gambler. At the resort, to his staff and guests, he was also quick with an answer and sure with his instructions and always delivered with a smile. The problem with Eldin was he thought he was able to keep his feet in both worlds and had a Teflon personality. He didn't drink at work, he didn't smoke, and he went to church on most Sundays, to see and be seen. He had little time to socialize and although women found him attractive, he always seemed distracted. His staff thought it was the burden of running such a beautiful resort, taking care of its needs and the needs of its guests, but the truth was, Eldin was thinking about hitting on a brown horse with white stockings, running in the third at Santa Anita, not to mention the occasional chaffing by some well-worn sequined thongs. There was also a deeply hidden part of Eldin that wanted to find Carlos again.

Sometimes, when he would stand and be talking to someone, he would do a short, almost unnoticeable squat, a cheap man's curtsey only just a few inches followed immediately by a sway from side to side, as if he was stretching. It was due to one or more of the dislodged sequins cutting in to his Happy Playground. The move helped dislodge them.

He made it his business to know each of his guests by sight. A noble feat since most of the resort completely turned over every week. He walked around the desk and came up to June and shook her hand. "We are so glad you could make it down to visit us. Your aunt called and told me to take personal care of you."

June smiled. "I don't know whether to be honored or concerned."

Eldin returned the smile. "I assure you, you will truly enjoy your stay here. The issues with your aunt were, well, a simple misunderstanding. If you have any concerns, wants, desires, I have informed my staff you are to be given the utmost in service," he said with perfect diction and in the traditional colonial English accent.

"Well, I think right now I want to just get my bearings and see where everything is, maybe sit on the beach for a while."

With that, Eldin directed June to the beach through and around the pool and gardens filled with hydrangeas and jasmine. "Of course, I will send a waiter to take your drink order and bring you some fresh towels." He made eye contact with one of the porters and gestured him to come to him. He told the young man to go to the bar and have a waiter immediately find Mrs. Hersher on the beach for a drink order. The young man nodded then turned on his heels and moved quickly to the bar as June walked the other direction towards the beach. She made her way passed the Dragonfly Restaurant and Jammers outdoor bar to the beach where blue lounges rested under a canopy of coconut trees filled with actual coconuts.

A waiter spoke as he came up behind her. "Hello, Miss," He was carrying two beach towels and a tray. As June sat down, he draped one of the towels over the back of her lounger, the other at the foot of the lounger, and moved a small table next to where she was sitting. "Would you like a beverage?" he asked, again with a smile. "Mr. Cornwell wanted me to take good care of you."

It was starting to bug her, everyone smiling. *Why is everyone so happy? No one is this happy? I've seen where they live.*

She took a deep breath. "What do you recommend?"

The waiter thought for a second. "Do you like rum?"

"Sure, if it's the same drink they greeted me with at the door." She thought if she answered 'all liquor' it would give the wrong impression. She actually couldn't remember the last time she had rum other than when she arrived.

The man smiled. "Ah, I will fix our specialty rum punch. Very good—*no problem*." He turned and left before she could have told him she had already had the drink. She liked that drink, if it was the same one she had when she arrived and she suspected it was the resort specialty. If she stayed long enough, she could probably like it too much. He returned quickly with the pink drink in a plastic beach cup and a small pineapple and maraschino cherry on top with a matching straw.

Her first sip was like the one when she arrived, burning all the nerve endings shut, slamming down her throat and then rebounding and melting her cerebellum. After she stirred the drink with the straw after eating the cherry and pineapple garnish, the second sip was like pure warm medicinal honey. She sat looking out over the small bay the resort was protected in, while the back of her skull began to warm from the inside out, traveling down her neck and shoulders, causing her to notice them begin to slouch. It was quick, instantaneous almost. She didn't realize the waiter was still there, standing next to her, smiling. She nodded. "Yep, this is just fine."

"Good, I am so glad you like it," he said.

"By the way, what is the name of this bay?" June said, gesturing with the hand holding the drink.

"This?" The waiter said looking back over his shoulder at the water and nodding his head in the same direction. "This is Labrelotte Bay, Mrs. Hersher."

In front of her, was a roped off swimming section of the bay, just off shore, complete with floating slide, sun tanning platform, and an inflatable climbing wall for the children or adults with children's hearts and ability, all, anchored in place.

To the south of her lounge chair was a boat dock supporting the water sports shack where the snorkel trips left from and water crafts rentals were housed. There were three children, between eight and twelve years of age playing on the slide in the water, about fifty yards from shore, well within the buoyed roped off swim area. They were English, or at least June thought they were from England. She could hear their accents from where she was and they were waving, to whom June thought, was their mother and father on the beach just towards the south on the other side of a cluster of empty loungers. No one was between her and the couple and as she looked passed them, there was no one in view all the way to the water sports shack.

About one hundred yards from where her parents were sitting, the older redheaded girl yelled, "Mummy, Daddy, look at us," waving both her arms high over her head as she tried to stand on top of the slide.

Daddy was as white as an Englishman would be expected to be with a growing pinkishness to the skin from unprotected sun exposure, and Mummy was in a billowy one-piece flowered swimsuit under a large-brimmed hat. Both had on, what June suspected to be, about a quart of zinc oxide on the bridge of their collective noses. This couple, June surmised, had been there at least a day longer than herself. She realized there can be a lot of sun damage in just one day.

The boy yelled as he waved hard to his parents like he was signaling a rescue ship two miles away and his life depended on them seeing him. "Look mummy—daddy. We're on the slide,"

Mother looked up from her magazine and waved back. "We see you, Love. Be careful."

"Don't drown your sisters," dad said, spoken in a voice only he and his own wife could hear, with the exception of June.

June looked to the north on the beach, which was virtually empty. Back behind her, was one other couple walking down from the bar to the center of the beach. They had the entire beach, about a quarter mile of it from her guess, to themselves. She also noticed the beach had been raked, from one end to the other, from the surf line to the retaining wall near the buildings, a span of about sixty feet. The surf itself wasn't really any kind of surf. It was just high enough to flop over feet if the person kept them flat on the sand. The beach sloped gently up, away from the water, all the way to the back retaining wall holding the mountain the resort was attached to, back from falling into the sea.

June had trouble fathoming the whole beach had been raked.

The couple she saw moments before walking down towards the beach were now in full view. The yapping of a dog, some kind of toy Yorkie, also helped draw her attention towards the couple.

"How 'bout here Honey-Bunny?" the buxom fortyish blond woman asked her husband as she made her way down to the water line in what June was sure were high heels. She wore a leopard-print, high-cut one piece bathing suit with the front and sides cut away, exposing large sections of her body for those few on the empty beach to see, low enough to include her caesarian incision. Her hat was a Fontana style, at least three feet across, and a bright white with a slice of leopard ribbon to match her suit. Her sun glasses were designer and so were her breasts, cheeks, back of the thighs, and jowls. June wasn't sure why the woman didn't at least try to repair the caesarian incision or pick a different suit. Maybe, June wondered, if it was a like a mother's battle scar. Men have old football injuries, women have birth scars, seemed fair to June. The woman wore diamond stud earrings and French nails. She had a copy of *Vanity Fair* in one hand and the dog in the other. The dog shook uncontrollably, like most of her breed, yapping at the trailing waiter, hushed and soothed by its owner with its nuzzle to the woman's jowls and a calm voice saying, "it's okay, Beauty, my little Snooky-lamb. I won't let you drown."

Her husband followed with the towels and supply package. He could not have done better had he of been a donkey with a saddle. Behind Honey-Bunny, was the waiter carrying a tray of drinks. He stood a few feet back still on the landing steps from the bar, waiting to see where the couple were going to land. The woman holding the dog noticed June about ten yards away. "E'cuse me," she directed her call to June in what June thought was a deep-southern accent—very deep.

"Yes?"

The woman said pointing her nearly one inch manicured nails at the two loungers she was standing near "Do ya'll know if anyone is using these?" Snooky-Lamb was licking her master's chin. As she lifted her head in response to the dog, June could see the makeup line which followed her jaw line from ear to ear. It was a darker brown foundation than her already browned skin. June could also see the development of hanging skin under her neck, acquired after years of living. June was guessing it would probably be the next item to be repaired and made to look twenty-one again.

June looked left towards the English couple and back to her right as if she was looking for anyone around who might have been using the beach lounger in question. Other than her and the English family, there were no other guests on the resort's expansive beach.

"Yeah, I think so." She felt bad lying, but she just had to do it. She then put her head back on the lounger as if to sleep. She didn't see the waiter smile and then hide his face from overhearing her comment.

"What about these?" The woman in the high-cut suit asked again. Her husband stood by her side, looking on as well. His arms still full of supplies. She was pointing to two other loungers right next to the previous ones.

"No, I think you're okay with those."

June assumed the man was the husband. He had perfect jet black hair and a swimsuit to match his wife's. He had the beach bag, towels, snacks, more magazines, a book on *Latent Economics and the Latent American Male,* and he was wearing dark socks with his sandals. The man and woman both seemed already to be carrying deep tans and when they fell on their loungers next to a table, the dark-brown bottle of baby oil fell out of the beach bag. June thought they could have saved some money and just bought some canola oil. The woman had a thick southern accent. The man hadn't spoken yet. June thought he was waiting to be asked something from the woman—allowing him to speak.

"Hoooney," did you get *my* towel?" She said to the man.

The waiter, the same one who first greeted June, was a few steps away, now standing next to the couple, waiting for them to park themselves so he could leave the drinks and remove himself. June could tell all he wanted to do was leave. He had a serious face on, different from the one he had with her. She assumed he had seen guests like this before, maybe even these guests, and all he wanted to do was leave their presence.

The dog looked at him and yapped then buried his body back in his mother's breasts while he quivered even more.

"Yes, my love-cake. All the way from *Mobile*," as he reached into the beach bag large enough to store and carry four full hams, and pulled out a beach-sized towel picturing Al Pacino in his role as *Scarface*. He looked up at June and nodded then smiled, showing his stark white teeth, June figured, were capped. She recognized the towel, she investigated a found body in the desert, rolled up in the exact same pattern. The death shroud was the killer making a statement. He even bragged about it later to the police snitch they put in his cell after he was booked.

Yep, it makes sense, June thought. *Mobile, Alabama with that accent*. It's far enough south.

The woman said to her assumed husband. "Honey Lamb, will you lotion me? I want to get tan; I don't want to turn in to one of Daddy's saddles."

There it is! June found herself nodding to her own thoughts. *Daddy's saddles. Which means 'Daddy' has horses—plural, and that means money.* June tried to watch, without being too obvious, how the woman was going to negotiate the sand and lounger with her high heels but she had already shed the shoes and was barefoot, while setting up her camp. The English couple were not paying attention to the show, the man had fallen asleep and the woman was reading some book—hardback with no dust jacket. The father's eyes seemed to open once with the shrillness of the dog's bark, then fell closed again.

The voice came from behind June. "Mrs. Hersher?"

She strained to turn around and see who was calling her by name. It was a long thin man she had never seen before. He was chocolate brown and the whites of his eyes and teeth matched his uniformed, starched white short-sleeved shirt. The shirt was adorned with brass emblems and tucked in tight to a pair of navy blue slacks with a wide red stripe down its side. His voice had a Caribbean accent with a flavor of proper British. He had his hat in his hand and from what she could tell from her vantage point, he was carrying a Glock in a polished leather holster on his hip. "Yes?"

"Oh, I am sorry Miss, let me come around here," the man said as he saw June trying to turn in her seat to see him. He walked around so he was standing in front of her. "I am Detective Nicholas L'Claire with the St. Lucia State Police. May I sit down?" he asked gesturing with his hand to a neighboring lounge chair.

The English couple next to her looked over when they heard the word 'police'.

"Please," she said and nodded. She took another sip of her punch then put it down on the side table. She really liked the punch, but thought any more lubricant on her brain pan needed to wait until after her discussion with the police.

The detective moved over and sat on the neighboring lounger, holding his hat with both hands and resting his arms on his knees. "I was informed by the manager you are a homicide detective from the United States."

"Yes, with the Phoenix Police Department in Arizona. What can I do for you?" June had a bad feeling she was going to be asked to go to work. Something she desperately didn't want to do, at least officially.

The Detective smiled and looked down. "Yes, well, I wanted to ask you for a favor."

She could see this conversation leading to the swift completion of her vacation. "Oh, detective, in the States, that sentence would bring frowns. Especially to someone on a vacation, a vacation they just started—today," she said. She pulled her sun glasses down to get her point across.

The officer smiled. "I understand and please believe me when I tell you I would not be here troubling you if it was under almost any other circumstance." The detective paused for a moment before he continued. "We have been called just a short time ago to this resort by the director. He was contacted by a guest who wanted to report her husband missing."

"'Missing'? Not dead, right?"

"No, that is correct."

"What does it have to do with me?" she said. She looked over at the table where her drink was sitting and thought about taking another sip but decided to wait. She could already feel its effects rolling over her cerebellum and making it warm and comfortable like a soft blanket in the winter. *Gosh, I like this drink.* "My cases usually start when the victim stops. If we don't have a body or have a good chance of there being a body, I usually don't get called."

The officer was looking into the well of his cap and nodded. "When we arrived, the wife was almost hysterical. We examined the room and found what we thought were small amounts of blood in the lavatory. When we asked her, she claimed she knew nothing about it. We were then approached by another man, a private investigator, by the name of Macomb McCain. He was hired by the husband's family to follow them here, from their home in Bishop-Stratford, England. It is a small town about an hour outside of London. It is where the husband and extended family are from. They are concerned he married this woman and she wants his money, apparently he is fairly well off. So they hired this McCain fellow to follow them here, on their honeymoon. The private investigator is the one who told us about their background. The husband is seventy-eight and the wife is forty-three. The family is concerned their marriage is not one of love and there might be a more devious nature to the wife's agenda."

"So, let me finish the story," she said, still eyeing her drink. "They come down here, the new wife does away with him, buries his body in the rain forest, claims him missing or dead and eventually inherits his fortune. The P.I. is here to document and report back to the family, who, in lieu of his will giving the young woman everything he owns, they now have grounds to argue the document and get their hands on their respective share. Does that sound about it?"

He nodded his head and smiled. "It seems to be the picture I am getting."

"What does the island's finest want with me?" June said while she looked up and down the beach. The Alabama couple was trying not to look. The husband was busy with laying out towels and setting up their camp. The dog was yipping mixed with a low growl and a spasmodic twitch. It was still nuzzled by the woman who was holding the dog in one hand and allowing her husband to begin the lotion rub application to her other arm. The mother for the proper English couple was still reading, but then realized there was a police officer sitting near her and without showing any desire to eavesdrop, did just that, or at least tried to. Her proper husband began to snore.

The detective looked at the bay then back at June. "I have been a police officer for almost fifteen years. I have worked all types of crimes including murder. Once I found out an American detective was here, it is not beyond me to look for expertise on things. We have not had many homicides and frankly, we have not had one this year for the whole island. I don't want to miss anything and this private detective could prove to be an *issue.*" He said the last part with a look of a metallic taste in his mouth. "I am asking if you would merely look over my shoulder and tell me if what I am seeing might be something."

She dropped her head back on her lounger. "Gee, detective, I really don't think—"

A Cockney voice emanated from behind June on the beach behind her chair. "So, this is the great American homicide detective." June was watching L'Claire as the yet faceless voice spoke. She noticed a look, like a hammer, slapped the detective's face as he looked in the direction of the new voice. It told June the sound was owned by the private investigator in question and not to the liking of the detective.

"I told you Nicky, you don't need no help from any Colony detective. I can supply you with all the expertise you need."

June could see L'Claire watch the man as he stepped around the chair in to her field of view. He was a short man, about five-seven, with a tropical shirt unbuttoned to the third button, shorts pulled up the tip of an abdomen which looked like it had housed too many beers over the years, and black dress shoes with black socks. He wore dark glasses that clipped on to reading glasses and flipped up. On top of the man's head he wore a flowered visor which looked to June, from where she was sitting, like the price sticker was still clipped on the back of it. He wore two gold bracelets on each wrist along with a silver watch band that was too big for his wrist so the watch slid up and down on his forearm every time he raised or lowered his arm. On his left forearm was an old tattoo, about three inches long, depicting a dagger and a cape wrapped around the hilt, the cape appeared to be blowing in a breeze.

The man reached out to shake her hand. "You must be Hersher, I'm Detective Malcolm McCain. I think detective L'Claire and I can wrap this thing up spit spot without bothering your vacation," he said thumbing his finger at Nicholas. "You don't need to trouble your pretty little head about this thing."

If there was one thing which bothered June, was anyone referring to her *pretty little head.* Another thing was shaking the hand of someone soaked in sweat. "It's nice to meet you, Mr.—McCain?"

"McCain, Det. Malcolm McCain," he finished shaking her hand and didn't notice her wipe her own hand on her shorts. He placed both hands on his hips. He flipped up his sunglasses and June could tell his black horned rims were for a man with bad vision. The lenses magnified his eyes like they were sockeye salmon on a salad plate. "Like I told Nicky here, I think with my help, he and I can wrap this polliwog up, sure as Nelson was a sailor. It's pretty obvious foul play was afoot."

June turned to Nicholas who was looking down at his cover in his hands and shaking his head. "'a foot'?"

"Foul play a foot? Yes dear. It's pretty obvious the wifey was behind our boy going over the wall and winding up in a hole in the botanicals. She's been a black widow ever since she crossed his path. No offense, Nicky."

"It's Detective L'Claire and there isn't anything obvious so far with this case. I was talking to the officer here about it and —"

"Look Nick, when you've worked as many homicides as I have, you get a feel for these things, kinda a sick sense. Like a tingling sensation in your all-togethers, if you get me meaning," he broke into laughter and June watched his eyes squint shut. "He's dead and she killed him. Pretty straight forward."

"I didn't see that at all."

"That's what I mean, you didn't see it. What about all the blood in the bathroom?"

Nicholas turned to June. "I mentioned that to you. There were two small drops in the sink and a couple on the floor."

"Huge my good man, its huge! Probably nicked an artery."

June's head was moving back and forth between the two men like she was watching a tennis match. As they spoke, she was able to reach her drink and took a healthy sip. She nodded her head to give the impression she was listening. "Detective from England, huh?"

"That's right dearie, ain't nothin' new here I haven't seen a dozen times before. I've been following these two since before their wedding," he said with both hands on his hips inverted with the thumbs forward. His head was bobbing up and down like it was a bobble head one would put on the dash board of their '65 Ford Fairlane.

June shaded her eyes, "You worked a lot of homicides in England, Malcolm?" She stole another sip. The more she had of this drink, the more she liked it. It also made the conversation between the detective and the private investigator more fun.

Malcolm looked up to the sky and back down with a cock-eyed smirk on his face. "Dearie, let's just say I've worked enough murders to impress a chuckwalla out of its Banyan tree."

There was a pause for a beat of five where no one said anything.

She turned back to the Nicholas. "There you go Detective. There's your expert. This man is able to talk mammals out of large trees." She put her sun glasses on and leaned her head back on the cushion. "By the way Malcolm, what police department did you work for in England?" She asked, already knowing the answer.

"Oh, dearie, there were so many."

"Humor me. If there were a lot, you must have been in high demand. No wonder the family wanted you to follow their daddy and his new wife. You could probably smell his *chuckwallas.*" She looked over at the L'Claire and raised her sun glasses and gave him a quick wink. Nicholas' face was one of pleading until he saw the wink. Then, he had to turn away.

"That's right dearie, got 'em all I have or Bob's yer uncle."

June looked up at Malcolm then at the detective. "Who's Bob?"

"I think he means —" Nicholas started.

"Oi—," Malcolm said.

"I don't have an uncle," June said.

"No, I don't think that's what he —"

"Oi—"

"I don't think I even know a 'Bob,'" June continued, ignoring the interruptions by the private investigator. She was actually distracted by her drink and the pretty pink colors as it clung to the side of the glass. She found herself staring at it as she spoke. She realized her diction seemed to have gotten better, at least in her own mind. "I know a Paul, a Gary, and about five Jose's, but not one Bob."

"I think it's just his way of—," L'Claire continued.

"Oi!" Malcolm said again, stepping in a little closer to get their attention, interrupting the detective. The two turned to look at him. "I'm saying I just have the inside track here. I've been following this man and his slag for a while and I think she moped him then got rid of the body."

"Moped?" June asked. "Why would she use a mop?"

Malcolm rolled his eyes. "Killed, dearie, killed."

"How do you spell that?"

"M O P E D," Malcolm said.

"In the United States, that's a gas-powered bike." June looked at Nicholas. He shrugged his shoulders. "You think she ran him over with a moped? I don't think it would kill a man. It might hurt a bit, but I don't think—"

L'Claire asked "If she killed him and got rid of the body, how did she do it?"

"Like I said before, simple," Malcolm started with a little voice of pride as if he had an answer no one else in the classroom had. "She rolled him up in the carpet and carried him off into the jungle." He stood for a moment as if the answer was as obvious as the day was beautiful.

June looked at Malcolm for a moment then back at Nicholas. "Detective, do these rooms have—"

"No, they don't have any rugs that large none which could cover a man," Nicholas said, shaking his head as he looked down at his hat. His frustration continued to grow. This was an answer already discussed before they arrived at June's lounger. There were probably other questions and answers which had been asked and answered and no one was satisfied with any of the answers.

June looked back at Malcolm. “Mr. McCain—”

“Please, dearie, you can call me Malcolm. May I call you June?”

There was a pause in June’s response while she took a deep cleansing breath. “Sure, why not. Okay, Malcolm,” the detective said. “There isn’t any rug in the room large enough. If there wasn’t any in the room, how did she roll him up in it?”

Malcolm was not to be discouraged. He had an answer. “She found one.”

Nicholas let out an audible sigh while the swing of his shaking head appeared to grow in a wider arc.

“I see,” June said. She turned to Nicholas. “If I turn down your request for assistance, is it my understanding you will be working, some or even exclusively, with Malcolm here?”

Nicholas again nodded his head as he looked down at his hat. “Yes, my Captain wants me to coordinate with the closest representative of the Motherland to maintain good relations and so on. If you are not willing to help, it will just be the two of us.” He looked at her with the eyes of a Bassett Hound.

They were pleading eyes, screaming for help. June had a soft spot in her heart for Bassett Hounds. “Okay, I’m in. But now look fellas, I am here on vacation and I am starting too really like this rum punch of yours. If I drink any more of this, and rest assured I plan to, I will wander down suspect paths that might find me pointing my finger at the Prime Minister. If I see this going nowhere, I am back here doing what my family told me to do—with more rum. Do we understand?” Malcolm looked like he had been kicked in his all-togethers and Nicholas looked like he just won the lottery.

L'Claire said with a smile "That is excellent, really really excellent! Well done!"

Malcolm had his hands on his hips and shaking his head "Dearie, you really don't have too. I got this all under control." He reached up and flicked the sunglasses down on their frames.

June left her head on the lounger. She was having trouble lifting it. "Oh, I know you do, but there are a couple of things. I want to see where your suspect found the carpet to roll up her husband; what this strapping woman must look like, big enough to carry her husband into the jungle rolled in said carpet, all without being seen. And I want to see how someone as astute as you, can sort this thing out. Call it professional development," she said with a smile. "Besides, I might now be able to write this whole trip off on my taxes, being work related and all."

Malcolm's first reaction quickly faded to the perceived complement. "Really? Well then, let's get sorting, dearie!" June looked at Nicholas who was smiling. He now had someone to share the misery.

"If you said 'yes' I was going to ask if you wouldn't mind coming now to look at the scene," Nicholas said while putting his cap on.

June took a deep breath then let it out slowly. She then struggled to get up from her lounger after the drink she was quickly falling in love with. "Malcolm, there's another thing," she stumbled just a bit, the rum finding her brain stem as it migrated to the rest of the body from the base of the cerebellum, where it had found a nice home. She didn't think anyone noticed her slip.

"What's that, dearie?"

"I really don't like being called dearie."

Malcolm frowned at June, as if he didn't understand. "Really? For a police detective, seems to me you're being a little sensitive about the matter, quite." He looked her up and down twice. "I'd think a woman of your age would like a complement thrown at her every now and then, giving you some hope, if you know what I mean. For example, I like your gams. Ya got nice gams," he said with a smile. "Calling you 'dearie' is what I have found women love being called. When I date women back in the motherland— and I date *a lot* of women," he said to her with smile and a wink, pulling up his flip down sunglasses, "They swoon! When I call them 'dearie,' they absolutely swoon." flipping his glasses down again to better punctuate. "Not sure if Detective L'Claire told you any of my background." He looked at the detective and then raised his sunglasses again. "Part of the reason I was hired is I got me a pretty nice reputation with the opposite sex. The ladies call me the 'Dragon Master.'"

June turned her head as far as she could. Her neck was going numb. "Are we still talking women who are part of the mammal gene pool?" June asked. She looked for her towel to wipe off her feet before she stuffed them back in her shoes. Her hand was resting on it as it laid draped on her shoulder where she placed it as she got up, a fact she had so soon forgotten—realizing her hand was on the towel, actually holding the item she was looking for. At the same time, her feet did not have any sensation of the ground. They were numb. She had no feeling of contact with the sand, or much else from what she could tell, from the knees down. She liked it. For a moment, it gave her the sensation of floating.

Malcolm gestured while he spoke. "Oi, was that a dig you Yanks are so known for?" pointing at her with the middle knuckle of his pointer finger. "You're poking the griffin is what you're doing." His head bobbed again in agreement to his own answer.

June turned to Nicholas. "'Gams'?"

"I think he was complementing your legs."

"Oh, sorry, dearie. You got nice *legs*. Especially for a woman your age and, well, occupation. Probably not a lot of fellows throwing themselves at your door step knowing you to be a murder investigator. You always have, that odor. Fear all the blokes have who might be a smidged interested in those gams is ya might got something in a mason jar on the shelf next to the cereal and the bloody lid might not be screwed on too tight. Boy doesn't want to see anything in a jar next to the cereal when he is trying to sneak out after a night of the Queen's loving if you get me drift. No sir, dearie. If you, somehow, get lucky to land a mate in the shallows, you want to be able to net him with a six pound test on a spindle reel. But the jar, those smells—"

"Hey, I bathe." June thought about shooting him, but she left her gun at home and she couldn't feel her trigger finger anyway.

"Seems it would kind of take the sap out of the old maple log, eh what? No worries I bet. You being so busy moving from case to case. Bet ya got no time for herding the sheep through the thistle."

When Malcolm turned his head to sneeze without covering his mouth, June saw Nicholas mouth the words 'I'm sorry' to her.

"Oi—" Malcolm said more out of habit than to get anyone's attention.

June frowned. "Why would he complement me on my—"

"Oi—"

"Why would he pick my legs? And then why wouldn't he just say le—"

L'Claire spoke to June as the three moved off the sand and with L'Claire's direction, towards the villa up the hill. "I'm not sure. I think it's the term for legs in the homeland." The two appeared to ignore the third.

June looked down at her feet and pushed them through the sand.

"Aye," Malcolm said in agreement with Nicholas' definition with a smile. He followed the two police officers up the hill and off the beach.

June made sure she didn't forget her drink. She really liked her drink. She also liked the fact her feet felt like they were walking on air. Only when she got to the warmth of the pool deck did any sensation come back.

As she was walking, she stopped in mid-stride and looked at her watch, walked over to the house phone next to the bar and dialed four numbers. "Hi, this is June Hersher. I need to cancel my spa appointment."

THE CRIME SCENE

Crime doesn't take a holiday, unless of course, it's Columbus Day

—Author

The three of them with June and Nicholas leading the way off the beach with Malcolm following, walked back up to the lobby and from there took one of the resort shuttles up to the villa where the couple was staying. On the way up, June noticed the place was just above her villa, on the almost sheer vertical portion of the mountain holding one of the white plaster villas reflecting something seen out of the Greek isles. She also noticed this was about where she'd heard the sound of voices earlier in the day. June was briefed quickly by the Detective L'Claire and Malcolm as they rode up the hill to the villa.

Nicholas pulled out a note pad. "Mr. Hollingsworth was a self-made, very rich, widower. He made a fortune in textile manufacturing and oil speculation in Scotland. He also pocketed a nice sum from his second wife's death from cancer. He was seventy-eight and had met his new wife at a party thrown by the Minister of Resources."

"You said 'was'," Malcolm said almost in a whisper.

"So?" Nicholas shot back.

"Just thinkin' you might be tinkering on the idea he might have had a gasket blown out 'is 'ead? Eh?" Malcolm none too quietly whispered, "There's the slag," Looking up to the villa as they drove. Malcolm could see, in the corner, next to the French doors leading to the sundeck, a dark-haired woman watching them. It was Frances Jue-Petri Hollingsworth the suspect and newlywed wife of Jonathan Hollingsworth III, the alleged missing husband.

As they arrived at the villa, there were two small police cars outside the door, clinging to the side of the narrow road and one police officer at the front door. The detective approached and gave the names of June and Malcolm to the officer who wrote the names down on a clipboard before the three entered. The villa was actually four floors if you counted the roof top sun deck. It overlooked Labrelotte Bay and on a clear day, the edge of the island of Martinique to the north.

They gathered on the narrow road, just outside the villa. "So, who is this woman?" June asked. She really didn't care to know but it made sense to ask as she looked at a parrot in the tree above her.

"Aye, I got this one Nicky," Malcolm said holding up his hand to the officer. He pulled out his own note pad that looked like it had been dipped in coffee, a faded tan color had crept over the paper. "Frances is forty-one and just coming out of a long term relationship with a Frenchman she had living in her flat in London by the name of Marquis Williams, a self-described fashion designer working for one of the downtown London fashion houses. She met him at a cocktail party, an art gallery opening where Marquis was there with his friend, Jacque, who was showing his art made exclusively of soup cans. They saw each other from across the room and were tingly with desire."

"Wait, how do you know that?" June asked.

"What?" Malcolm said.

"There was tingling? How do you know there was tingling?"

Malcolm shrugged. "Well, he *is* French. They have that effect on women. May I continue?"

"Sure," June said. She forgot by this time what she asked.

Malcolm turned the page. "Marquis had a temper and after his third firing for 'creative differences' as he would call it, Frances decided it was time to call it quits with her French designer. He begged her not to leave him, which initially surprised her since it was her flat and he would be the one leaving. She changed her mind several times, each time Marquis was able to seduce her with his French ways as well as a newly designed blouse and silk skirt with its own *'signerie'* he would say in French. She had packed one of those particular skirts, the last of the Marquis designs for her, for this trip she liked it so much, avoiding telling her new husband where it was from. Marquis had a look he used and with his one, dark eyebrow, he could break her down to forgive him with tears. This was always followed by physical gratification, usually ending on the kitchen table among the freshly washed cantaloupe. She was paying for everything on her administrative secretary salary as she also worked in the Ministry of Resources, while he continued to promise her the buyers just didn't understand his level of design. After all, there was the *singerie.* It was truly a relief the first night she was in her flat alone. There wasn't a need, anymore, to save soup cans."

"You're making this crap up," June said. She had stopped looking at the parrots when Malcolm mentioned 'freshly washed cantaloupe.'

Malcolm didn't stop. "There were rumors Frances, the skank that she appears to be, also supplemented her income working as an exotic dancer at a high end strip club called The Kitty Cat Club, where she went by the name of 'Blaze' and specialized in pole dancing upside down, but I couldn't confirm it as I expanded my search by going to every strip joint on the east end as well as countless hours at the club itself. Marquis, between jobs, would earn a little cash being a step dancer and part time mime. But even his French aura couldn't buy him a third trip home to her. His anger sealed the deal and Frances had found herself living in her flat—alone, and she discovered she liked it, until she met Jonathan at the party."

June had gone back to the parrots and the flowers and Nicholas was talking to one of the officers. No one appeared to be actively listening to Malcolm. So, he continued his narrative.

"Jonathan, Mr. Hollingsworth, saw her standing at the fruit tray in the buffet line at the aforementioned party and made his way over to her. The introductions were slow but kind, and Frances found herself listening to him—listen to her. His eyes said he cared, his voice confirmed it. She couldn't remember how it happened—he was that good—that suave, but she found herself giving him her number for him to call. She wasn't looking for a date. She found herself very content in her flat, overlooking Camden Square, at the top of Hampstead Heath. She was very content. He was older than she—by decades, but she didn't seem to care and he seemed to enjoy the idea. There were two dates of kindness and fun. She laughed until at one point, she had to excuse herself to the restroom. On the third, however, she wanted him. She took him, landing him like a salmon in a hand net. It was then Frances found out Jonathan Hollingsworth the III, was a kind man, an older man, a fun man who 'knew things'. New, wonderful, fulfilling things of tenderness and compassion, filled in between with naughtiness, teasing, guava jelly and the perfect cup of tea in the morning. She had never traveled to Mars before. But in Jonathan's arms, she went there—every time." He finished his narrative and looked up.

June just starred at Malcolm. "You ever write letters to those naked magazines?"

Malcolm didn't understand what she meant. "Sometimes, why?"

June looked over at Nicholas who was wiping his own brow. She wasn't quite sure how much she remembered of the details given with the spiced rum punch kicking the crap out of her cognitive abilities. She remembered words like *naughtiness* and *things* and tried to make a mental note about coming back to the island to figure out the guava jelly. She also was kind of stuck on the age difference between the two newlyweds. She had found herself doing the math in her head and with her finger on the handrail that led to the front door from the road to figure out the difference in ages between the two. Because of the rum, she had to do the math several times, each time ending in confusion, just before starting the equation over again, drawing the outline of numbers on the white-painted wooden rail, but seeming with every breath, she found herself carrying the one and then needing to erase what she had written and started over.

She was more concerned about how she presented herself as she arrived at the scene. From the outside, she looked fine, at least she thought so. She did still have the big blue towel draped over her shoulder and had forgotten it was there. The feeling in her shoulder turned off, adding to the growing list of body parts beginning to lose their ability to feel and thereby work the way god had intended them to work.

They entered on the main floor consisting of the living room, its own private pool, and a step up kitchen. At the far end was a wall of windows open to an unobstructed view of the Caribbean. The villa contained a half bath just around the corner from the kitchen and a wrap around sun deck connecting the small plunge pool to the sunbathing area overlooking the bay. The living room was tiered with the dining area and kitchen on the upper tier and the living room sitting area on the lower level overlooking the deck and pool as well as the expansive tropical view west over the Caribbean. The interior was white stucco with soft brown Saltillo tile covering the floor and adjoining stairs. The furniture was overstuffed floral set in tropical white wicker. Tables and walls were adorned in paintings and vases depicting the islands and island life. The adjoining kitchen was modern with stainless steel appliances and white ceramic tile counters inlaid with granite. Two steps down connected the dining area to the sitting area. They were also in Saltillo each inlaid with a small square ceramic tile with a parrot painted on it. June looked around the room and found lots of parrots in the room, paintings of parrots, curtains with parrots, coasters with parrots, parrots hiding in the fake silk plants.

From the same main entrance, a set of stairs went down one level while another set went up to a master suites on each floor, complete with their own bath and sun decks on the upper and lower floors. The upper bedroom connected via an outside stairwell, to the fourth floor sundeck. The suite was impeccably kept, as if a maid had just finished cleaning for the day. A part of June was a little jealous Aunt Eleanor didn't buy one of these units. *She had to have seen these. Why wouldn't she pick this one or one like it? I mean, don't get myself wrong—that's funny—what I just said to myself—'don't get myself wrong.' That was funny. Sometimes I can be really funny. Or is it the rum punch? Maybe I just think I'm funny and people laugh when I say something funny and they think they need to laugh so I don't get upset they didn't think I was funny. Geez, there I go again with myself. 'You should be a stand-up comedian June.' No, I shouldn't. I know I'm not that funny and I'm just funny now because I'm think-talking to myself. My voice sounds funny when I do this—deeper, like in a cave—Hello? Hello? I never think-talk unless I'm drinking, this punch. God I love this drink! Where was I? What are we doing? Hey, what a nice painting on that wall of a parrot!*

She was working on focusing on the events in the room. The rum punch warmed her whole body. It had moved from her brain stem and made her skull feel warm besides making her feet numb as well as other general body parts. She tried to make a mental note to order more of the drink as well as a concern she could, by the end of the week, have a real, legitimate drinking problem she would need to seek help with when she returned to Phoenix.

Frances spoke as she walked across the room to greet the three as they entered. "Detective," she directed her greeting to Nicholas. She was tall, about five nine, a good two inches taller than Malcolm, with long dark hair, deep chocolate brown skin and crystal green eyes. Her white teeth almost glowed. She was in a crimson red one-piece bathing suit, with a deep 'V' cut top accentuating her very large, credit card-purchased breasts, and a beach wrap split up to her hip. She wore high heels making her the tallest thing in the room. The woman was within two years of June and looked half June's age. "Have you discovered where my Johnny is?"

she said wringing her hands. The long, polished nails got in the way with each other and made a clicking sound as she rubbed her hands together. She was from St. Lucia and still had a noticeable creole accent under a fine layer of proper English.

"No, Mrs. Hollingsworth, not yet. However, we are working diligently. We are in luck to have an American detective also staying at the resort and she has volunteered to help. Mrs. Hollingsworth, this is Detective June Hersher."

June walked over to the woman, almost falling from the step she didn't see. The ceramic parrot design in the tile step was supposed to help people see the step. She was sure the punch had nothing to do with it and that no one noticed. Somehow, the towel stayed on her shoulder—the same towel she had forgotten was even there. *Gosh, that drink was good, and why would they put a step there? Oh look, another nice painting!* June shook Frances' hand and looked the wife over as Frances walked up to her. June found herself immediately jealous. *I need to get to the gym.*

Malcolm cleared his throat, catching the attention of Nicholas.

"Oh, yes, right. I suppose you might already know private investigator Malcolm McCain." Malcolm didn't walk up to shake the woman's hand. He simply nodded his head with his hands folded in front of him.

Frances looked coldly at Malcolm. "Oh, yes. The man who's been following us since before our wedding," Frances said with an air of coldness.

Malcolm frowned. "What do you mean, following you? I have no idea what you are talking about," he said with a short nervous laugh, looking at the detective and June, who never looked his way.

"You were in the bushes outside our window last night. Johnny saw you. It is why in our love-making, he said we should not have the sheets on, to give you a show like in London. We always saw you in the elm tree across the street from Johnny's flat. You were always on that lower branch with your binoculars, watching us. Johnny always wanted to leave the curtains open so you could, you know, enjoy yourself. He felt sorry for such a lonely ma—"

Malcolm nervously snickered while looking back and forth between his two new colleagues. "I assure you, Detectives, I have no idea what she is talking about. I'm not lonely. I have friends, lots of friends. I go to the pub and stay until it closes almost every ni--"

"It's alright," Nicholas said as he raised his hand to stop Malcolm. "Mrs. Hollingsworth, I brought Detective Hersher here for another look to see what might or might not have happened. If you don't mind," Nicholas spoke with all the manners of a well-schooled Englishman. Malcolm just rolled his eyes.

While Nicholas spoke he looked at his new colleague. June was walking around and looked at the villa. He smiled, seeing the American detective, already at work.

June slowly walked around with her hands behind her back and was sizing up what she didn't have. *Why is this place bigger than mine? How do I get to stay in one of these places? Oh look at that vase! That's a nice vase! It can go with the parrot picture.* "Mrs. Hollingsworth, I am confident the St. Lucia Police will move heaven and earth to find your husband—?"

"Jonathan. I call him 'Johnny' or 'the mad bovine' in our more intimate moments," she said as she combed the underside of her long hair with her fingers.

The room was very quiet for a moment.

"'When was the last time you saw your husband?" June asked, still eyeing the vase. *I would really like that vase. Where would I put it? I could keep candy in it next to my bed! No, that can't be a good spot.*

"Like I told these officers over here, we fell asleep in each other's arms last night. Actually, it was early this morning. Mr. McCain can attest to that. He was in that bush right there." She pointed to a group of bougainvillea's, directly in line with their bedroom window.

"Aye," he hesitated. "Maybe I can vouch for myself. Bastard bushes cut me like a Slovak consonant." Malcolm said, nodding his head.

Nicholas looked at the man then back to Mrs. Hollingsworth.

June kept looking at the vase.

Mrs. Hollingsworth looked at the P.I. and frowned before she continued. "I fell asleep and when I woke this morning, he was gone. I thought he might have gone for a walk but when he didn't come back for several hours, I got terrified something might have happened to him. Maybe he's fallen and can't get help. He is in wonderful shape. I can attest to that, but he is, well, mature. I feel like something might have happened to him. I understand they have deadly vipers here. Maybe one of them fell out of a tree and—I don't want to think about it!"

June was stroking the lip of the vase. *Do you suppose they would miss it? Would it fit in my suitcase?* "Mrs. Hollingsworth, were you and your husband having an argument this morning?" June didn't look at the woman. Not because June didn't want to, but because her eyes had gotten lost in the sparkly shiny object of the vase like a hypnotist using a watch.

Mrs. Hollingsworth straightened up. Her arms wrapped around her indicating defense. “Why—how did you know?”

June didn’t respond. Not because she didn’t want to, but because she had forgotten what she had just asked.

Mrs. Hollingsworth continued without an answer. “Well, if you must insist, I did talk to him this morning. We woke and when I looked up at him, as I was snuggling him, wrapped around him in our naturalness, he had a look of thought. I asked him what he was thinking about, what was on his mind. He said it was nothing important.”

Malcolm whispered to Nicholas. “Ya sure it wasn’t the rat poison you slipped in his cereal and he is now rowing his boat to the other side of the River Styx?”

June looked over at Nicholas and Malcolm, missing what was said, but she figured it was the private detective who probably said something inappropriate by the look on Nicholas’ face.

“He was distant and I asked him what was wrong. He just got out of bed. I followed him to the kitchen. He finally said nothing was wrong, took my face in his hands and kissed me. I could tell he was upset. I could see it in his face. I was upset he was upset so I went back to bed. When I woke, he was gone.”

“Pish posh,” Malcolm said under his breath.

June heard Malcolm’s comment and was quickly becoming annoyed with him waking her from her coma. It was a nice coma. “What does that mean?” She asked Malcolm, quickly forgetting others were in the room.

“What?” Malcolm said with a questioning look.

"'Pish posh,'" she said.

"It's just something I say."

She nodded. If he could read her mind, he could tell she wanted him to stop talking and with the rum on board, if he stopped breathing, it would be even better. The more the rum punch worked on her, if he could read her mind even further, he might read she wanted him on a leaking raft about a half mile out to sea surrounded by sharks, but she wasn't sure he could read the paper let alone her mind.

A voice from one of the first officers on the scene in the corner of the main floor called Nicholas. "Lieutenant," "Could you come here sir?" The three detectives walked over and looked. The officer pointed to the floor. "Do you want us to sample this, sir?" The officer said, pointing at drops of what looked like blood on the floor in front of the pedestal sink with a two drops in the sink. It was the blood they wanted June to look at.

Malcolm started, looking between the arms of the police officers standing in front of him "Just as I thought," he began in a slight whisper. "F*oul play.* She probably slit his throat and then buried him up in these hills somewhere," gesturing with his hands to the sloped hills outside. "If we looked around, we'd probably find his *twigs and berries* stuffed in an envelope as a memento of her kill, stowed away in her hat box, the She Devil!"

"What?" Nicholas said.

"'She Devil'?" June said.

"Do you not understand the English Language, my dear?" Malcolm said to June.

"Bad form," Nicholas said as he looked back into the room. "This is what we were talking about," he said pointing at the drops on the floor to June. "What do you think?"

"Well, that is blood. We'd need to test it to see if it's our vic or someone else's." June said as she turned back into the room just as Mrs. Hollingsworth walked up and looked.

"Oh, no, is that from Johnny? Is that my Johnny's blood?"

"We don't kn—" Nicholas started.

"As if you didn't know," Malcolm said.

"Mr. McCain," June said. She felt the pleasant buzz begin to wane and reality fill its place. She liked where she was and didn't want to come back to the reality which was her life, finding her here on this island as a homicide investigator. It was making her angry along with the towel continuing to slide from her shoulder. She tried putting it on the other shoulder, thinking there was less of a slope on that one.

Mrs. Hollingsworth clutched her chest. "You think I—"

Malcolm smirked. "I've thought that since I found out you were a pole dancer off of Piccadilly Squ—"

Nicholas interrupted. "Mister McCain. That will be enough for now," he said with the look on his own face of sheer frustration. He looked back for June. She was looking out the window leading to the private pool under a very large bread fruit tree. He figured she was thinking through the case, listening to the evidence and conversations, maybe seeing something outside which might impact the case. He decided to let her focus. He had never worked with an American detective before. He had heard they were the best, somewhat quirky, but could see things normally not visible to the common eye. Nicholas had a lot of respect for them and gave her all the room she needed to work. He didn't know she was wondering what kind of tree she was looking at and wondering if it would grow in her back yard at home.

He was an observer, Nicholas was. He got along with his peers, he was smart, educated by St. Lucian standards, and found himself on the promotion list early. He loved his job, no two cases were the same and the opportunity to get to work with a real American homicide detective was a chance of a professional lifetime to fine tune his own skills.

June was distracted, again. A bird was singing happily outside, brightly colored beautiful birds the size to fit neatly in the palm of her hand, hitting soft notes on a scale adding whispers of sound to the palate of this place. The bird's song was taking the anger away and back to the happy place she was just before Malcolm spoke. She frowned at the last note. It seemed squelched, ending a song prematurely. "Detective Hersher?"

She heard her name and turned around, the blue beach towel starting to slide off her shoulder, again. "Oh, yes, sorry." June addressed Mrs. Hollingsworth, "Ma'am, we need to properly search your villa. The officers need to take some samples of the material on the floor as well as anything else. Will it be all right with you?"

"Yes, yes, of course. Whatever you need to do," she said, ringing her long, gorgeous hands. June looked down at her own hands. The nails were short and worn, like she wrestled cows for a living. June couldn't remember the last time she wore polish. She carried a scar from a rope burn when she was fourteen trying to lasso one of Dad's mares. *It almost took the finger off,* she thought as she rubbed her ring finger on her left hand where the scar could still be seen just behind the wedding ring. She still wore the ring.

There was also a crescent-shaped bite mark on June's right hand where Antagonis Rucker, a self-described cowboy rapper, bit her as she tried to handcuff him. It was early in her career while she was still in uniform and after her and her partner were called to a bar fight down in the Deuce before the deuce was bulldozed and restaurants and high-rise apartments went in, before it was renamed, 'The Deuce'. She still remembered the smell of the bar in the lobby of the Hotel Harrison, a combination of stale garlic and old urine. Antagonis was in the middle of hitting some man passed out on the floor for what looked like a series of blows when he looked up and saw the two officers. She was the closest to him, so the man headed for her with drunk rage in his eyes.

She took a step forward and gave him a knuckle strike to the throat.

Somewhere in the flood of the polyester pile on, a wave of blue shirts pouring in like a foamy tide on a pink beach- somewhere, June's hand got too close to Antagonis' mouth in the cuffing process and he bit down on the only meat he could find. Another officer booted him in his forehead, breaking his grip of his teeth on her hand.

June got tetanus shots and tested for AIDS. She remembered it was a long night followed by another long year, waiting for the AIDS final.

Antagonis got booked and released in six hours. Three years later another downtown unit found him dead under a dump truck. He had passed out and slid under the truck for shelter. The next day, the driver, not knowing there was a human under the rig he was driving, got in, started up, and promptly and accidently drove over Antagonis' head.

She has gorgeous hands. I bet if she got bit she wouldn't have gorgeous hands, June thought. She looked at the woman again, her long legs, her beautiful body and deep eyes on a frame not much different from her own only looking more fit. *Maybe she would.*

While the other officers searched, Nicholas and June stood on the pool deck and talked about the evidence or lack of evidence and what they wanted to look for. Malcolm wandered into the kitchen and looking around, writing something down on a note book, the pen appearing to fail. With a frown, he finished on a small white board in the kitchen after he wiped off its small space with a paper towel. He wrote on it as if he was doing a calculation then talking to himself and writing something down again with another pen he found in his pocket on a small spiral note pad he forgot he kept in another pocket. The small pad looked like it had lived in that pocket for a long time.

June whispered. "I'm not sure you have a murder here."

Nicholas responded. "I have to say I'm not seeing much either; however, a little bird keeps chirping in my ear that there is one. Then, there is the blood or what looks like blood, on the floor."

June looked over Nicholas' shoulder at Malcolm who had returned from the kitchen and was trying to look inconspicuous at not hearing what the two were saying by tending to the silk flowers on the table and picking them up and smelling them. "What about him? Is he the chirping bird? Your boss is saying you got to work with him?" June said.

Nicholas saw her look and glanced that way himself. "Yes, a very large, nasty, squawking bird. I have to tell you, I truly appreciate your help. I know this is not something you wanted to do on holiday." He looked around again. "Do you think she carried him out of here and buried him in the jungle like Mr. McCain alluded to?"

June shrugged her shoulders, "No, I don't think so." She said as she helped the towel to settle back on her shoulder. She looked back at Malcolm and saw him sniff the fake roses again and watched his eyebrows go up as if he liked their smell. Mrs. Hollingsworth had moved a few steps away and had taken a phone call on her cell. "Besides, she couldn't get him out of here without help. She looks strong but her hands, her nails, she hasn't worked a day in her adult life, at least not standing up and not recently. If she did get him out of here she would have signs on her—somewhere.

Malcolm chimed in from just inside the door. "This place is as full of accomplices as a Limey pub on a holiday."

"Like?" June said. She knew the wife could probably hear and was listening. She didn't care. June now wanted her nails done to look just like the wife's. Somehow, Mrs. Hollingsworth III had quickly become her mentor, a benchmark to reach or to at least try to reach. It was like looking at a department store catalog. You see a blouse or a dress on the model and you want to look just like them. You know you're not going to look like the beautiful model who is one-third your age and half your weight on a diet of small carrots and a broth made of grass clippings, but you want to try.

Malcolm said, gesturing with his hand as if he was waving off a flock of geese "Like half the clientele at this god-forsaken place. A place like this is the perfect place to get rid of some poor sort, especially one as transfixed on such a black widow as Mr. Hollingsworth was of his new wife." He spoke those last words as if he was spitting vile. "She could get anyone to help her, once she got her talons into them. Anyone, all are suspects. I just need to figure out who. Once you two could see what she could do behind these windows, well, you would agree with me."

"Did it involve talons?" June mumbled under her breath.

"We just need to figure out what happened to Mr. Hollingsworth," Nicholas said. "We are conducting the inquiry."

"Who?" Malcolm frowned.

"We."

"Who is 'we'?"

"We—we, the St. Lucia Police," Nicholas said as he tapped his chest.

"I think there is a restroom you can use over there," Malcolm said pointing to the half bath next to the kitchen.

"Why?"

"I thought you needed to—"

"Gentlemen," June interrupted. "I think my work is done here, at least for today. Take a sample of the blood, pictures, if there is a razor or comb he might have used, and hers as well. Ask the neighbors if they heard anything. Who do you use to process your evidence, like DNA?" she asked.

Nicholas took in a deep breath. "That's part of the problem. We have a crime lab here but the nearest DNA lab is Miami. We express mail it there, but it still takes weeks for a response."

Malcolm was shaking his head. "Why do we need DNA? It's either hers or his and why would it be hers? There isn't a cut on her?" Malcolm said. His face contorting into a look one would see on a man just a few hours after finishing week old sushi on a summer Cambodian night.

Nicholas sighed. "Mr. McCain, we don't even know if it is either of theirs. It could be from the maid, or a prior guest."

Malcolm answered with his fists on his hips, "Well, that's just bad housekeeping," realizing his evidence might not be evidence.

"In fact," June started, winking at Nicholas, "you should ask Frances Hollingsworth if she is menstruating." Her face was stone-cold as she looked at Malcolm.

Malcolm's face flushed. "Ask her—"

"If she's menstruating. It could be her menstrual blood in there. Or, maybe she cut her legs shaving. I'm sure with all the cases you've worked, the issue has come up a time or two."

Malcolm swallowed hard. Both June and Nicholas could see his very large Adam's apple move. "How, ah, how do you spell that?" He said trying to find an empty page in his notebook then shaking his head. "Well, I think that is a job for the police department. I don't think I should be involved in the direct interrogation of the suspect."

Nicholas said, "Oh, no, I'm fine with it, Mr. McCain. You can ask her. We could tie up that loose end right now, shut the door on that point, so to speak."

Malcolm dropped his head and turned towards Mrs. Hollingsworth who was standing on the far side of the room, looking out the window towards the bay and still talking on the phone.

Mrs. Hollingsworth seemed visibly upset. She saw Malcolm approach with his fedora in his hand. June and Nicholas couldn't hear what Malcolm said to her, but

Malcolm's back was to them and the wife turned to face him as he approached. She looked down to close the phone as he began to speak. They could see her face from where they stood. He gestured with his hand towards the restroom and she covered her mouth in astonishment, her one dark continuous eyebrow clumped in the middle, as the question was asked. Her facial expression gave June and Nicholas their enjoyable answer. Frances Hollingsworth spoke in a low voice, still not loud enough for the two detectives to hear until the end. "No, Mr. McCain, I am not," was the only part of the conversation the two heard.

Malcolm nodded to the woman and then returned to L'Claire and June. "She said 'no' to the mensta thing. She also said she does all her shaving in the master bath room. Her husband," he swallowed hard again. "Her husband likes to watch and sometimes help," Malcolm said.

That must be one of those 'things' her husband is known for, June thought. "Well, thanks for clarifying it for us. The DNA test will do the same thing but it speeds things up," June said. "If you get anything else, need any more help, I guess you know how to get a hold of me. I will be around." With that, she adjusted the towel on her shoulder and flipped one end of it around her neck like a feathered boa. As she left the main floor and headed back up to the driveway, she heard Malcolm talking to Nicholas.

"Anyone with a pair of sticks and fruit, she could get anyone with a wink and a nod to help. Not a doubt in my mind."

Malcolm was right about one thing, June thought to herself. If Mrs. Hollingsworth wanted to, she could probably get anyone to help her with just a look. She had seen suspects with equal innocence in their eyes turn out to be sociopaths. Her body language was an indicator of a woman desperately worried about her husband. But could also be an indicator of a devious player. June hated the idea of Malcolm being anything close to right. That fact made June cringe more than the wife being a killer. If she was a killer, she was a stone cold murderess. If she was the killer, she would not stop with her husband to get what she wanted. Whatever it was, probably his personal fortune, however much that was. June had seen murders over ownership rights to a half used cigarette pack.

June walked back towards the front and the driveway beyond. By the time she got to the front drive and the shuttle waiting for her, June had a headache. She got the shuttle driver to take her back to the hotel lobby, still slinging the blue towel around her neck. She wondered if the headache would ever leave or if this would be the state of affairs for the rest of the week. She decided she needed some medication for it and wondered what the shortest route was to the Jammers Bar for some medicinal spiced rum punch and maybe a plate of French fries, 'chips' they were called here, all with the British influence.

She walked through and then out the lobby and across the patio by the pool. She decided she might want to find the corner seat all cops sit in at any bar, mark her territory with napkins and empty drink glasses, and spend the rest of the day right at that stool and watch the sun set and her brain stem go numb—again.

As she climbed the two steps up to the bar before crossing to her seat, June didn't notice the mottled colored tail slither back under one of the yellow hibiscus bushes surrounding the mango tree which rose magnificently over the bar and pool, leaving three colorful feathers on the walkway just before June passed. In a second, the bush had shrouded the thing so it could finish its new meal in peace.

THE RUSSIANS
AND
THE PROPER BRITSH COUPLE

Knowledge is of no value unless you put it in to practice
-Anton Chekhov

The next day, when June came down to her chosen seat at the bar, the Russians—a mid-thirtyish couple named Natasha and Boris, were already there. They sat at a table in the bar. The fact was they were South African with South African passports, but no one bothered to ask about them, not just yet, which was part of the reason for the confusion of them being Russian with such traditional Russian names. The two had been married for three years and ran an insurance company out of their den in Johannesburg, specializing in recreational vehicle policies. Neither knew a thing about Russia beyond finding it on a map.

The couple was in deep conversation, sitting at a corner table across from June's roost, on the other side of the restaurant, occasionally interrupted by the now incessant yapping of the American couple's Yorkie on the beach. Boris looked past the raven-haired Natasha and frowned in the direction of the dog, which was now sporting a little red and green doggy vest.

June was hoping she was early enough to get the corner stool on the end of the bar and was visibly happy when she discovered she was. Of course, it was breakfast time and there were not a lot of drinkers at that time of day. Realizing a victory with the empty bar stool, she now tried to figure out how to claim it for her own personal use entire stay. She began to think of the possibilities for the week. She didn't care who was there, at the bar, or even the resort. All she knew it was just her, her chair, maybe some magazine reading time, a nap—*god, how long since I had a nap? Wait, I had one on the first day. Okay, so how long has it been since I've had two naps?* She was beginning to get excited about those simple things.

She had her towel, a *Cosmo* and *People* magazine. She got them in the Miami airport and tucked them into her bag to read on the beach. She wanted to read the article about '*What Men Want and When They Want It*' in one magazine and about the new Prince of England in the other. She had skirted the pool and stopped off at Jammers and ordered her drink from Stefan and sat at the corner stool while she waited for it.

June heard the voices, it was too late to hide from the two men not so much Nicholas, but he would not be around if it wasn't for Malcolm. They had spotted her before she could flee. She looked at either side of her seat as if for a place to hide. There was none. So, she sat in her seat and waited for her order, focusing on the far end of the bar. She thought if she didn't look in their direction, she wouldn't be sucked in to their world. The only thing she wanted to suck on was the straw to her rum punch, in her lounger, on the beach, in the soft sand, under the shade of the coconut tree-shaped umbrella, before the true breakfast hour.

As they entered the area where June sat, they were already in a conversation the last part she was just starting to hear. "...really, I saw them yesterday," Malcolm told Nicholas walking passed June, sitting down at the bar two stools away and around the corner turn of the bar on June's end, while tilting his head in the Russian's direction as the two men sat across the restaurant from where the young couple was sitting. Malcolm pretended to drink tea he had brought with him from his room and looked at the breakfast menu he picked up from its holder on the bar. It was upside down.

Nicholas, again in full uniform, knew he just didn't want to be where he was, at this point in time, in his career, with this man.

Malcolm glanced over at Boris and Natasha again before he spoke. "They were seen talking to the Hollingsworth couple the day before the old man disappeared right over there, just beyond where they're sitting now. Then, when the Hollingsworth couple left, they had a whispered conversation about our victim and his skank," Malcolm continued. Eventually, he could tell the words on the menu didn't make sense so he turned it to its right side.

"How do you know they had a whispered conversation about the Hollingsworth's if they were whispering? That does not make them suspects," Nicholas said. He looked at June with a face reflecting his hard morning.

"I can read *whisper* lips," Malcolm said with a serious look on his face.

Nicholas frowned at Malcolm's words as he glanced at June, not quite understanding what the man said. June was in a stare, focused on the far end of the bar. If he didn't know better, Nicholas would have described her as catatonic. "You mean, you can read lips?" he said back to Malcolm.

"Aye, I can do that as well. No, I said I can read 'whisper lips'. I studied it in Nepal with the llamas."

"You studied lip reading with the Dahli Llama?"

"Well, not necessarily with him, just the regular llamas. They all whisper, you know. Very hush hush society."

"So, you read their 'whisper lips'?"

"Aye."

"And what did their lips say?"

Malcolm looked from side to side to see if anyone was looking at him. "I'm not exactly sure. They're Russians, so they were speaking, you know, Russian."

"The llamas are Russians?"

"No. The Russians are Russians."

Nicholas just nodded. He was in pain and just wanted this man to stop talking. "Are you sure they are Russian? They could have been from the Ukraine. They are different in the Ukraine, or how about Siberia? Moscow, now there is a dialect!" Nicholas said while counting each region on his fingers. Malcolm nodded as if he agreed. Nicholas was sure the look he was seeing on the man's face was one of an overloaded brain pan trying to figure out where or what the word 'Ukraine' meant.

June tried to ignore their conversation. The whisper lips story was intriguing, but only because she had never heard of whisper lip reading and spent two minutes thinking about it while she waited for her drink. Once the drink arrived, she just wanted to get to her lounge chair in the sand.

"Have you seen them around?" Malcolm asked.

Nicholas glanced over his shoulder at the Russians. "No, I have not. Why?"

Malcolm frowned as if Nicholas' admission was a sign of an amateur. "They have all the markings of criminals. He is as hairy as a jackanapes in the wintertime while she, well, she is a seductress with her one eyebrow and high cheekbones, a trained observer can just tell. There was a woman similar to her in a little pub in Slough, a quaint little hamlet full of taints like her. She looked very similar to that one only missing both her upper front incisors. She was a seductress that one, with her ability to suck olives down her windpipe without unclenching her teeth." Malcolm was staring in thought. "One time, she did this thing with her big toe, some marmalade, and a straw which made me arch me back and—"

Nicholas, now desperate, "Is that how you tell if they are criminals? Hair on the back and a big face?" "And frankly, one eye brow doesn't do it for me."

"Then you have never dated a Yorkshire wench!" Malcolm's eyes twinkled. "Crazy! Like a Nubian lioness. Every time, Nicky, every time the hair and the close set eyes give them away. They're like jaguars, ready to pounce on you like a Serengeti safari," he said with a wry smile.

The sound of the American couple's dog yapping caused the two men to look in the direction of the new sound. The wife was nuzzling her dog while she wore another one piece, sequined, leopard print suit, but different in color. The husband was addressing her two-towel need on her lounger and talking to the waiter about the wife's desire for more ice in her drink. She was wearing a pair of sandals which gleamed in the sun light.

June said as they looked towards the American. "Do I want to know what you two are talking about?" Nicholas made eye contact first and started to shake his head.

"Of course you do," Malcolm started. "You wanted to know how we are so successful with our investigations in the U.K., take note. We're talking about the influx of commies into our picture of murder and debauchery here. There are Ruskies on the island!" he said as he looked to his left and then to his right, his voice slightly lowered as if the secret was enough.

"Ruskies? You mean Russians?" June asked, trying to make the connection. She also realized it would be a good time to get several rum punches on board before her rescheduled massage later in the day. She ordered the drink while the bartender gave her the breakfast menu. She paused for a moment about what time it actually was, whether she should just stay put at the bar, actually try to finish her trek to the beach and set up camp, as well as the fact she was drinking hard liquor before her breakfast chips.

Malcolm nodded. "Exactly. I was just explaining to old Nicky here we have Russian spies staying at the resort. Russian spies, in the middle of a murder investigation, isn't a coincidence."

Nicholas said forcibly. "And again, I ask, how do you know they are spies or even Russian?"

"I'll do you one better," June started. "Who cares? Spies need vacations too." She made eye contact with Stefan who came over and took her order. She thought about breakfast, then decided she would just drink it. "Besides, was Mr. Hollingsworth worthy of the Russians following and doing away with him clear down here? If he was, there was bigger stuff in this show than just a marriage of—whatever this is."

Nicholas said to Malcolm. "Go on, tell her what you told me."

The bartender handed June her drink, "Geezus this can't be good." She took two quick sips and told the waiter she wanted another. It was not quite nine in the morning. June looked down and Malcolm was now wearing sandals with his black socks.

"Gladly," Malcolm said and laid his fedora on the bar. He looked around again before he spoke in another hushed and guarded tone. "I think they could be after the swag."

June took another sip. "Swag? What the hell is a swag? You think they could be after Mrs. Hollingsworth?"

Malcolm nodded looking left and right—again.

June stirred the rum off the bottom of what was left of her drink. "How does it affect your murder investigation of Mr. Hollingsworth if Russian spies are after Mrs. Hollingsworth?"

Nicholas' head was bouncing back and forth between the two.

"I'm not quite sure. I have to noodle that for a wee bit. But my venture is she was their only competition and they had to eliminate her."

June just stared. "You didn't sleep much last night did you?"

Malcolm squinted his eyes in curiosity. "No, how did you know?"

"You have got to be high," June said with a look of amazement. "Do you take any prescription medication?"

Unfazed, Malcolm followed the question after some thought. "No, no, nothing except the wee drams as I close down the pubs and the occasional little blue pill if you get my meaning, dearie." And with that, Malcolm made himself openly laugh—hard. "Get it? The little blue pill. You might be a bit surprised this man in front of you is a bit of a hound in the homeland."

"Must be at night while hanging from a tree as everyone sleeps," June mumbled in her glass.

"What's that, dearie?" Malcolm said with an upbeat tone, unaware of June's meaning.

"I was just acknowledging your blue pill use. Bet they can't keep enough on the shelf for you."

"Well, I might just add—"

Nicholas interrupted. “Can we get back on the subject at hand,” frustration and fatigue in his voice. “Mr. McCain, you have no information leading to the involvement of our visitors and I do not want you to voice your opinions in public, or frankly, anywhere. When it comes to our guests, all are our friends until proven otherwise. Do I make myself clear?”

“But—”

“Do I make—”

“The slag has—”

“Clear?”

“Accomplices. Ruskies!”

“Ah-hum?”

“Commies.”

“We call them ‘guests’. Well paying, meaning to have fun, ‘guests’. Are we clear, sir?” Malcolm adjusted his hat with a ‘humpfed’ noise as he turned on his heels heading for the beach. Nicholas turned towards June who had finished her first punch and was just putting her lips to the next. “That man will kill me,” Nicholas said.

June nodded. “That man is a piece of work. Careful though, he might be right. I’ve seen homicides with less evidence.” She took her first sip of the drink from the straw almost pure Bounty Rum. The brand the islands were famous for.

“Do you now think there is anything to what he is saying?” Nicholas asked, watching Malcolm walk away.

“Ruskies?” June said through her straw. “I mean Russians? God, he’s got me saying it now.”

“Yes.”

“Who cares? You’re not even sure if you have a crime, let alone a murder. The husband just went missing. There could be a lot of reasons other than that wife of his killed him. For all we know, he could be out for a walk—a long walk mind you, but still."

"Let me ask you this," Nicholas said as he put his hat on the bar. The bartender delivered a glass of ice water and with the humidity, the outside of the glass appeared wetter than the inside.

"Fire away," June said. Her second drink half gone. She, bulldozed her way through the pain of the rum.

Nicholas paused for a moment. "You saw his wife, correct?"

June nodded, while sipping. "You're talking about Hollingsworth?"

"You saw a picture of him, correct?"

June nodded again.

Nicholas slowly shook his head. "They seemed somewhat mismatched, wouldn't you say?"

June shrugged her shoulders. "It seemed to me he was somewhat lucky to land such a beautiful woman. But you have to remember, women, on the average, like the romance and the security. Men like the looks and need respect. So, maybe it was perfect."

Nicholas nodded. "I would agree. Then tell me why would he leave her? I would think he would want to die, clinging to her nickers." He paused and shook his head pointing with his thumb in the direction of the private investigator. "Now the man has me speaking his dragon slang."

June thought for a moment. She couldn't ponder much. Her brain was warming under the influence of the rum and starting to warm the rest of her spinal column. Her feet were clinging to the foot rest on the stool and they were turning numb. "Maybe he ran off with another woman." It was all she could come up with at the moment.

Nicholas looked at her as if she had two heads.

"It could happen. He landed this one, why couldn't he land another? And still, what does it have anything to do with Russians, spies in general, or if there was any foul play at all in that villa? By the way, how do I get upgraded to a pool villa like the one they have? If I had my own pool I wouldn't have to run the risk of running in to Malcolm."

Nicholas smiled. "I will inquire for you." With that, it was his turn to leave, walking out and just glancing at the couple who had been identified, rightly or wrongly, as spies instead of owners of an insurance company, working out of their den, specializing in recreational vehicle policies.

After her early unexpected meeting with the two men, June went down to the same place on the beach from the day before, set up her camp complete with her magazines, sun lotion with a PF of 45, and two towels. She made sure there was a table next to her lounger and plenty of shade from the constructed wood canopies, looking like large wooden umbrellas of dried palm fronds covering a wooden stand attached to a center post. An hour later, when she was done with the magazines, she folded the last one across her chest and closed her eyes. She woke later to the yapping of the Yorkie and *Mr. and Mrs. Alabama*.

Today, the husband wore a leopard print speedo complete with the leopard face in front, the cat's nose perfectly aligned with his body parts to match his wife's suit, cut way up on her hips, exposing her tanned stretch marks, and way down between her cosmetic breasts. The suit was held together by a gold chain. After about fifteen minutes of the dog yapping like finger nails on a chalkboard, June picked her magazines and headed for her room.

Housekeeping had just left so everything was freshly cleaned and the bed was freshly made. It beckoned her to crawl in. She gave in, stripping off her suit and finished with a three hour late morning nap, waking up to the cold air-conditioning and finding herself snuggled under covers.

She opened her eyes seeing the trees move in the light rain shower as it came and went on the island throughout the day.

She smiled. She pulled up her covers and went back to sleep for another hour.

When she woke, she laid in bed and thought about what to do next. Since the sun was out again, she decided to lay by one of small pools up on the hill near her room instead of walking all the way down to the beach again. She bounced up and tossed her suit back on and sandals, grabbed her room key and made her way down the short walk.

She had the nearby pool almost to herself, except for one of the workers doing maintenance to the pump. The peacefulness of the place, the plants, the sound of waterfalls cascading down from rock walls in to the pool, almost put her back to sleep. Rain, again, came and sprinkled her. It was a warm, soothing rain and she merely covered her face with her towel so as to not take a direct hit in the eye. The sound of the rain hitting the plants, especially the palm trees or the soccer ball sized leaves of the bread fruit trees sounded like someone was playing the drums, hundreds of drums, all around her getting wet, she didn't care. And just as quickly as it came, the rain stopped, like it was connected to a valve and someone had turned it on and just as quickly, turned it off. She laid in peace and finished her magazines.

That night, starting at dinner, June found herself comfortable and relaxed, her shoulders not so high and tense around her ears. The murder investigators had left her alone most of the day except for the brief encounter in the morning at the bar, to the point where she had almost forgotten about it—almost. It was a warm night, but the breeze blowing in off the water, was relaxing. A slight sprinkle of rain fell, then stopped, then ten minutes later, started again.

She found her place at the end of the bar, her back to the corner, and she was on her second punch as she watched Stefan push some sticks and dried plants in to an amber bottle as he stood behind the bar. Then, he poured in some clear rum. June couldn't read the label but figured it could probably be used for rocket fuel. She was witnessing the making of the spiced rum the island was known for. Stefan finished and put the bottle back under the counter, pulling out another one similar to it and raised it up to look at it. The liquid was a darker mahogany, it had fermented long enough.

She had a full view of the bar and restaurant. The bartender, Stefan, was pulling a double shift. Without her asking, he had brought her two drinks instead of bringing her only one. He smiled and winked She could look out across the bar to the open sea. Labrelotte Bay was beginning to reflect the setting sun with strips of orange and gold hues painting the water those same colors then expanded in to a shade of pink, running up to the beach, and the front side of the coconut palms being painted a silverfish-tan deepened as the light darkened in color with the setting sun.

The bar had three levels and tiered itself down the beach. Tables surrounded the bar deck and sat on the two decks below. The lowest two decks were outside the roof line and exposed to the sporadic rains.

Past the bar deck was one of the three upscale restaurants at the resort, rightfully called *The Upper Deck* and was only open at night for dinner. As June sipped on her drink, the staff was just setting up for the night's dining. She thought about moving to a table, maybe having dinner, but her legs were starting to go numb—again, assuming it was from the punch or just the way they were tucked in under her seat, cutting off the circulation. Or maybe it was some type of pulmonary illness. She didn't care, she was comfortable. She had somehow gotten some sun and the sundress she was wearing, which she never wore in Phoenix, felt good against her skin, allowing the warm humid breeze to drift over her shoulders and down her back, soothing the light sting of the beginning of a sunburn.

Behind her and to the side was another English family, different from the one next to her on the beach. Mum, Dad, and three small children appearing to June to be in stair-stepped age from about five to eight.

The youngest of the children asked. "Mummy?" He had yellowish blond hair and sat tall in his chair with his feet swinging freely under it. His mother wore a flowered print dress and father was in slacks and a tab-collared shirt. She noticed many British on the island, like the family on the beach earlier. It was a commonwealth of the motherland which explained the three flights from Heathrow each day.

The mother looked with a gentle smile. "Yes, my love?"

He looked at his mother while he stabbed another French fry with his fork. "Will we be able to go swimming again tomorrow? I so loved it today."

June watched from her place at the bar. The French fries looked good. She signaled Stefan and ordered a plate. She didn't remember seeing this family on the beach before and figured she had missed them when she left the beach herself. The other two children chimed in agreement.

"Of course, my darling. You and your brother and sister are, most certainly able to swim tomorrow. Daddy and I will, again, watch you from our chairs."

"It was grand fun today, Mummy," the sister said.

The father sat at the head of the table, watching and not saying much. He was a large man with a barrel chest, rosy cheeks, and mustache—enough to make a walrus jealous. When he smiled, his eyes squinted shut. He commanded the area with his presence and it seemed to June he commanded the family. He did not appear to be a man of much mirth, but when June saw him smile again and again, highlighted with an occasional snicker at what his children or wife were saying, she realized he might just be letting himself enjoy this place as well.

Behind June were the Russians, at a table, next to the steel-drum band setting up for the night's musical entertainment. June watched them, dark and brooding, but looking like they were about to jump each other and make a baby right at the table they were at. *They are Russians,* she thought.

She didn't pay much attention to them in the morning. They were sitting so far from her on the other side of the bar, they were hard to see and frankly, June didn't care. Now, she thought, watching them was like watching the *Lifetime Channel* only from a soft porn point of view. He was bald, shaven clean, wearing a dark shirt open to below the table line. She had jet black hair and a blouse cut almost the same length—just to the top of the table. Being a resort and, June noticed, most people were in their bathing suits, shorts, and casual shirts, the Russian couple were way over dressed. Even the couple from England seemed a little too proper.

June looked a little harder this time, since they were sitting so close she could hear them speak. June looked on to make her own evaluation of who they were and what they did for a living, just like every other case she worked where the victim was unknown. She contemplated they were German, maybe Russian, June surmised, at least that's what the third glass of rum punch was telling her. She didn't even consider South African, their real home country which no one knew.

June could hear them speaking in what she thought was German. *It could be French Canadian for all I know,* she thought to herself. She tried to be objective, trying to see if these two could be Russian spies Malcolm was talking about. Having never seen a Russian spy, and the lubricated state of her grey matter, she was at a disadvantage, but she kept trying.

It was what she does.

Their voices were not as sweet sounding as the English. The words cut and spit. Something both of the couple seemed to like—cutting and spitting. *There's a lot of saliva with whatever they're saying,* June thought. They seemed infatuated with each other and June wondered who they were, where they came from, and what they did to earn their way here. The cutting and spitting appeared to be in close conversation interrupted intermittently with deep, passionate kisses, touching bordering on foreplay, and then there was stuff with the feet under the table. She liked to play *Guess the Profession.* She did it with homicide victims all the time when she was on scene, before the background would confirm who they were and what they did. She was hardly ever right but it didn't keep her from trying.

'Let's see, Hersher, who do you think they are?' She started saying to herself, smacking together her now dead as a flounder's lips. *Maybe he's a doctor and she's a teacher and they saved for years to make this trip, sometime after their third child.*

She actually prided herself on hardly ever being right. The game almost always allowed her to rate the couples higher than what she found them to be in real life. She tried to see this couple as the Russian spies Malcolm insisted they were. It made her feel better knowing they fit the stereotype for the profession. The more she drank, the more the description Malcolm gave made sense. There was also a part of June which desired the woman to not have had three children. The idea of her having children and that body after having said children, made her own self-assessment even sadder. The woman was at least ten years younger than June. It could explain her beauty and she probably didn't have children to have distorted her body from the one of her youth, but it didn't help June much.

She took another sip. She felt the need to untie her legs from under the chair, just to let them circulate some blood if for nothing else. The random thought of a fire and resulting stampede of customers also entered her mind. Forget the idea there were only about seven family clusters in the three tiered bar and restaurant, all but three were already sitting outside the edge of the roof line and thereby, technically, already outside. The fear of a fire and stampede was never a threat. But June wanted her legs untied, just in case. As she did so, they let go of each other and hung uselessly from the chair. She left them tied too long. It would take her a few minutes to circulate some blood for them to work like legs again. Stefan came over to her and smiled. "You like our punch, huh?" He was smiling and that made her smile.

"Yes and I think I want another. This time make it with the hand crafted spiced rum in the water jug you keep under the counter. I think I would like the spiced rum." *Are my lips starting to leave the planet? They're flapping. I think there was a little breeze which made them flap!* She thought to herself. She tried to focus for a moment and reached up to touch them without drawing any attention to herself. Of course, Stefan was still standing in front of her, looking right at her. He smiled as she squeezed her lips and pinched her upper and lower lips together with her thumb and forefinger.

"Ah, how do you know our island secret? In all the years I have made this drink, we never used the spiced rum. Very potent!" he said continuing to smile.

"Yeah, well, you're lying. Why else would you have an old medical jar with twigs in it under the bar? Besides, I saw you pour it. I want to live on the edge here, Sparky, so let's see if I can handle it. Besides, I think you might be fibbing so you can keep some yourself for after work. I can't be the first one to ask for the homemade stuff with the punch. There is something about consuming a drink you have to strain between your teeth." She stopped for a moment and looked up like she was thinking. "Oh, and how about those fries to eat?" she said trying not to blink. It was her professional opinion, based on years of objective observations and training in the keen art of observation, her eyes were not closing and opening at the same time. It would be a dead giveaway on a traffic stop indicating something was not right. Someone here, maybe at this very bar, might notice her incapacitation and report her to—*what am I saying? Damn it.* She felt the need to put something absorbent in her stomach to soak up the rum that was now, somehow, going to be added with the combination of twigs and sprigs from a remote rain forest on a small island in the lower portion of the Lesser Antilles, kept in a warm jar on a shelf behind a bar. *Sounds like good drinking to me!*

Stefan turned to get the fries and start her drink. She slid her glasses on her face and tried to read the menu laying in front of her. It took her a minute to realize the menu *and* her glasses were upside. *Damn it.* She looked around to see if anyone was watching. Then she sat the menu down and decided to just go with the fries. It appeared no one in the bar cared about her level of drinking sophistication. The fact her optic nerve was beginning to fail and she couldn't see much past the bar level helped. It also helped that the Russians were doing something under the table which would have distracted anyone close to them. She was close enough to see more cutting and spitting, apparently on purpose and involving two carrot sticks and a dollop of ranch dressing.

She was plucked from her happy place by a voice. "Oi, I think those Gaelic heathens had something to do with the missing Mr. Hollingsworth." Malcolm had squeezed into a niche behind her near the trash can. No one was supposed to be behind her. Cops never let anyone sit behind them. *Damn it.*

"Malcolm, what are you saying? And why are you sitting in the trash?" if she had the next spiced rum punch—the one Stefan was actually pouring for her at that very moment, other parts of her body, she predicted, would start to experience catastrophic failures and shut down or relax so much she would start to leak fluids. As soon as her lips went, she knew she was in trouble and they were gone. *I need to stop and focus, focus June, focus.* "Who? What are you talking about, Malcolm?" she said, not that she cared what he said. She thought he actually said something about 'the heavens have some things two cars worth'. She didn't think that was right and just needed to hear it again because she thought her inner ear canal was now calling it quits.

He nodded his head in the direction of the young. "Those two Hun bastards. Like Hampstead Tigger's they are. My sources tell me they were seen talking to the Hollingsworth's day before yesterday right here in the full light of day. Then, when the Hollingsworth's left, those Russian commies were seen to have a whispered conversation. Very suspicious." Stefan saw Malcolm and walked over to him. "I'll have whatever she's havin', mate."

Stefan looked at him then at June.

"Ah, Malcolm, Stefan and I just kind of made this drink up. It's pretty strong," June said with perfect diction.

The big man laughed. "Oh, please, I'm from Liverpool. We start drinkin' whiskey while we're suckling mum's teat." He looked at Stefan and nodded with confidence. Stefan looked at June.

She shrugged. "Make sure he gets some of the sticks and twigs in his glass," she said and then a wink that felt more like a spasm.

It was all Stefan needed to know. "Very good, ma'am."

He's not going away, she thought and then began to realize the feeling in her legs, all of her legs, has started to come back with a spidery tingly feeling after she had unlatched them from the rail on the bar stool. She reached up to scratch her nose and realized the outer edge of her nostrils was without feeling—once she found her nose actually had the nostrils attached to them. *Damn it.* "Okay, for the sake of a real bad conversation and since I am waiting here to eat, why would they be suspect?"

"Look at them. Their *theatrics,* trying to get people to think they are lustfully in love with each other. Their hot, glistening bodies rubbing all over each other. Their taunt, undulating, arms and legs in a writhing dance of heated passion—"

"What's your point?" June said as she tried to shove what little thumb nail she had on her right hand into the palm of her left. Nothing. *Damn it.*

"It's obviously a ruse. They want us to think they want each other—to throw us off the track of their depraved plan." The bartender returned with Malcolm's drink. He took three large swallows before his throat constricted shut. "Wow, that's—good," he said with a small cough. "Full bodied—earthy." He reached up and pulled something out of his mouth and looked at it. Then wiped it on the napkin which came with the drink. From where June was sitting, it looked like a twig.

"Yeah, it should taste *earthy,*" June said while still evaluating her extent of feeling loss. "Again, what are you trying to say?"

"I'm not trying to say anything dearie. I am saying they are on the 'TFSL'."

June saw the fries coming from the other end of the bar by another waiter. Stefan was bringing the drink.

French fries which might absorb some of the rum in her system and give her the ability to function just a wee bit better than she was now. The drink Stefan was bringing would most likely cause her to be found on a garbage scow heading for New England as the galley bitch. With any luck, if the fries could counter the alcohol, it maybe would allow her to be able to return to her villa later that night under her own power. She had some pride, although it was draining from her in the silky love she was finding with the drink, this bar, and as she looked around, this place. She knew there was no hope. Like a life ring thrown to a drowning man when the man had already, well, drowned. But she tried to listen, tried to concentrate, tried to care. "'TFSL?'"

"Aye, Top Five Suspect List," Malcolm said while he looked into his glass and pulled out another piece of what looked like bark. He flicked it off his finger. "It might surprise you that couple is a real life Boris and Natasha, and they are real spies, on holiday. If you remember our conversation of my research this morning, her name really is *Natasha.* If you remember your INTERPOL flyers on international spies, you will remember one identified as *Natasha, the Red Herring of Vladivostok.*"

"What? INTERPOL doesn't have flyers on international spies. Nothing we could see anyway, especially you. You're making crap up—again." June took another sip. The rum was giving her spine a slow, warm massage as well as shortening her patience. There was a slight spill of liquid outside her lips, catching on the corner of the mouth and beginning to slide down to her chin. She left it alone. It wanted to be free and June thought she would allow it to flee the conversation, *flee, my little drip of drool, flee!*

Malcolm ignored her comment and just kept his eyes on the couple in the corner. "Why else would she be named—*Natasha*?"

"Maybe it was her grandmother's name? A family favorite name? Maybe her mom randomly picked it out of book." She stopped for a moment, distracted by the shiny edge of the bar. There was blessed silence for a moment. "Go on," she said, spinning slightly in her seat, causing her knees to knock together. "Whoa—this kind of feels good."

"What does?"

"Spinning."

"Oh, pish-posh."

She continued in a full circle in the chair. When she came back to center, she reached out and grabbed the passing bar, then spun the other direction, stopping long enough to take a sip. She decided to try to see how close she could come back to center on one spin. It was a contest—with herself. "Spies?" She said a little too loud and figured it was good enough to make Malcolm grimace, she wondered if the couple heard. She looked back over her shoulder at them as she spun the other way. As far as she could tell, they never looked over at her. There was still something going on under the table. "If they're spies, why are they here?"

Malcolm frowned. "Spies need vacations too. My sources tell me they flew in from Uruguay after meeting with a former Nazi party member known as *Mr. Sandals* who was drawing attention to himself and his small cottage industry of investing Russian gold for some Russian big wigs who were skimming from the shelves. These two escorted some more gold and had to explain to this Sandals bloke, he needed to keep a lower profile.

They made their point by cutting off the tip of one of his little Nazi's fingers and then forced him to swallow it."

June just looked at Malcolm. She didn't want to ask, but found herself not being able to help herself. "Why do they call him 'Mr. Sandals'?"

He took a drink. "Wow, this is good." He smacked his lips and blinked his eyes twice—hard, and then paused and stared at the glass. "Have you noticed it gets better the more you dr—"

"You just made that shit up."

"What?"

"The Mr. Sandals story. You made it up." She spun again.

"No, not at all. I got on the blower and called my friends in the motherland and they confirmed it. From what I gather, Boris there liked to go to resorts with that Hunnish bastardized name and hunt down women on their honeymoon who just had a late night tiff with their significant other. He would console them, fill them with drink and then park his schooner in their harbor of love, if you know what I mean." He took another sip as if he just ordered cable TV. "His wife there, would photograph the whole event, then put it to music, and then post it on the internet. Most of it was quite tasteful."

June sat and listened as best she could, her mouth slightly open. She realized she was mouth breathing. "What's a blower?"

"A phone."

"Why didn't you call it that?"

"I did."

"No you didn't."

"Yes, I did."

"You called it a blower."

"Yes?"

"That's not a phone. If you would have said the word 'phone', for you to have actually used the word 'phone,' I would have known what you meant. Geez, it's like you have a different word for everything."

"We are in a British Commonwealth. I think our words hold the bane."

"See, there ya go again," she said as she spun two complete circles in her seat again now going in the opposite direction. "What the hell does that mean, 'hold the bane'? Look, wait, never mind. Who do you know in England who has that information?"

Malcolm looked left then to his right, his traditional method to check for eavesdroppers. "Look dearie, my sister-in-law has a cousin. The cousin has a father-in-law whose nephew works for one of the papers, the Piccadilly Insider."

June thought for a moment. Part of her brain was still on line remembered standing in line at the grocery store and seeing it just below the gum and Tic-Tacs. Unfortunately, it was not the part of the brain which controlled her bladder. She found herself really needing to go to the restroom. "The one that had a picture of a lizard on its cover with the story title having to do with something about dinosaur aliens? Weren't they also in the bidding war for the princess's photos before the car crash? It's a friggin tabloid."

"And a very good tabloid—well respected. No one ever proved the lizard wasn't from Neptune's moon. So, this contact said those two are in the game."

"So what if they are spies. It doesn't mean they whacked the old man."

"Now, there you go. What does 'whack' mean?"

"Kill, it means 'kill', Malcolm." She spun in her seat again. Malcolm finished the drink just at Stefan brought another. Malcolm didn't remember ordering another but it didn't matter. He would drink it.

"Why didn't you say 'kill'? You said it twice. Whack means something you do, you know, with your twigs and berries —in a quiet place, alone, after you got stood up at a late night pub—again. The fact she was missing a good amount of her teeth and three fingers on one hand was no matter to you, you even told her so as well as the mustache and ear hair were totally reasonable on a person of her age." June noticed Malcolm was staring off in to nowhere, reliving a distant and sad memory.

"Geez," she said. She looked up at the English family then she looked back at the young, undulating pair who now might be a Russian spy couple the more the rum was talking to her. They appeared to have mellowed some, being distracted by the Rastafarian steel drummer who was setting up about three feet away and who began to tune his steel drum. Whatever was going on under the table earlier—involving napkins, a fork, and some ice cubes, appeared to be over. She looked again at the Brits then back to Malcolm. "What about those people?" "What about them? Why couldn't they have killed her?"

"The Sergeant Major? Oh, he most *definitely* could have, but he didn't."

"Why?"

"Because—he's *the* Sergeant Major. Sergeant Major Gerald Fulbright with His Majesty's Fusiliers, and his piano teacher wife, Nancy. They bleed the Union Jack."

"You sure it's not likely they did away with one of their own, just for spite?" June said pokingly. "Maybe the Sergeant Major needed a little confidence building, you know? Something which could remind himself he still had the gummies to corner the jackrabbit," June said, just wanting to stir the pot at the same time she stirred her spiced rum punch, getting all the rum up from the bottom of her own glass. She tried sucking the remnants through the two small straws which came with the drink, but they were plugged with refuse. So, she drained the glass traditionally, allowing the ice to rest on her lips while the last of the earth-ladened liquid filled her mouth, just before she reached over and started on the fries.

"Oh pish posh."

She shrugged her shoulders up, telling the seed was planted now in Malcolm's mind; however, she was not able to put the shoulders back down again. Apparently, that switch was also off-line.

She watched as a young woman walked over to the British family's table when the meal was done and escorted the children away. She appeared to be their au pair, June couldn't tell exactly. She was young, appearing in her mid-twenties. Each of the children went from mother to father and kissed them on the cheeks before they left with the younger woman.

It was the Manager's Welcome night and everyone began moving out from around the bar or tables they were at and gathered around the pool, just outside the confines of the bar and restaurant, where the steel drum band was and seven aged men sat with fiddles next to them. There was a brief introduction and welcome by the resort manager, Eldin Cornwall, welcoming all and encouraging the guests to enjoy their stay. He appeared to curtsey and role his hips from side to side, a move wasted in meaning to the entire group, but it made him feel better. No one could tell he lost a thousand dollars that day, chasing white stockings in the third. He also introduced the rum punch table and adjacent wine table.

Waiters began circulating with trays of or 'devours. June stayed with her fries at the end of the bar and made an occasional spin in her chair while watching the events ramp up around the pool. Local craftsmen who had carved bird feeders out of coconuts, or jewelry out of seeds from a plant with no consonants in its name and coral from a local reef for earrings and necklaces, sat at tables around the pool while wearing their best and cleanest attire. They smiled with respect while the guests of the resort moved from table to table searching for the one item they didn't need. All the while, the band of older and seasoned men played classical island music. The old men in the group didn't smile. You would see these same men, sitting outside any gas station outside of Chattanooga, playing, just waiting for someone to stop and use the restroom.

June had a great vantage point, up a little higher than the area surrounding the pool, in a comfortable chair. Plus, she did not have confidence her legs would work to carry her over to the party, thirty feet away. Thirty feet was a long way from where she was in her growing condition.

The band began to play and people began to dance, including the Sergeant Major and his wife. He being a retired sergeant major and she being a part-time librarian and a piano teacher, June didn't think would witness enjoyment on the part of the couple. There was a perception of tightness and formality, even though June saw him smile, actually smile, as he sat with their children at the dinner table, staunch conservatism. When the children were away from the bar and out of sight of their parents, the two morphed into something June could not have predicted, first toasting each with their gin and bitters, drinking them down like addicts dying of thirst, preparing to take their glasses with them as the Conga line formed by the pool, led by Diane, one of the young managers who might not have volunteered for the job, but accepted it with zeal. She was followed by four other staff members in Carnival dress. It was the islands big event of the year and the staff displayed some of the costumes of the festival and of their heritage, for those in the crowd who would not be around for the annual event. Everyone that night, was, for a short time, at the island's annual festival.

"Here we are, all alone at last, my little salt lick," June heard the Sergeant Major say in a deep, baritone voice as he and his wife prepared to join the party from their table. June took a double take in the direction of the words she was hearing, fearing she was starting to hallucinate word combos such as 'salt' and 'lick' in the same sentence.

The wife smiled. "Yes, my handsome oaked stallion." As she walked by June from the table with her husband, she held her arms over her head, still holding her glass in one hand, and whooping in an octave not heard. The Sergeant Major, as they moved about the floor, kept pinching his wife's bottom and kissing her sweaty neck. She was truly the salt lick. His own sweat ring forming under his large Caribbean shirt. June would have joined the line except her feet, clear up to her knees, were useless and she wasn't sure she was ever going to feel them again. For a proper British couple, June thought, they weren't very *proper*.

The last she saw of Malcolm, he was walking his glass over to the line, blending in like the rest even with his black dress shoes and black dress socks, one pulled up over his calf and the other down around his ankle, getting in the forming Conga line of guests and staff, dressed in traditional island Indian attire, feathers and beaded leather everywhere, some flying through the air and finding his mouth, causing him to attempt to spit them out, followed by chugging the last of the spiced rum in his glass, then reaching and grabbing one in each hand.

June noticed his gait was a little skewed to the left. She ate another large bite of fries and another sip, shook her head, "I really like this drink."

ANDY, THE SERVICE WOMEN, AND THE POOL GUY

He enjoys true leisure who has time to improve his soul's estate.

—Henry David Thoreau

Somehow that night, June found her way back to the resort shuttle just outside the lobby, and back up the hill and to her villa. She woke the next morning dramatically early for what she'd done the night before. The sun had cut into the room at just the right angle and landed on her face. It helped she was laying perpendicular to the side of the bed, having fallen on the bed sideways in the same clothes she was wearing at the party. Her dress was partially unzipped, leading her to believe she made some effort to get out of it,

She rolled her head the other direction. The hammering of the rum seemed to have sloshed from one ear canal to the other as she rotated her head. The dampness of the pillowcase felt good on her warmed face. She thought at first she might have a fever. Then she thought of all the fevers she could get on the island, a tropical island no less? Malaria, Typhoid, or Dengue. She didn't like any of them.

She opened her mouth and breathed in, sampling the taste of the air streaming over her tongue, finding herself smacking her lips, trying to free the rancidity of whatever was camping there on her taste buds. Something had obviously crawled into her mouth and given birth to a whole herd of offspring. "Geez," she said sitting up, fighting her dress twisted tight as she slept, and stabilizing herself first before moving off the bed to a near a standing position.

She went in and washed her face. Leaning against the bathroom counter, June looked at herself, watching the water fall from her face. "God you look tired," she said. But not just physically, to her core. Not tired from the play the night before, although she would admit it would be part of it, but tired from life. She could see the youth of her life gone and the long lines of wear replacing it. It was here, in this mirror, her fatigue became exposed to her. If she were honest, she would have seen it a long time ago. When she was honest with herself, like here in the looking glass, truly honest in the light of this day, she knew it was so. She knew she wanted to be just herself, and not feel the weight of life, but over the years, it had become the new normal. She wasn't sure what it meant to be *just herself* anymore.

It wasn't as if she wasn't happy, happiness came and went. At least she thought it had come over the years. After a while, the function of life seemed to step in the way, taking over herself and everything around her. She laughed, she smiled. She even told the occasional joke, but there was, at her core, a lack of joy. Now, in this mirror, she could really see it. It was as if the history of her life was worn as a mask for everyone, except her, to see.

She shook her head and dried her face off on the towel still damp from the night before. She wondered what it was damp from. Apparently, she just didn't come in and crash on the bed. She figured she made some effort to prepare for bed, with some form of face washing and an attempt to remove her dress. She thought for a moment and was kind of proud of it, She wandered into the kitchen and pulled some fresh pineapple off the welcome tray the resort left for her then sliding a coffee pack in the coffee maker and turned it on.

Looking out the window, she could see the edge of the jungle as it came down to the small bay. Waiting for the coffee to finish, she shuffled into her bedroom and opened the louvered windows, then closed her eyes and allowed the breeze to run over her. She took a deep breath in, filling her lungs with the warm, moist Caribbean air. Even in the early morning, the air wasn't much cooler than the middle of the afternoon.

Just outside her window was one of the smaller pools and next to it was the Italian restaurant. Both the pool and the restaurant were parked farther up the hill from the main pools and the rest of the resort. The restaurant's placement allowed for incredible views of the sea and the lower parts of the resort while guests dined outside. From her room, about forty feet away June could clearly see both the restaurant as well as a section of the pool deck and blue loungers. She noticed someone laying on one. She went out to her patio, backing up to the restaurant but had a better view of the pool deck and the lounger in question. There, curled up on his back, lay Malcolm. He was clad in native ceremonial wedding outfit one of the staff had modeled for Festival. She remembered asking one of the waiters about this exact outfit she had seen on someone other than the unconscious P.I. It was the traditional St. Lucian marital head dress complete with peacock feathers as well as plumage of the St. Lucian Amazon, a parrot on the endangered species list. It was worn when the French and English were fighting over the island. Malcolm himself was wrapped in a hand woven headdress complete with shells and beads, the whole ensemble now sitting sideways on his head. June could hear him snoring the fifteen or so yards they were apart. She stepped over the short wall that separated her patio from a small lawn and the restaurant pool area and took a few steps towards him to get a better look.

Malcolm was completely naked except for the headdress and the shoes and the standard issue towel. It appeared to June, much of Malcolm's body hair had been shaven off except for half a mustache. A necklace of chicken bones was around his neck, the appetizer wings from the night before had been tied together, braided actually, with some palm fronds. His shoes had also been tied together. There was a blue pool towel covering his happy-go-luckys, but he had rolled over and the crack of his backside was fully exposed to the maintenance man cleaning the pool. Stripes of back hair were missing from his very hairy back as if someone tried to shave him in not a very organized fashion and then simply gave up. Much of the cut hair seemed to have landed in clumps on the pool deck next to the unconscious owner. *Maybe the razor broke,* she thought. The pool man ignored the carcass in the lounger, stepping around it as he continued brushing the pool walls, the snoring fell on ears plugged in to headphones.

"Geezus," she said, finishing with a grin.

She returned inside, got some coffee, and jumped in the shower, trying to wash off the smell of stale liquor. The smell oozed from her pores. She brushed her teeth as well as her tongue. She went into the kitchen and poured some cereal and ate it dry, hoping it would absorb some of the toxicants in her stomach. At the same time, she was wondering if it was too early to have another rum punch, maybe without the twigs.

June put her swim suit on and grabbed a new book, some new author was writing crime fiction with Phoenix as the setting. It was better than romance, but she thought it was a little too close to what she did for a living. Maybe she would pick up one of the trash novels at the small market. She rubbed on sun block, missing parts of her body completely and leaving globs of untouched white lotion on other parts as if they were ladles of sour cream. She grabbed her sunglasses and again, headed for the beach. "It's a new day, let's try this one more time," she said to herself as she made her way down the hill in the early morning. Malcolm was gone when she walked out front again, down the path to the driveway next to the restaurant and pool.

As June got to the narrow cobble-stoned street in front of her villa Andy, one of the resort shuttle drivers, was just dropping off a newly arriving couple to the resort. He shouted, "Heading down me-lady?" His striking white teeth shown like a beacon as he smiled and looked out his window at her, his arm draped over the door. He wore a pair of headphones and appeared to be jamming to some heavy beat music June could hear.

"Yes, thank you," she said and he slid the van door open for her. He released the brake and the van slid down the narrow cobble-stoned path, gathering speed as he came to a turn, one of many on the roads connecting the villas on the hill with the rest of the resort. June was glad she caught a ride. The idea of walking in the early morning sun, even in this paradise, was enough to begin to create waves of nausea, especially after the night before. She was already sweating and wasn't sure if it was from the humidity or she was detoxifying. She came to the conclusion it was probably a little of both.

"I'm Andy. You can call me Andy," Andy said with an ear to ear grin she could see from where she sat in the back seat, his smile, with those blindingly white teeth, reflecting in the rear view.

As Andy drove the van with its one occupant down the hill, June noticed he began making machine-gun noises with his mouth, forgetting he had a rider or he just didn't care. From the passenger seat she could see what he was doing. Andy would sequence his machine gunning noise, which June had to admit, were very good, with his right thumb on the steering wheel, activating an imaginary trigger on the imaginary control yolk of an imaginary fighter airplane. June figured the van was the imaginary fighter. It moved with too much agility to be a bomber.

"What ya got going there, chief?" she said while watching him. She needed to reach up and grab the handle above the door to keep herself from sliding across the seat and bouncing off the other side of the van as they came to another turn and Andy kept the speed up. The van picked up speed and brakes and lower gears were, apparently, only a suggestion. "Are there seatbelts I should be wearing? She asked, looking around while still gripping the handle.

"Yes, if you need to use them. Most people do not. It makes for a quick exit," Andy answered. There were seatbelts in these small, shuttle vans, but no one wore them. The turns were tight and steep and whatever speed Andy was at, it needed to be cut in half. It made the rides at Disneyland truly child's play.

Andy said "Oh, sorry. I'm a frustrated pilot," as he seemed to come out of a dream, as well as off the gas pedal. "I like driving these roads and machine gunning the enemy planes. I especially like your ZZ Top on my headphones while I am doing so. " He looked at her again and smiled as he down shifted and the van lurched into the lower gear as well as a slower speed.

"Enemy planes?"

"Yes, the other cars, people along the road, animals," he said nodding and shifting the van down another gear again as they made the climb over and then down the other side.

"ZZ Top?"

"Mostly, but you can't fly missions to Bob Marley. One can only take so much of Bob Marley. He is too soft. You need the beat of the boys."

June nodded. She knew what Andy was saying. When she was pushing a patrol car she would often want to launch make believe rockets at stupid drivers. "How do you know they are enemy planes and not friendlies?" She said, playing along.

Andy looked at her with a questionable look.

June continued. "They can't all be enemy planes, you'll run out of bullets before you get down to the bottom of the hill, then those planes will kill us both. You got to pick your targets, and then just tap the trigger." She held up her hands so he could see it in the rear view, like she was holding the steering wheel and then flexed her thumb. "See? Just a tap. We call it trigger discipline."

"Trigger dis—"

"Discipline."

"Discipline," he repeated. "I need to remember that. I can't out fly them in this thing if I run out of bullets."

"Of course you can't. It's a shuttle van," June said.

She held on to the overhead handle as he took another turn, thinking what other piece of sage advice she could offer. Then, she realized she was talking to a van driver about shooting a make believe machine gun at hotel guests and resort employees as well as other shuttle vans. She also realized her nose was running. She quickly wiped it. Ah, good point," she said.

Andy looked back over his shoulder. "I did not pass the physical," he finally said.

"Oh, sorry, that's pretty common with pilots. Their eyes aren't—"

"My feet."

"Excuse me?" She frowned. She thought she didn't hear what he said. "Your feet?"

"I have too many toes on one foot." He changed gears again to take the last downhill. There were two gardeners trimming a set of bushes along the road. He didn't pull the trigger. He looked in his rear view and into her eyes. "Friendlies!"

June smiled. "Very good."

"Yes, I was born with six toes on my left foot. My parents thought it was cute and so they didn't do anything about it when I was young, not that they could afford it. They couldn't. My parents said it was my very own dewclaw, like our dog, Banshee. She was part mastiff and part Labrador. It didn't bother me much since we all usually run on this island with sandals or even shoeless." He paused to shift, turn the wheel, and then look out his side window at a hummingbird flying next to him. "But when I tested for the military, I could not fit into the flight boots. Very disappointing. So, I work for the resort and machine gun guests or staff along the road. I will not machine gun you. You will be a friendly this whole week!"

"I appreciate it. Remember the rule," June started. "Only enemy aircraft, ground units and people you don't like. Especially people you don't like."

He looked in the rear view and smiled at her. June held on to the overhead hand rail and the other hand on the top of the back seat. "How do I know who are enemy and who are friendlies?" Andy asked.

"That's the best part. It's your flight. You can shoot whoever you want," June responded.

She smiled at him and he saw her.

June said, "Your machine gun noises are pretty good," leaning into the turn, wondering what the rollover possibility was at a forty-five degree pitch. "You ever hit what you're aiming at?"

Andy looked over his shoulder at her as he came to a turn. It was a hairpin to the right and what seemed to June to be a definite rollover possibility. "Oh, yes, all the time. I never miss. I have always wanted to fly airplanes." Andy punctuated his sentence with another hairpin to the left and another increase in elevation. "Sharp dressed man...." he sang out loud and about ten decibels above normal speech, from the music in his headphones. ZZ Top was setting the pace for this flight to the lobby. June began to feel a slight wave of nausea one gets on roller coasters. She searched for the horizon. She knew it was out there, somewhere, in the jungle of trees. She just had to find it.

The van shifted again as it lurched around a turn, trying to miss someone from housekeeping carrying down a load of linens bound in a sheet and balanced on her head.

Andy continued with the line of questioning. "Yes, it was my feet. I told them I did not need to wear the boots, but they said it was part of the uniform. They said I could not fly one of their planes without shoes."

"Well, that makes sense then."

"Yes, I think so as well."

"Have you thought about the army and being an army mountaineer? Bet you are pretty sure footed." As soon as June said it, she thought better of it, *but what the hell, you can't have six toes and talk about it with a complete stranger and not have a sense of humor.*

"Yes, unfortunately, St. Lucia does not have an army. I am very good at climbing coconut trees. My nickname is *Panda.*"

June frowned in thought. *Do pandas climb trees?* "Well, it looks like you landed on your feet and you're doing all right." *Stop it, June! You are an insensitive bitch.*

"Yes, I am very happy here. This is a good job and I get to meet nice people every day." Andy pulled up to the front of the open lobby as he cruised into the shuttle breezeway to a full stop. He quickly got out and opened the sliding back door to let his single passenger out.

"Thank you for driving me," June said with a smile.

"Oh no, thank you for talking to me. I think sometimes I can scare people."

June looked at her driver with an inquisitive look. "Why would you be scary? Other than the drive is like a ride at Disneyland only with no safety harness."

"Well, sometimes, I lose track of where I am and there are people in the van and sometimes, well, I—how do you Americans call it? *Spray and pray.* People in the back sometimes do not know what to make of it."

"Oh, I thought it was the toe thing."

"Oh, no, they cannot tell because of my 'comfortable custom orthotics with the high arch-support soles.' They are the ones with the company emblem of some kind of marsupial on the inside of the heel." Andy said as if he was quoting an ad, then he pointed down to his shoes which look like they could be paddles on an old butter churn.

She looked at his feet and then back into his eyes. "Good luck on your next mission. Remember," she held up her thumb. "Trigger discipline," she said smiling.

"From now on, I always will, thanks to you." He paused for a moment and smiled. "You are a good woman, a nice woman. Thank you for coming to my island. I hope I will be of service to you again," he said and slid the door shut behind her. Just as he got in the van, he held up his thumb and flexed it like he was operating the trigger on his steering wheel.

June turned to walk into the lobby, cutting through the open area on her way to the beach. She was halfway across the pool deck before she remembered she wanted to go to the restroom and check her nose.

As she came back out, Malcolm stood in the breezeway her head spun left then right, looking for an alternative path, but it was too late. They had already made eye contact. He looked better than she felt and dramatically better than he had about an hour before, unconscious and naked. She could smell lavender and Brut cologne as she approached, the breeze catching him from behind and right towards her. She could still smell the odor of alcohol oozing from his pores and Dentine gum, lots of gum, coming from his mouth. His face appeared washed, but June noticed his eyebrows were drawn on with some type of brown felt-marker. *Maybe, he figures, no one would notice.* His hair line over and around his ears had been shaven to where his hat rested. His shirt was miss-buttoned and his socks didn't match, neither did his shoes for that matter. But he was standing, almost without swerving. *He must have a much higher tolerance than I do.*

"I see you met Andy," Malcolm said with emphasis on the name. "I can't figure out why he hasn't been picked up by the authorities and questioned."

June said, not breaking stride as she walked past him. "Good morning to you too, Malcolm," and to the two service women she walked passed on the pool deck on her way to the beach, "Good morning ladies."

Malcolm was at her shoulder trying to keep up and not fumble in to the coconut tree with the wrong shoes, June now noticed, were on the wrong feet. One shoe, June noticed, appeared to be a woman's business flat, a very large woman's business flat.

"Good morning Ms. June. How are you this morning?" One woman asked. They both folded pool towels and stacked them on a corner table next to a set of yellow hibiscus bushes.

"We'll see," June answered the woman with a wink then rolling her eyes and surreptitiously nodding in Malcolm's direction. The two employees nodded uniformly in agreement each with a slight smile on their face. Malcolm had been lingering around the counter and pool area on a daily basis.

Malcolm just kept talking to her as they walked, swearing in an inaudible mumble after glancing off the white plaster wall. June had time to think it was the party, the summary of which dictated somewhere on this beautiful island—a poor woman, she assumed it was a woman, was now laying claim to her new married identity of being called 'Mrs. Malcolm McCain' based on his ceremonial head gear she saw him in earlier this morning. "It's pretty evident Natasha or whatever her real name is—if she *has* a real name, is here with her partner to discover something, find something, kill something. I bloody well know it." He was able to dodge another coconut tree with a swaggered two-step to one side, but he almost stepped on a small child in the process.

June noticed Malcolm burped slightly as he spoke. She stopped in her tracks just next to the pool. One of the deck assistants was vacuuming out this pool. The morning sun hadn't fully crested that part of the mountain which held this section of the resort. The shadows still fell on the pool and surrounding area. "I tell you—"

Malcolm interrupted her, almost in a rush to quiet her. "Shush, not so loud. God knows who they paid to listen in for them," he said nodding his head three times in the direction of the assistant still vacuuming out the pool.

"Okay, I am going to the beach. If they show up, I will keep an eye on them. By the way, where's your necklace?"

"My what?"

"And your new feathered hat? You had a new necklace and hat this morning when you were at the pool by the Italian restaurant. Not much else but hey, you're in the Caribbean." She smiled when she spoke.

Malcolm looked over at the deck assistant then lowered his voice as well as his head, looking at her out of the top of his eyes sockets. "I had a lead on that pool worker and his involvement in this whole debacle of sin. I was working undercover, dearie. I wanted him to think I was unconscious from too much spirits so he and his associates would share their combined plans." He nodded. A man convinced his cover story was a good one. It dawned on June he might have done something like this before, scary as it was to her to imagine. She started to think he might have pulled such an operation and have it wind up just like this—with his eyebrows shaved and the wrong shoes on the wrong feet.

"Well, if your cover story was to be naked, in a headdress which means you married someone or something last night while eating a plate of barbeque wings, resulting in you naked on a lounger, you were successful. Oh, by the way, you have no eyebrows."

He reached up and felt his face and eyebrows or at least where his eyebrows were or at least use to be. He then frowned as if he had forgotten something. "Drat, I didn't think anyone would notice. It was all part of the plan."

"Yeah, I'm sure no one will notice today. It's the shoes I would be worried about. They're a dead giveaway you're not a native."

Malcolm looked down and frowned again. He had forgotten the shoes didn't match. "Why would Russian heathen spies go to the beach?" Malcolm asked, trying to get back on track of the mission at hand.

"Why wouldn't they?" She said coming back to her thoughts and what was left of her senses but her eyes moved from eyebrows to shoes. "You think they would want to blend in. This place has a beach. It's where I would be if I were a spy; wanting to kill someone or learn important security data. Wouldn't you? I tell you what, if anything happens, I will let you know." June turned to leave when he called to her back.

"How?"

It took her three steps to stop her forward motion before she turned back to him. "How—what?"

"How are you going to let me know?"

"I will give you a signal." She turned and walked away again.

Malcolm's head bobbed up and down in agreement. "Okay, now me twigs and berries are all a flutter," he said as he too, turned and walked away in the opposite direction. He stopped in a couple of steps, turned and called to June's back—"Oi," he said, almost in a yell. June thought about not stopping, pretending she didn't hear him, but she knew she couldn't get away with it. She stopped and slowly turned. She tossed her head slightly to indicate she was listening.

Malcolm yelled into cupped hands, "What's the signal?" Even the boy cleaning the pool heard it and thought the man was talking to him so he took off his head phones to listen. Two other cleaning staff came out of a side door to see who was yelling about what, standing next to the two women folding pool towels. Malcolm was oblivious to them.

She took a deep breath and let it out slow. The beach bag she was carrying, all of a sudden, got very heavy.

She closed her eyes and bowed her head. Then, raising it again, she cupped her hands around her mouth and shouted back like she was yelling at the home plate umpire from the third base dugout in Yankee Stadium, "I will waive my towel and whistle."

Malcolm nodded and gave her a thumb's up. The pool attendant went back to cleaning his pool. The two women went back inside where they came from. The other two continued to fold pool towels.

June found the beach and the lounger under the same coconut tree she rested under before. It was now like seeing an old friend. Just having the sand under the tree raked and the area around it pristine and welcoming actually made her feel joyful.

About the width of two loungers from where she made camp, was the proper British family from the night before. The Sergeant Major was slathered in white skin block. It was already too late for him, his skin already taking on the redness of a nice first degree burn. June hadn't noticed it at the restaurant the night before. He was reddening up nicely. With a large wad of zinc on his nose but now, he was sporting a hat. The wife was in a one-piece with the skirt with a stack of magazines on a small plastic table next to her.

All the children belonging to anyone were in the water playing, including the children June saw from the first day. She was surprised how well she could hear them scream. She looked a little farther down the beach and there was the couple from her first day on the beach. The mother and father were just passed the Sergeant Major and his lovely wife. They owned the children who were screaming.

The man looked the color of a pimento painted in a white wash of lotion. His wife was wearing the exact style of swimsuit the other woman was wearing only a different pattern. She was buried in a magazine as well. The husband looked like he was sleeping off the effects of the night before, contrary to the Sergeant Major who was watching the children playing, seeming to always be on guard, June observed based on his body language, always diligent of his duty as the Sergeant Major, finding and transferring those skill sets to his duties as a father and husband. He was a warrior, with a warrior's heart. He was a sheepdog of the highest degree, guarding his flock. June looked at the way he looked and talked to his wife. He was a lover of her, a fine woman and their love was deep, sensual, and at times, a bit—robust. June was a witness.

The Sergeant Major spoke, his hands folded across his large lap holding a hardback book of some kind. “Look at the children, would you Nan? They’re having a spot-on time, what?” June thought it could be a British thing. Then again, maybe it was just that men like the Sergeant Major didn’t use dust jackets-not proper.

“They do seem to be having a lovely time here.” The two adults waved like royals to the children who climbed up on the floating sun deck.

The Sergeant Major reached over and took Nan’s hand. “I do believe *we* had a lovely time last night, as well,” he said to her with a smile and a wink. The smile was buried under the huge mustache but the face contorted so she could only tell it was a smile because his eyes squinted. “By the by, that suit you’re wearing drives me absolutely insane.”

Nancy looked at her husband from under the wide brim of her sun hat and through the dark, wrap-around sunglasses like people are issued from the doctor after getting their eyes dilated. “Oh, Gerald, you are such a *wild fox,* you are.” She began to giggle. She took a moment and scratched her nose, smearing some of the zinc oxide which covered everything from where here eyebrows merged all the way down to her flared nostril openings, then to her cheekbones under her eyes, but only her right eye. She forgot she was wearing it. Her husband didn’t seem to mind. He had some on his head, causing beads of sweat to form and sit quietly until enough had gathered weight to slide down the hill’s forehead.

He reached out and offered his hand to take. “I have to be when I’m in the presence of a little *minx* like you! Tugging on the General’s collar like you did!”

There was more giggling. "Oh Sergeant Major, you *conquered me*, trimming my hedges like you did with your sword of thunder! You launched your invading armies and they—"

June grabbed her towel, magazines, beach bag, and the small plastic table and moved three loungers over, away from sound of the couple's conversation.

Berman and Stefan were on, working the front and back of the bar. Berman working the bar and Stefan taking orders.

Stefan approached June as she resettled. "Miss, June, I just want to say it was fun watching you last night. The staff have talked. You are in the running for one of our all-time favorite guests."

June looked up at him from her lounger, shielding her eyes from the glare of the sun. "All-time favorites? Did I do something last night I shouldn't have? Not a lot of memory about last night. I hope I didn't embarrass myself, my family, my country, my God what did I do to warrant such a vote?"

Stefan laughed. "Oh no, Miss June. You were wonderful. We know who is real and who isn't. You are very real. We want you to have a good time here. We think you could use it."

"You do, huh?"

"Yes Miss. Now, what can I get you?"

She ordered a soft drink, her stomach still a little queasy from the night before. A light breeze started and the clouds moving over the top, barely above the island, added more protection from the sun. Even though it was humid, the air felt fresh, moist. Raindrops started to fall in one of the island's daily events. It would rain for a few seconds or even minutes then stop. June didn't move. She figured she was at the beach and she was supposed to be in some stage of wetness. She did nothing other than pull her legs up to support a towel draped over the back of the chair and her head to form a tent to protect her magazines in her lap. The rain let up after about thirty seconds. Removing the make shift shelter, she looked to the north and the beach was nearly empty. Three security guards walked the freshly raked beach, down by the water line so as to not leave foot prints. The resort was, if anything, well patrolled.

She laid her head back on the lounger and looked out over the deep blue bay. There were no waves, just the simple lapping of water onto a gently sloping beach. One couldn't hear the water rolling slowly up on the beach. Other than that, it was silent, and strikingly beautiful. She heard the wind cutting through the coconut palms and witnessed the clouds pulling in front of the sun with the intermittency of giant hands, causing fades between cool and warm, light and shade. Her mind wandered back to her life and the years in the past. Images, like snap shots and home movies, played at random intervals and in random order. It had been a blur, passing years one upon the other, it got her to this point in time after her husband died, years alone, aside from Maggie, and pushing herself to live each day until she fell asleep from exhaustion. She didn't want to think about it. Now, years later, his death was like it was just yesterday.

She tried to read one of the magazines she brought with her but she couldn't focus. She looked long down the beach again. She fought back a wave of emotion she had been feeling since she got to the island where she cried herself to sleep.

She was hoping she wasn't going to curl up in a ball and sob like that again. When her husband was murdered, she stuffed her emotions quickly, got caught in the focus on the killer and then rolled into her job and raising Maggie. It kept her safe from the one person who could really hurt her, herself. She wasn't supposed to cry, she was supposed to be strong, if not for herself, for Maggie and besides, *she couldn't have a homicide detective sobbing like a, well, girl.*

Now, on this stretch of beach, it was just her, alone with herself. No one to protect her from the only one who knew her. She felt the emotions and thoughts, memories, were all just below the surface. They never went away, they never were processed and dealt with. Now, the island seemed to strip all those things that kept her from that.

Her head slid to the side, still resting on the lounger. Her look turned to a stare as she started to fight back her emotions again coming deep from within her. The wave of it passing, then rising again and sweeping over her. She could feel herself, the weight of which became noticeably heavy, press down on the chair as if gravity itself was changing.

Quietly, a light rain started again. She had just enough time to cover her head and magazines with the towel, adjusting her legs so they leaned on each other, touching at the knees, Just before June fell asleep, as the rain began to fall.

LABRELOTTE BAY

HAFFU THE RASTAFARIAN AND THE GOOD-LOOKING SURGEONS

Free speech brings with it some freedom to listen.

—Bob Marley

June didn't sleep long in the lounger. When she woke, her head was still turned to the side. She wasn't sure how long she had been asleep but based on the pain in her neck, it could have been for a while. She hadn't had a nap in years until she came here and had never fallen asleep on a lounger. She couldn't remember when the last one was and now, since she's been on the island, she has found herself napping, daily. It felt good.

She slowly lifted her head, the movement hurt. "Ow, ow, ow," she said to herself. She turned her head and focused her vision. Just passed the Brits were tables and stands of people from the island selling their handmade crafts. After first pushing her head with her hand to an upright position, she left her towel and magazines and walked in the surf line to the tables with the crafts. The sand was like powdered sugar under her feet, and cool to the touch.

Under a huge magnolia tree next to the craft stands was a black man sitting in a white plastic chair, the kind one buys at the grocery store and can be stacked, ten of them, then carried to one's back yard for the family barbeque. It had a cracked arm and looked like it had been cracked for a while. He was talking to another man, sitting in another similar chair behind him, just behind a woman rolling corn rows in the hair of a small girl with very blond hair, also sitting in the same kind of chair. The man in the chair and the one behind him had carvings from some kind of wood, coconut carvings, and other items made out of sea shells all hanging from what looked like an IV stand.

The two men sat behind folding tables on the beach, directly in front of the small beach-supply shed. He wore an old pair of shorts; a tank top with the face of Che Guevara; and a red, green, and black knit cap stuffed with what looked like a volleyball size amount of hair. On his tables, three of them, two were covered with well-worn table cloths and the third in a beach towel. He had then covered them with beaded necklaces and bracelets, clam shell necklaces, and small carvings out of abalone shells and coconut carvings. He smiled at June with a smile of calm sincerity and she was able to generate one back to him. She had seen the look before. It could be from true peace, or some really good island pot. Both had the same look. After a moment, she voted for the serenity.

"What is a pretty woman looking for at my humble tables?" The accent was so thick and fast, June understood about every third word and simply nodded and smiled. She moved from his three tables to others around him and at each table the maker of the wares smiled a gapped tooth smile of sincere friendliness. She looped back to the first tables and the man in the plastic chair stood up. She stopped and picked up some earrings and a matching coral necklace. The Rastafarian said "That is a very fine selection you have made, Love. I think you need a pretty dress to go with those pretty earrings."

She smiled again. She understood the line. He sounded like his accent had changed. "Oh, you think I need it all, do you?"

"A pretty woman like you does not need any more adornments than what god has already given her."

At first, she thought it was a well-rehearsed line until she really looked at the man in the cap. He was at least appearing sincere. It wasn't as if she needed a compliment, needing any affirmation at all. She was content with who she was, who she had become, she had convinced herself of it. At least it's what she convinced herself over the years. But here, on this beach under this magnolia tree, as big as the main resort building, this man said something which seemed to have clicked. At least at that moment, he was another example of the peace owned by the island and its people. June certainly knew Evil. It lived here as well. It lived everywhere. But the idea of a place which seemed, as a natural tendency, to be at peace with itself and pass that peace and tranquility to all those who wish to see it and embrace it, made her want to believe, even if it was just for a short time, the words he expressed, words and smiles she was getting from everyone, was a sign of hope that maybe—just maybe, was real and still existed for people, maybe even her.

She bought all three pieces. The Rastafarian's friend, who sat behind him had never gotten up, finally struggled to his feet and showed her some of the dresses and then referred her over to his sister sitting next to the woman constructing the corn rows in the girl's hair. It appeared to be a family operation, a loose family operation. The garments were bright and happy and June knew one wash and they would probably run to a grey, but for a time, for a moment, they would capture the pleasure she was feeling.

After spending a few more minutes hunting the tables, and for a very short time contemplating the corn row idea, before canceling it in a wave of better judgment, June decided she was hungry and it was time to eat. Without looking at her watch, she walked back the few hundred feet to the outdoor restaurant She sat at her newly adopted corner table. She picked a table, which plastic legs appeared uneven, causing it to rock, not enough to spill her drink, but enough to cause her to feel comfortable with the place. It was just a table, a brown plastic table at a five star resort, but it made her feel at home for some reason. Its plastic, like the higher end plastic chairs that matched it, wobbled just a bit, not sitting firmly on the uneven wooden deck. It was not pretentious, just life. There was a comfort of home here and one she was beginning to feel solace in.

She tucked her linen napkin in her lap and glanced at the menu. The crisp, starched-shirted waiter came and took her grilled chicken order and just as quickly left her alone again. She kept looking at the beauty of the empty beach. She sat back in the plastic chair and felt her body relax in to it.

It was not quite the tourist season and the weather was warm bordering on hot but, she thought, to get an empty beach like this, she would tolerate the heat. Her eyes were drawn back to the man down the beach, sitting at the table with yards of hair stuffed up into a well warn and faded knitted cap. A few minutes passed, maybe it was longer, June couldn't tell and was beginning not to care about the time when the waiter brought her lunch.

The voice coming from behind her was familiar, like nails on a chalkboard familiar. "Oi," June turned around and saw Malcolm leaning against the white wood rail that separated her from the upper deck of the open restaurant. He was actually trying to peak through some palm leaves, as if he was hiding. He wore a different wrinkled floral print shirt, the same shorts, and black socks with black dress shoes. *At least this time they matched,* she thought. "I didn't give you the signal," she said to him over her shoulder.

"Oi," he said. His eyes looking over the beach.

"You know, Malcolm, you, in no way, look like a local in that outfit."

He looked down at her and then back at himself. "You think so? Eh—that was a little jab, eh? What's wrong with what I got on?" He actually sounded serious and wanted to know. "I might admit I look a little disheveled after last night. Gad that was fun, what I remember of it." He felt his forehead and shaved eyebrows, shaking his head a little from side to side. As his hand slid down over the missing eyebrows and realizing June was watching, he quickly removed it, pulled the brim of his hat down, and turned his head slightly to one side as if he too, was looking at the beach, in an attempt to hide his freshly shaved forehead from her. Unfortunately for him, the sun highlighted the bare discolored spot of skin like a white highlighter and caused the brown marker to shine like gold in the sunlight.

June put her fork down. She figured she would probably regret starting the conversation and open the door to her own taste of non-compliance, but she couldn't help it. "The shoes—you're wearing dress shoes at a beach resort. Poor form. Of course, they are better than the combination you had on earlier." She thought she would leave the eyebrow issue for another time.

"Oi, can't worry about that now. Conspiracy's afoot."

June picked up her fork and stabbed at her lettuce. "Well, we are talking about shoes."

He looked down at his shoes. "Really? What should I be wearing?"

June quickly took another bite of her saffron rice and a piece of chicken and then moved the chair next to her with her foot and lifted her leg, showing the pink flip-flop sandals she had on. "Something like these."

He looked at her foot and then frowned. "Not a lot of calling for flippy-flops in England. I figured if it is good enough for the Queen Mum, its good enough for me. Besides, yours are girly. All sandals are 'girly.' If you haven't noticed, I'm not much of a girly-cue kind of fellow. The women back home call me a 'Tasmanian'! Do you know what it is?"

June looked at her plate while the man talked. She nodded "It's a large rodent in Tasmania. The natives shoot them and make stew." She had no idea if she was even close but figured Malcolm had no clue either.

"Exactly" But it's a wildcat it is, crazy! The women like me 'on the edge' so to speak. Those shoes would take away from my *aura*."

"So leave the flip flops here. No one said you have to wear them in England, unless you want to wear them as shower shoes or if ever you go to a pool and go swimming. Do they swim in England, Malcolm?"

"Aye, like a pack of fish, we do. Some of us swam halfway back from Dunkirk before the lads were picked up. They were even carrying their kits. Strong swimmers, we are. Nimble too, like a sand crab." He went back to his notebook after pulling one of the palm fronds from his mouth. "I got the hairy legs though so is it part of the whole look as well?" There was a questioning tone to his comment. "I don't see a lot of hair on the men here. Do you suppose they shave their legs? I'm drawing the line at shaving me legs. The damn French don't shave anything. Hairy bastards."

"Just think about it, okay? If you don't want anyone to know you're here, then don't look like you don't at least fit in." As she spoke, she rubbed her own legs resulting in a frown.

"Aye, I can do that. *When in Rome,* eh?"

"Exactly. When at a Caribbean beach resort, look like a tourist instead of someone riding the short bus." June said while still rubbing her leg. "Or, in your case, less like a tourist."

"Aye, I'll do you one better, I'll look like a native!" He started to nod his head as if he had just discovered the great answer to his undercover duties.

She didn't want to tell him he was the wrong color to be a native. He might try to do something about it as well. He might do it anyway, even without her pointing it out.

"I see you found Haffu," Malcolm said. He started panning through his note pad.

"Who?"

"The man you were talking to over there under the large tree. He is known as *Haffu, the Rasta*. In reality he is Thomas C. Cunningham. He got the name, Haffu," Malcolm thumbed through the pages in his little book, "when someone asked him what his name was at the same time his friend sneezed. The person asking thought it sounded like Haffu and it stuck."

"How do you know?"

"I asked him."

June nodded again, took another bite and a sip of her soda. "Direct, good. I'm sure he thought you were just talking and asking out of pure curiosity and not what you really were doing."

"What's that, dearie?"

"I have no idea," she said with two shakes of her head.

Malcolm continued from his notes. "His mother was St. Lucian and his father was from the Miami, Florida area when he came down to St. Lucia on his Spring Break from college and met his future wife at the Castries market. They fell in love and the week after he graduated, he moved down to the island, married, and then just as quickly moved back. He got island fever not to mention missing everything else the States provided. A month later, he got a letter saying his wife was pregnant. A month after, he had divorced her and three months after that, married another graduate student from the University of Miami where he was still enrolled. Thomas was the bastard child and grew up around the island and became a part of it. Somehow, Thomas' mother thought the father pulled some strings and had their son scouted by the Hurricanes and recruited to be a wide receiver for the team."

He turned a few pages in his notebook and read again from it.

June used the time to take two more bites of rice. *Saffron rice, hmmm.*

"Thomas and his mother saw this as a chance to get the education he couldn't get here. So, he went; found success, and graduated with honors in three and a half years. He truly had some honey in his pear tree, what?" Malcolm said, tapping the side of his own head. "He stuck around and got a master's degree in Economics, finishing up his schooling defending his dissertation on—" he turned to another page,—the *Economic Parables and Fluid Dynamics between Eastern and Western Agricultural Commodity Acquisitions.*"

June's eyebrows went up. She thought Malcolm just made up the thesis.

He looked back at June then down the beach, towards Haffu. "His mother was so proud she bought a real nice binder and put a copy of his thesis in it and keeps it on the coffee table in her house."

June sat back in her chair. She was surprised. Surprised the man she was looking at had the education Malcolm was describing. It surprised her, but she found there were constant surprises by the people and life here. She liked it. "Then what happened?" She was a little mad at herself being interested in anything Malcolm had to say.

"He decided he had enough of the American dream and came home to mum, dabbling in some small company human resource departments until one day, he landed on the beach after an all-night bender with some mates of his. When he woke, he was here, on this beach, under that tree," Malcolm said, pointing to the magnolia tree Haffu was currently sitting under. "The story goes there was a shell on the beach and he picked it up, tied a string through a fluke hole at the same time an elderly couple from France walked by, seeing the man working on what they thought was a hand-made, bracelet, offered him one-hundred dollars, St. Lucian dollars, of course." He turned a page in his notes, then pointed to the bar. "That's his sister and his former girlfriend at the end of the bar over there."

June looked in the direction Malcolm was pointing. There were two women sitting at the bar, one long and young and the other wearing glasses and a few years older than the young one.

"Nicole and Carolyn, they are. Both doctors. Nicole is Haffu's younger sister. Both of the women are traveling surgeons, bouncing from island to island helping with general surgeries for those who can't afford it. Conspirators I wager! *Mules* like you Yanks like to call them. Carrying notes, I wager from one drug lord to the other."

"How do you know?" June asked.

He spoke, pointing at his own chest with his thumb. "How do I know? How do *I* know?"

"Yes, enlighten me."

"Look at them. They are beautiful. When was the last time you saw a 'doctor' that beautiful? Hmm?" He shook his head. "Doctors in the U.K., they all look like sheep with the Willys if you ask me. Short, frowny faces-scowls like a sucky lemon face. Don't even get me started on the Germans! Pesky Hun Basta-"

"What's your point?" June interrupted.

"Look at them. The one can't be in her twenties, the other, maybe thirties, a little old for my taste, mind you, but I wager they are no more surgeons than Bob's me uncle."

June smiled. She forgot how much fun it was to play with the insane and Malcolm was falling deeply in to that hole. "Getting back to—"

"Haffu.'

"Then what happened?"

"To who dearie?"

"To Haffu and the French couple."

"I asked him. He said he looked at them and—," Malcolm turned a few more pages. "'Smiled'. It meant he found his calling. A con artist he is. It's pretty obvious about him. He drives a 2011 Ford Taurus." Malcolm bopped his head.

June looked up. "What's 'obvious'?"

"The man is a swindler, a cheat, a conniver of the trusted. He very well could have done in our victim just for the money in his pocket." Malcolm squinted in thought towards Haffu down the beach. "It's only a matter of time before this case breaks wide open. I perceive there is more to this bewildering land than meets the humble eye. I'm getting close, I can feel it in my nubbins. I think we are swimming, swimming mind you, in a nest of villainy. And with your help in assisting me, I know I will find the vile individual who buried our poor victim in the jungle of this god forsaken place!" His eyes fixed and firm. His head, nodding in agreement with himself.

June looked at her plate and sighed. "Waiter?" she called, catching her waiter's eye, she held up her finger and quietly spoke. "I'll take the spiced rum now."

THE GARDENER

Nature is just enough; but men and women must comprehend and accept her suggestions.
—Antoinette Brown Blackwell

There was an army of gardeners on the property, but there was one, in particular, who caught June's eye. The next day, she watched him while she sat on the short wall, waiting for the shuttle to take her down the hill to the main lobby for breakfast. In the distance, down below her villa, towards the resort lobby, she could hear the yapping noise of Mr. and Mrs. Alabama's dog which had fast gained a reputation of being a pain in everyone's mental ass.

June was going to walk around the main resort area for a while, trying to get some exercise before she started her day beach side. She thought maybe she would even try to get some snorkeling in. She had never been snorkeling, at least not in the Big Pool. From what she had heard from a few of the guests, it was worth the short trip and more importantly, it was free. Apparently, being an owner at this resort, or the owner's 'wound pretty tight niece,' allowed you to have many of the traditional resort activities, free of charge.

While the other gardeners seemed to work in pairs or groups, this man liked to work alone. June figured it was because he seemed to be the boss of a crew, giving instructions while working the side of the mountain, trimming trees and bushes back from the roads and paths. The jungle seemed to encroach daily. The state of affairs at this place seemed to be a constant struggle with the jungle for ownership of the ground the resort rested on, the island constantly wanting to take the ground back, and the gardeners were the tip of the sword or in the case, the machete, to keep the jungle at bay. The boss sent the others out in pairs and he worked alone, plugging in his headphones hanging from his pocket.

Where the others had hair shorn close, he had Dred-locks with colored beads woven in them. He didn't stuff his locks into a woven basket like Haffu, but let them hang around his shoulders.

June remembered seeing him before, around the resort. She couldn't place him until it finally came to her, he was the man on the beach sitting under the magnolia tree talking with Haffu when she walked up to examine the items for sale on the tables. He appeared today to be wearing the same tan pants and worn white shirt as he did then. Today, he was wearing boots and carrying a machete. If one of these gardeners had to wear shoes as part of their job. She remembered he had his feet up on a neighboring chair under the large magnolia. Today, he had his tan pants rolled up about three rotations from the bottom, exposing the high-rise boots which were not tied all the way up, flaring open and fitting loosely.

In the lawn space around and between the units and road, the gardeners worked a slow but deliberate pace. They never stopped, just a slow temperate movement of work. Some would be raking, some would be trimming, all would be talking and laughing about something, June could never make it out because it was in *islandese* as she named it herself, a combination of Creole, English, French, and Caribbean island street slang.

In the heat, the boss—Gardener, moved from coconut tree to coconut tree, trimming them up, removing the low palms from getting any lower. They would fall and he made a neat pile, stacking them one on top of the other as if the pile was the important thing. The other crews worked near him and eventually, they all stopped and picked up what they had globally cut, loading it onto large canvas sheets the men had spread on the ground. They would then tie the four corners up and throw the whole load on to the back of a small truck before climbing on themselves, hauling it off to a large compost pit near the tennis courts.

The resort was so large, it had its own plant nursery. June had seen it when she went for one of her morning walks, making a right turn down a dirt road, she figured wasn't for the guests. Huge piles of trimmings, limbs of trees, grass trimmings, just about anything which had been living ended up here in the nursery's compost pit. The eventual compost would find its way back into the ground around the resorts hundreds of flower beds. Even on a tropical, former volcanic island, every bit of the recycling helped. The Gardener moved to his own rhythm. He took long slow strides and when he struck a branch or stooped to pick something up it was slow, but steady. It was the only way one could work in the climate they were in. Sweat, started when you walked out the door, even in the shade of the large magnolia, mango, or coconut trees they were working under, the air moved like a warm, heavy blanket.

What she really noticed about him was his use of the machete; a machete with a duct taped handle, held on his hip by what looked like a leather, hand-tooled sheath to carry it in.

From where she sat, he was an expert in the large knife's use. Watching him operate it efficiently and with care, each time branches would fall. June determined it was very effective and very sharp in the hands of someone who knew what they were doing, it could be very lethal.

The Gardner was taller than the rest. He seemed to have always been around where she was during the week, working the side of the hill near her villa which put him near where the Hollingsworth's were staying. There were many gardeners, but she kept seeing him. He was everywhere and yet, when she turned back around, he was gone. First, he would be standing in an area on a hill or in a flowerbed or along a hedge, then he would be gone when she looked a second time, vanishing with just a turn of the head. It also looked to June as if he was watching her. She would sometimes catch him glancing at her out of the corner of his eye. She figured her past wasn't a secret here and word traveled quickly about the American detective helping with the disappearance of a guest quickly after she got to the resort and discussed it the first day on the beach.

She noted his use of the machete and that he was very good with it. He would reach up and with the leading edge of the blade, poke the underside of the branch once and it would cut free from the tree. June hadn't seen any homicides where a machete was used. A couple of shovels, lots of guns and various knives, an ice pick, and on one occasion, a toaster oven, but never a machete. If there was foul play somewhere on this island, or this resort in particular, this man could well handle its execution.

She watched the Gardener with his large knife. She quickly realized the working part of the machete wasn't the long blade, but the curved front. It appeared to be the sharpest point. With one strike of the front curved edge of the blade, the whole limb would come down.

And the Gardner would make a neat pile.

"Oi, I see this case has perked your interest now," Malcolm said as he walked up to her as she waited.

She hoped Andy was still on. June tried to count the vehicles driving that morning and believed there were at least three shuttle drivers at any time. She wanted to see how Andy was adapting to the new weapons tactics as he flew the shuttle van. She smiled at the thought. It was a steep downhill drive and she just wanted to move to the beach and check a few things, like maybe snorkeling, without losing her cereal. She didn't want to get her stomach upset with the twists and turns, before the boat for the snorkel trip had its chance to do it for her. Malcolm popping up like he did, was making her stomach upset.

"What? Oh, him. I was just watching him with that thing he's using."

"It's called a machete," Malcolm helped. "Pop your 'ead clean off like a Guernsey in the lowlands it would."

"I know what it's called."

"Oh, no worries. You just kind of looked like, well, you had a look on your face," he said as he buried his hand in his breast pocket of his very wrinkled tropical print shirt and pulled out a note pad and short pencil, and scribbled a note with it.

There was a pause as the two watched the Gardener move to another tree, stand under it, reaching up with his arm, punching the palm frond from underneath with the machete, cutting it like butter and causing the limb to fall free.

"What look?" It finally hit June what Malcolm said.

"You know," Malcolm said, not taking his eyes off the Gardener. He shrugged his shoulders as he spoke.

"No, I don't. Hence the reason I asked. 'What look?'"

"You know. The one which says 'Oi, what the blimy 'ell is the thing he's swingin' o'er his 'ead*?'* look."

June looked at Malcolm as if he was speaking a foreign language. "I didn't have a look."

"Aye, ya kind of did."

Maybe I did, she thought. "I knew what it was, I've never seen it used, not like that."

"Like how, then?" Malcolm asked.

"More like a Hollywood slasher movie—crazy guy who was dropped on his head too many times when he was younger and now lives in his burned out house of his youth with the remnants of his dead mom's hair he keeps in the pillow he sleeps on and organs of the missing neighbor kids in a freezer bag in the basement."

Malcolm stared at her for a moment, taking low and slow blinks. "Sorry, I'm not familiar with that form of its use."

There was a pause as they both watched the Gardener and his crew farther down the road, before June spoke again. "So, is he on your list as well?"

"He is moving quickly up and with little effort, towards the top of the list, yes."

"Why him and none of the others? What happened to the wife? You are all hell bent to convict Mrs. Hollingsworth of the alleged murder of her husband, what happened to that theory?" June asked.

"Oh, no, the She Vixen is still the number one candidate as far as I'm concerned. I have no idea why Nicky hasn't picked her up for questioning and given her a real Jack-O-Lantern interrogation, if you get my meaning. It must be political. She is the puppeteer and these men, well, they just don't have the where-with-all to reject her coming on's like sophisticants such as myself. They are weak of mind and can't see through her Mata Hari ways. She's a witch I tell you. If you don't have a strong aversion to beautiful luscious women, like me, you're bound to fall."

June looked at him. She just let the last couple of sentences roll around in her mind as she watched the Gardener work. He nailed two more branches. "What are you, some kind of Shaman?" she said over her shoulder to him.

"Not familiar with the term. Does it have anything to do with being an officer in the Labor Party?"

"Never mind," June said and went back watching the Gardner as she waited for her shuttle.

"Funny you bring it up though," Malcolm started with no break in his thought process. "Well, I haven't eliminated any of the others, you see. They are all very suspicious. But he," he nodded in the direction of where the Gardner was working. "Well, he is right there at the top."

"So, like I said. Why him?"

Malcolm looked again at her and this time with an inquisitive look. "He's the bloody gardener, that's why, and he uses a machete. Do I really need any other reason?" The two stood for a moment before June spoke.

"Actually, that is about as sound a reason as any of the others you have listed in this case."

"See? I might be on to something with this one," Malcolm said, bobbing his head in agreement. "The wife, or should I call her the 'She Vixen from Hell' has a way of tangling the minds of the simple in her web of treachery and vile. She's a Siren I tell you. She sings and the males can't resist her call."

"The Gardener has a simple mind?"

"Of course he does."

"Why?"

"Because he's the bloody gar—"

"—dener. I understand. It doesn't take a lot to get on your short list," June said.

About then, Andy came around the corner, shifting down to take the hill. The van was empty except for two girls from housekeeping he was shuttling up to the area. He was wearing a WWII cloth flying helmet complete with goggles. He pulled up and smiled. "I thought it would be you," he said as he jumped out and slid the back door open for June who herself was smiling and shaking her head. "I heard the radio call for a pick up at this location and took it quickly. I wanted to say 'hi' and show you my father's old flying helmet. I think it's pretty appropriate for missions, don't you think?" Malcolm seemed frozen with his pencil still pointing at his paper, looking at the driver with the head gear. His mouth was slightly open. Then, he smiled and began to nod, an equation was being somehow calculated in his brain. He flipped a page in his little notebook and wrote something down.

June watched and knew Andy just made the short list. "I was hoping you would pick me up. I wanted to see how well you're making your target acquisitions," she said. The van was tilted at a steep angle due to the road angle and she climbed in the back seat hand over hand as if she was climbing up to Camp One from the Himalayan Base Camp. She plopped down in the seat while Andy slid the side door shut and climbed back in to the driver's seat. The maids were exiting on the downhill side waving goodbye to their driver whose attention was focused on June. "What are we flying this morning, Andy? P-51?"

"Oi." Malcolm called. His lips finally moving.

June spoke with a smile while pointing in the direction of the Gardener. "Oh, Malcolm. Keep an eye on that one. But not too close. He will stack you with the rest of the palm fronds," It caused Malcolm to turn to look in the Gardener's direction, then back at June as Andy released the brakes and coasted down the incline.

"No, Miss June, we are flying the Messerschmitt 109," Andy said as he turned the wheel hard to avoid hitting the restaurant building next to him.

"Why that one?"

"It was a very good plane."

"Ah, does the helmet help?"

"Tuesday morning," Andy said back.

June frowned. "What?"

"It is open Tuesday morning."

June realized Andy was in another world by just living his life, but the headgear covered his ears, muffling her voice. He couldn't understand what she was asking. She let the question go since he probably couldn't hear her repeat it anyway.

It was mid-week and June was more tired now then when she first arrived on the island, but it was a different kind of fatigue. She was starting to feel some form of relaxation, even with the pestering noises of Malcolm and whatever he was looking at around the resort, she was feeling—*alive, What the hell does that mean? 'Alive' and does it mean something different coming from a homicide detective compared to my mother or aunt or anyone else?* She rambled the conversation in her mind. She didn't know. The debate would stop between distractions, like the fresh smell of jasmine, the smiles of the staff, the hammer of the spiced rum or the beach or the water of the bay or a shuttle driver wearing World

War II head gear just to please her—the list was looking like it would be endless.

The trip down the hill with Andy that morning had two pilots flying, one of them driving, and many targets shot between the two. Andy pulled in to the parking bay by the lobby entrance and June got out after he opened the door for her. He had slid the cap off on the last turn just before the arrival at the lobby. June was sure his cap was not resort management approved. "Have a pleasant day Ms. June. I will see you later," he said.

She walked the beach and around the pools on the lower resort, with no real destination in mind, losing track of time. She walked out to the boat dock and checked on dive times. Finding she had about an hour before the morning dive, she decided to look around again. June walked the other direction to the tidal break which made the shape of a 'comma' allowing the Caribbean surf to bounce around the corner of Labrelotte Bay, minimizing the effects waves would have on the beach. She stood there for a moment and watched the surf and rocks meet. She then turned and walked up to the tennis courts, nursery, and across to the hillside toward the villas, working her way back she deciding to walk up the side of the mountain to her room rather than ride the flight simulator Andy or any of the other Gemini pilots were driving. She took every road, serpentining back and forth across the mountain in beautiful tropical foliage and deep shadows. Every turn showed the sea, trimmed in view with flowers and greenery. She would stop at those turns and look to the green water. In the distance, sailboats made their way from Castries to Rodney Bay or Gros Islet or going back the opposite direction after a tourist's night of partying in the two small villages north of the main capital city and north of Windsong.

The distant horizon was usually a blur in humidity but on this day, she could see the island of Martinique to the north. She looked at her watch. It had been almost three hours since she had left her apartment and watched the Gardener and discussion with Malcolm. She had missed her dive time, but knew there were others. She was in a full on sweat by the time she got to her room, walking in and dropping her clothes as she made her way to the bedroom where she was greeted with the sixty-five degree air temperature recorded on her room air-conditioner. She was tired and crawled naked under the cool covers and mosquito net and curled up around one of the pillows and breathed a deep, cleansing sigh and was quickly whisked away to sleep.

When she woke, it was almost four. She startled herself awake, a fear of missing something—forgetting something important. That was her life, always fearful of missing something. But where she would have woken up quickly and sat up, moving to put her shoes on and go somewhere, June just laid in place. She opened her eyes, falling on the open windows and the sunlight coming through. She pulled the covers up over her exposed shoulder and feeling the warmth of its cover calmed her again. After a few minutes, she sat up slowly. She was going to make dinner reservations at the Upper Deck, the restaurant next to the outdoor bar, but the woman who answered when she called told her she wasn't competing with many people and since Europeans ate later than Americans, June would dine, almost owning the whole restaurant if she picked an earlier time, which she did. June didn't mind eating alone. She was used to it.

She went in and brushed her hair after taking a quick shower, and thought about putting on makeup. *For who?* She thought. She compromised on some lipstick and pulled her hair, which began to become an uncontrolled mop from the humidity, up into a ponytail. She found the sun dress she bought at the beach in her closet and decided it would be the attire for the evening, a step up in attire from the shorts she'd been wearing all day. She also needed a new set of underwear. She couldn't remember if she had changed them the first two days she had been there and that occupied her mind for some time, concerning her she forgot to change it and wondered if this was the only thing she had forgotten or any indication of her world as she got older.

When she had decided she had done enough damage to her hair and her looks and there was nothing else she could do to make herself look more human, she grabbed her small purse and headed for the door. She decided to walk down the flower lined path from her unit to the main resort and to the restaurant, skipping the shuttle.

The waitress came and took her drink order. June thought about ordering something other than a rum punch, but then she thought why change a good thing? There were only a couple of minutes before half-price happy hour was over so, she ordered two. She felt good about the order, like she found a bargain at the dollar store.

Her table in the restaurant was on the next deck up from the beach. The plastic table with the wobble was just below her. Her table was of a higher quality, covered in a linen table cloth and a small glass vase with a fresh cut set of hibiscus flowers. She could look and see the whole beach and the sun set in the bay directly in front of the cove out in front of her. There was no music playing yet, no sound other than some light conversation from a neighboring table, some talk by the wait staff, and a gentle breeze blowing through the coconut trees overhead. The surf made no sound because there was no surf. Just the gentle lapping of the water against itself and the powdered sand of the beach.

After a few minutes, the sound of music, steel drum Caribbean music, made it to the beach from the Booze Cruise—a catamaran, from the local singles resort down the coast. The lights of the boat, running without sales, silhouetted the forty or so people on its deck by the golden sun setting behind it. June could see them singing, dancing, waving their arms in cadence with the beat and following the lead of someone on the bow of the boat, a tour guide, she surmised. The heavy beat music faded as the boat eased down the coast around the north point on its way to Rodney Bay. It was then she felt something alive rub against her leg. She instinctively pulled away, feeling something furry. Looking under the table, she was looking eye to eye with a small cat. "Hi puss. You startled me."

The waitress came back with June's drinks "Oh, I am sorry ma'am. We have several of these cats around and they gather and wait for someone to drop their food. Scat you cat, scat," she said as she moved one of the three other empty chairs and tried to brush the cat with her foot. The cat, already aware of the possibility of being chased off, was way ahead of the foot, moving down off the platform and back into the jungle plants right behind June.

"Oh, that's all right. They don't bother me."

"They do keep the mice and lizard population under control," the waitress said.

"Lizards?" June asked, sipping her punch.

"Lizards and Geckos, ma'am," the waitress said as she turned to look at the beams and exposed rafters of the roof. "There. See?" she said, pointing at a corner of the beam.

June had seen the gecko lizards before and even had them at home in Phoenix during the summer, but these lizards were over a foot long and nothing that looked like a gecko. There was something even more tranquil about it being here. The mice, however, she could do without.

The waitress replaced the chair she had moved to shoo the cat and took June's dinner order, the seafood crepes with fried plantains—and another two rum punches, getting the order in just at the end of happy hour. "The lizards help with mice and other bugs, the cats help with the lizards."

June had finished the first one while the woman explained about the cat. She was thirsty. After the waitress left, June took a sip of her second drink and sat back in the chair, looking over the beach and the canopy of coconut trees next to her. Stars struggled to be seen through the openings in the palm trees and the occasional break in the clouds. She sat and relaxed in the chair.

Then, the thoughts and memories came.

Since her husband died, June had learned to be alone, aside from her role with Maggie. She remembered and ran the conversation she had with her mother, father, and aunt before she left. The look of her daughter too, all told a story she was well aware of. She knew it. After Maggie started to attend the university, June often went to dinner alone and after a while, she grew to like it—no one having to talk to, listen to their day's events, sharing friends or activities. She thought there were times, maybe more than a few, where she would delay going home to Maggie and stop and eat, claiming she was working. Losing a husband, a mate, a partner, took the wind out of her sails to be the mother Maggie really needed. It was nice just being, safe for her to just be in her own world. June found herself in so many other worlds as part of her work, it was nice to have her own—small, safe, existence made up of whatever she wanted it to be. Protective walls as high as needed to protect her heart from vulnerability—again.

Over the years, she learned to just be without a mate to share the pains and joys of life with. It just seemed simpler that way. She surrounded herself with Maggie and work and avoided the issues of feeling and anything close to love. She did that once and it got murdered. She could share with Maggie some things, especially as she got older and Maggie began to ask. She never lied to her daughter, but sometimes, she was slow at volunteering information.

After a moment and another half a glass of punch, she allowed herself to think what if she wasn't alone? What if there was someone there at her table, sharing the moment with her, his friends, his day, her telling him the randomness of events and discussions a day like hers might bring. *Who the hell wants to hear about that?* She immediately thought to herself. *Someone would want to hear that stuff to be with me,* she thought. *Someone who doesn't get squeamish at the thought of death.* She took another sip and felt the cat nuzzle her ankle.

She took in a lung-full of fresh air and let it out slowly, closing her eyes as she did so. She looked up and watched the coconut palms move with the light breeze which caressed the island. She watched the wait staff move from table to table, another coming and filling her water glass. They all smiled and seemed sincere when they did it. She allowed herself to think and ask, *what if there is joy outside what she had been living? What if? Do I have to move down here to have it?*

The rum was beginning to massage her brain again. She really liked this drink. She looked into the glass as she held it in her two hands in her lap and just beyond it, under the table, was the cat. It had come back and just sat there, looking up at her. She watched and smiled at the animal, which was looking into the bushes behind her. The cat's full attention was on a dark spot in the bush, then, while looking back over her shoulder, the cat moved away, leaving the area of June's feet all the while looking back into the darkness.

June looked in the direction of the cat's attention and saw only dark space trimmed with palms and long grass. She didn't notice the movement of the fronds on the back side of the clump of foliage.

The reptile had sat virtually motionless, its tongue sensing the air and waiting for the cat to come close enough to become this month's meal. The cat, however, was aware of the threat and decided to try a table for scraps farther away. The snake, decided to try another restaurant.

Tomorrow would be another day.

ONE-EYED SWILL

All the world's a stage and most of us are desperately unrehearsed.

—Sean O'Casey

The brochure said they offered snorkeling and SCUBA diving. For resort members, it was free. June rose with the sun the next day, had a bowl of cereal sitting on the patio of her small unit and watched a cruise ship approach Castries. She was a little disappointed she didn't find Malcolm on the lounger by the pool. She kind of liked seeing him there, splayed out like he was. She grew excited for the first time since she had been on the island about actually doing something like this. It was a fun thought, going snorkeling—in the Caribbean. Maybe she'd see something you couldn't see in the desert, like fish—weird fish, colorful fish, sea snakes and such, the kind you see on cable shows about fish and sea snakes— in the Caribbean.

She went to the phone and called the desk for a shuttle to come and get her. She washed her face and threw on her swimsuit, put on her Diamondbacks baseball hat, a pair of sandals, a cover up, some sunblock, and stuffed the loose items in a beach bag she bought from a vendor on the beach and then grabbed a towel on her way out the door.

She walked down the few steps to the road, just outside the Italian restaurant at her usual pick up location and waited. She could hear the whine of the shuttle's engine as it worked its way up the hill. As it came around the bend, there was Andy driving. He smiled at June as he saw her. He wasn't wearing his helmet, June assumed, because there were other people in the van.

They probably wouldn't understand.

He started to get out of the van to run around and open up the door like all the shuttle drivers do for their guests, but stopped as June quickly opened the passenger door next to his driver's seat and hopped in instead of sitting in the back. "No head gear today?" she said with a smile nodding towards the back.

"Good morning, Miss. No, not this run," he said graciously and a wink, also nodding at the four people in the back seat "but maybe later," Andy said as he reached down under his leg and pulled up just enough of the helmet so she could see it, then smiling back at her while looking out her window at the side mirror. "How are you today? Your face looks like you are in for adventure!" he finished as he shoved the van in to another gear and pulled away from the turn, backing up in the narrow lane until he could find a wider spot, then turned the van around and let gravity fling it down the hill.

"I thought I would try snorkeling today."

"Oh, very good and very fun. Capt'n One-Eyed Swill will take good care of you," Andy said as he came to one of the t-intersections, shifting down and breaking the van's speed with the gears before applying the brake. June looked out her window and saw a three hundred foot slide through the jungle if they missed the turn, not stopping until they came to another part of the road. A bouncy trip the van would make if Andy didn't make the turn, a true memory to tell the survivors' beneficiaries.

"'One-Eye'?" June asked, hanging on to the overhead handle as the van made another turn. "Why is he called 'One-Eye? Do I want to know why they call him that?"

Andy turned and looked at her with an inquisitive look on his face. "Miss. June—ah, the Capt'n only has one eye."

"Ah, I thought—never mind. Is that his real name?"

"Oh, no, his real name is Jesus Martinez Delagarza."

"So, why the name change; just for show?" She leaned into the next turn Andy took a little sharper than normal. She thought she could feel the two inside turn tires leaving contact with the ground. She glanced over her shoulder at the four people in the back. They had just arrived in the last day or two and had not had enough quality time with the shuttles to build their confidence in the drivers' abilities. They were white knuckling anything they could hang on to, including each other. Especially the little couple from Asia, June figured maybe Japan. They were a young couple, not having lived long enough to build confidence in anything, including their eternal love for each other in case of catastrophic van brake failure on this roller coaster of a shuttle ride. June smiled. She was confident by the end of the week, they too, would be seasoned to the ways of the van. June thought of the seatbelt issue. No one would want to use anyways while taking a header over any of the cliffs around the resort. The only chance of survival, June remembered from the first day, was to jump free. It was why she found herself sitting up front, in control of her own door. The Japanese couple in the back—they were screwed.

"I think, maybe. From what I heard, he was an Argentinian flounder boat deck hand who had to leave in the middle of the night because his new girlfriend was really that—a girl. He thought she was twenty but her brother, while he was chasing the Capt'n with a knife, was screaming she was only fourteen, an easy mistake if you saw the sister and knew anything about Argentinian women. It is the problem with the Argentinians; they start their love very young. Like that Romeo and Juliet couple." Andy shifted the van again before he continued. "He escaped and moved down to St. Lucia and worked the docks in Castries for a while then applied for a job here as a snorkel guide, but he wanted to give it some character so he showed up to the interview with an eye-patch and the name. He lives right there," Andy said and pointed, as they drove, at a white building behind the guest children's day care facility where the vans are stored and a small garage is maintained under a huge breadfruit tree. On the small white porch, were several workers, some were drivers, some waiters. All were sitting in chairs, talking. Four were at a small card table playing dominos. When Andy drove by, he honked, drawing a wave from several of his friends. In the window of one of the rooms Andy was pointing at, were four amber bottles with sticks in them. June recognized them as the beginning of spiced rum bottles like the larger versions under the bar she was at earlier. There was also a faded pirate skull and crossbones flag in the window.

"Apparently, he loves the spiced rum," June said pointing out the bottles.

"Oh, yes, miss, very much so," Andy said with a snicker. "Sometimes, when the bar runs low, it is his we sometimes buy to finish the day. He makes a very good spiced rum, Miss, very potent. He claims the best of his rum is kept under his bed in the dark. He said it ages better there." Andy shifted again. June watched two oncoming maids were walking in the opposite direction the van was driving and who waved to Andy. June noticed Andy's trigger was working without the sound of gunfire, just like they had practiced, short, quick bursts of pretend gunfire.

"Did you hit them? I thought maids were friendly?" June whispered. By this time in the ride, the four guests in the back in the back appeared to be reciting some kind of prayer. One appeared to be crying.

He glanced over to her and smiled. "Maids are friendly, just not those two. I was dating the shorter one until I found out she was seeing another man. I became really interested in her cousin, the taller one, but she was not interested in me and refused my advances. She told her cousin of my attempt and made her angry." He shook his head as if he was still trying to figure out why either would be mad at him. "Island women, who could answer their quirky ways." Andy paused again. "He really can see out of both eyes."

"What?" June said.

"The Capt'n. He really can see out of both eyes. He just often forgets what eye to patch to keep the story straight. Lucky, most of the guests only see him once or if they do seem him again, never remember which eye he has covered. At least they never say anything about it. When he needs to really see something, he lifts the patch. He doesn't think anyone knows." Andy, instead of pulling the van to the front of the lobby, drove around another corner to let June out at the top of a short flight of stairs that would take her directly down to the docks. "There, just follow the path. It will take you right to the dock. You will have fun today, Miss. You will see things that are wondrous!" Andy finished speaking and looked at June with a smile of years, forgetting, for a moment about the other passengers in the back, still glued to anything substantial as well as each other—praying.

June smiled at her driver. "Thank you, Andy. I will tell you all about it. Remember, trigger control," she said in a whisper and flexing her thumb before she got out.

Andy smiled again and gave her a thumb's up shoving the van into reverse and backing up to take the remaining guests to the lobby door. June glanced in the back of the van at the four. As soon as the van began to move, they latched on to the backs of their seats as if they were being launched on a ride at Disneyland. She knew, in actuality, they were just beginning to learn the ways of the resort.

She walked down the path, shouldered on both sides with tropical trees, wondrous smells, and flowers, through the Bird of Paradise and ferns coming out of the side of the hill, all the way to just above where the dock met the walkway.

There was a white wooden building, trimmed in Caribbean blue eaves, surrounded by a wood dock. On one side were bright yellow beached catamarans along with single and double passenger kayaks. On the far end of the dock were three, open-decked, motorized boats, June assumed, were what they used for the dives.

On three sides of the building, were horizontally hinged window shutters made of plywood and locked open with a chain. At one window was a sign advertising "SCUBA" rental and at the other window was the rental and snorkeling check in. Rudolfo, a former Castries night club singer turned resort rental and boating guide, was taking names and handing out fins and masks to the tourists.

Rudolfo had a short run on the island circuit of the local resorts singing and organizing karaoke song fests when karaoke was popular. He had milk chocolate skin and hazel eyes. When the karaoke craze died, so did his dream of making it to New York's Broadway to sing in *Cats.* He still loved to sing, even though badly, as he demonstrated daily. He was always humming show tunes—always. Sometimes, his singing would carry over to conversations he would have with the guests about rental fees, fin sizes, and where the restroom was. June heard him point around the corner to a young couple the location of the ladies room, his directions were to the tune of *Surrey with the Fringe on Top.* At the counter, standing in front of June signing up with Rudolfo, were the Brits, the younger couple June saw the first day, as well as the Sergeant Major and his family directly behind them. It sounded like they had found each other on the resort and hit it off.

One of the girls asked her burn-victimed parents "Mummy, Daddy, what do you think we will see underwater?" June was able to get up close to the four adults and saw the look of day old zinc on the young mother's cheek and the father's left ear, blisters where he missed with the sun block for too many days. Another day floating in the water allowing the sun to work on their solar flared backs, was exactly what they didn't need. Mummies and Daddies did not appear all too responsive to the needs of their children, let alone questions of wants and desires.

The Sergeant Major and his wife looked composed, the wife even smiling at her children and the questions formed from the other couples children, but the breeze shifted just ever so slightly and blew across the couple's face and then directly at June where she picked up a very distinct smell of stale liquor. She compared it with the look on each of their faces and although they stood with dignity and honor, stereo-typical of a British couple, it was June's deductive reasoning, given the set of physical facts presented to her, the young couple as well as the Sergeant Major and his elegant wife, were both hammered.

Daddy took in a deep breath of fresh Caribbean air before he spoke some form of an answer to his child, like the act of breathing itself was slowly killing him.

June noticed the odor, she guessed gin, emanating strongly from him, almost as if it was oozing from his pores, mixed with the smell of zinc oxide and what June could only identify as some type of eucalyptus oil, like one would use on sore joints. It appeared to her, it was not only the sun which was laying claim to them, but the consumption of any of the resort's creative drinks. It would not have surprised her if both daddies blew a .3 or better on a Breathalyzer. She found humor in the idea they were not truck drivers driving a load of fuel out of Tulsa. That wouldn't have been so funny.

Daddy held on to his wife as he answered. "Oh, I'm not sure what we will see. I just hope the boat ride is a quiet one," the Daddy said as he let out his breath. June noticed the wife looked at her husband's and smiled a weak smile and mouthed the words 'I'm sorry. Does Mr. Wiggles still hurt?' June decided she didn't want to know any more and just signed their pain off to too much sun.

The Sergeant Major and his wife, held tight to the sign-in table, it was helping him to stop his swaying. The wife was doing the same thing, as if they were on a rolling ship hanging on for dear life.

June looked across the dock and saw another worker pushing one of the catamarans into the water. There was a couple standing on the beach in floatation vests, waiting for the boat to be readied for them to take out.

It was the Russians.

He was wearing a black speedo, cut low showing his taunt and tanned abdominals, bracketed by his pelvis bone, indicating a body fat in the single digits; and she wore a crimson red one-piece French cut to her arm pits, a silver chain at the hip. June wondered why the Russians, or frankly anyone from the Ukraine region, always wore swimsuits like they were mounting the uneven bars. She needed more rum to sort the question out. The envious issue was this couple *could* get away with wearing these types of swim suits. *It was bad enough if you were overweight, out of shape, or covered in cellulite and still tried to wear one, but if you had bodies like this couple, well, that is just enough to piss me off,* June thought. Then, she heard a familiar voice.

"There they go."

June turned around. It was Malcolm. "Geez, there you are again. Can't you just walk straight up to a person and give me a chance to hide?"

"Why would you want to hide?" he said with a questioned look. "Besides, I'm like a ringed-tail Lemur. Cat-like," Malcolm responded chewing on the tip of his pencil, accidently having stuck it too far in to his mouth, causing him to gag. He stuck it back in to the pocket of his swim suit.

"A what?" she said shaking her head. "Never mind." She wanted to give up on trying to read anything in to what he was saying. "There 'who' goes?"

Malcolm nodded in the direction of the Russians. "I bet they're on their way to meet their handler." He pulled out a notepad from his wrinkled shirt, the pencil again out of his purple-flowered swim trunks, looked at his watch to mark the time, and made a note. He was still wearing the dress shoes. *At least they still match*, June thought. “Did you follow them down here?”

“Of course,” he said in a low tone. I figured I would kill two mackerel with one stick.”

“What?”

“Isn’t that what you Yanks say?”

“Kill two birds with one stone,’ if that is what you are trying to say?”

“Oh, right, well then, that’s sorted. Not quite sure why you would want to kill two birds unless they were good eating and the odds of doing so with one stone is simply too rare to make sense, but not a lot you Yanks do makes sense. I was by your flat and you were gone. The shuttle driver told me you were here. Do you know he makes airplane noises when he drives?”

June smiled. “He’s strafing and bombing targets along the flight. I wish he’d strafe you,” she said a matter-of-factly looking back to Rudolfo who was penning the names of the Brits on a piece of paper on a clip board while humming the tune to *El Solo, Migra*. The Sergeant Major and his wife looked at each other to see who might let go of the railing first. So far, neither of them did. They were lovingly encouraging in their competition with each other. Neither wanted to fail in hopes to hold the other up.

Rudolfo was fifteen years younger than June. *I’m too old*, she thought. But he was nice to look at, now humming something from *Funny Girl* or *Funny Lady.*

She was next in line. *I’m going to have to tell this man my shoe size. A nine and not proud of it.*

“Hello,” came Rudolfo’s sweet, very sweet voice. His smile and eyes matched his sincerity. He stood for a moment, neither of them saying anything.

June was temporarily lost and did not know why she was standing there, or where she was standing for that matter.

"May I help you? Do you need fins and a mask?"

His soft, falsetto voice caused her mental gridlock, then cracking her coma, she awakened with three quick blinks. "Oh, yes, sorry. Size eight please." June decided she would rather have tight fins than come clean about her swollen feet. She was sure they were just swollen, having been that way since she birthed Maggie.

"Here you go." The handsome man handed her a mask with attached snorkel and a pair of fins which had '8-10' written on the yellow rubber in blue ink. She smiled.

Malcolm was quiet until the British couple walked away from the counter and away from the other guests. "Strafing? That would make him a bit daft, what?" Malcolm said with a frown. He took out his note pad and wrote something in it. "Anyway, thought I would bring you up to speed on our—," he lowered his jaw "—*murder.*"

"Malcolm, I just think—"

"The communists there were seen passing another note to the large waitress at dinner last night. Very suspicious. I think she could be in on it as well."

"Who?"

"The waitress."

"What about the waitress?"

"She got passed a note."

"A note?"

"Yes."

"What was on the note?"

"I don't know. I didn't read it."

"Then, how do you know it was a note?"

"It was made of paper."

"How do you know it was made of paper?'

"Well—I"

"What if it was something else? Like a bill for dinner, or the recipe for dinner or something he dropped? Or, and I'm just thinking out loud here, what if it *was* the bill? Let me ask you, was it presented in a black leather case?"

"You saw it too!"

June looked past him to the beach. The Alabama couple arrived and their dog was yapping. It was a good hundred yards away and she could still hear it. She was glad she was going to be gone for a while. The dog caused June to spend mental quality time figuring out a way to remove its vocal cords with a butter knife and a straw.

Malcolm's face went blank for a moment, like it was being overloaded and frozen. Then, what was left of his eye brows went up as if an answer just rolled in. "Then today, they go sailing? Coincidence? I think not. Then, I get word about this man who runs this place, someone by the name of—"

He stopped when a bellowing South American voice came from a back room behind the counter where Rudolfo was filling out lists.

There was a show along with this snorkeling excursion, June imagined. The booming voice caused Rudolfo to flinch, forgetting where he was in the show tune medley. He heard this same introduction every day since he started with the resort. It still startled him every morning. Rudolfo was easily startled.

One-Eyed Swill was now on stage or in this case, the boat dock. He came out from the office from behind the counter, to see his charges for the day's snorkeling charter. "Arg, mateys, we be goin' on a dive trip today with a bunch of land lubbers!" He said as he slapped the back of the nearest staffer to emphasize his point. He was an eye-patched, deeply tanned man with hair sun-bleached yellow, going in every direction and that hung passed his shoulders, falling on his chest and back. He was shirtless and had on a pair of faded boxer–type swim trunks, pulled up to the base of a middle-aged man's gut, a man who drank too much beer and too much of his own spiced rum. He had on no shoes. As a matter of fact, June noticed, very few wore shoes. It looked like he hadn't worn shoes in years. He had on a faded black eye-patch with a white, hand-painted skull and cross bones in the middle of it. It was rimmed with rhinestones with some of the stones missing.

The man looked like he was almost sixty. There was an aged tattoo over his right breast. It looked to June like it was homemade, like the prison tats she had seen in her work, only this was a unique and a very old design, resembling a small image of what looked like a wolverine with a pixy riding on its back. The pixy had wings and holding two lightning bolts in her hand over her head and the control reins connected to the wolverines bridle in her other hand. The pixy also looked like the artist didn't quite line up the eyes correctly, giving the fairy a look of being cross-eyed. What June didn't know was the story behind the tattoo. So, she asked Rudolfo.

"The tattoo, kinda looks a little cross-eyed," June said in a low breath as the Captain walked the planks of wood making up the boat dock and his stage.

Rudolfo looked over at the captain who was busy and distracted. "Yes, three years ago, One-Eye had a pacemaker put in and it had formed a small, but a very obvious lump under the skin. So, one night, legend has it, with a bottle of Bounty rum, he sat at the kitchen table of his friend, Tulsa Tom. He was a former oncologist, tour guide, and budding tattoo artist. Tom covered the bump with the tattoo he could draw the best. It was either the pixy riding a wolverine or a famous mouse doing things with Cinderella."

One-Eyed stood with his fists on his hips as he bellowed. "Arg, I hope I don't go losin' any of ya's to the phantoms of the deep like me last group." He paused and looked around at everyone with his unmasked eye, tilting his head from side to side so he could get a better look and walking among his captured audience patting the men on their sunburned backs, disheveling hair on the tops of the children and eyeballing the women from bow to stern. "Breakfast cereal for the fishes in Dave Jones' locker, they is." His eye fell on June. "Arg, a beauty to behold, such a mature and handsome wench," he said as his eye worked June up and then down again like a beach towel before he turned back to the others.

June smirked.

The British couple's little girl said. "Mummy, what does he mean?" There was concern in the girl's voice as she tried to smooth out her hair from the crazy man's handling of it. She thought the man was going to make fish cereal out of her.

The Sergeant Major and his wife watched and listened but didn't let go of their moorings as their own children wandered down to where the boats were tied up, luckily getting out of the reach of the man with the patch.

One-Eye looked around with his one unpatched eye at this charges. "Prepare yourselves for the wonders of the deep. We be castin' off in five bells!" Then One-

Eyed Swill pivoted on his cracked and dry heels and went back into his office separated from the counter area by what looked like a well-worn towel in the doorway. If there was a door to slam, he surely would have slammed it swinging the towel wide for him to move through, for it was his character, but there was only the towel curtain hanging by a few nails in the opening, a curtain, June could see upon closer inspection as she walked by it, made out of what looked like an old saddle blanket.

Malcolm spoke up. "Yep, I' reading your mind already. He's another one. He's got warrants out for him in Argentina for "dating" the mayor's daughter," he said making air quotes around the word *dating*. "He claimed he thought she was twenty or so. He left the next day when he found out she was much-*very* much younger and the mayor told his brother-in-law whose background was even less honorable, he wanted to make a necklace out of the man's toes. Bad form dating a mayor's young teenage daughter, bad form indeed. I don't care what you say about the rampaginess of the Argentinians, I do, sometimes, admire their application of justice."

Malcolm looked passed June and saw the catamaran leaving with the Russians on it. The dark-haired woman, was sitting forward, her long bronze legs hanging free over the woven mat deck, highlighted by her colored swimsuit, like a beacon of color on the bow of the small craft, one foot dragging freely in the water, while the man worked the tiller and boom like an expert. He had sailed before. She looked like she had modeled on the bow of a boat before. Malcolm gestured with his thumb in the direction of the office One-Eyed went in to. "Keep an eye on One-Eye. Let me know what he's doing, you know, suspicious-wise. I'm going to follow them."

"How are you going to do that?" June asked.

"Come on Lass, how do you suppose?" He looked over at the other sailing boats.

June saw what he was looking at. "Have you ever sailed before?"

"How hard could it be? If the bloody Russians can do it, we Brits can do it much better. We're a sailing country. It's in our blood. Every Brit knows how to sail. We killed the bloody Spanish Armada and the Nazi's with their Bismarck. Humph, there isn't a Russian alive who can out sail a Brit."

"Maybe," June said. "Unless the guy is a sailor. Like maybe this guy."

With that, Malcolm turned on his Oxfords and walked over to the other counter and started making arrangements to take out a catamaran in pursuit of his Russian quarry.

June carried her flippers and mask and made her way to the dock by the boat they were going to take out, an open wooden rig with benches running down both sides, an open bow, and a helm in the back by the very large Mercury motor and drop ladder.

Just as One-Eyed Swill promised, he was herding the guests to the boat within five minutes, once aboard adjusting the large group in the confines of the boat for balance. He then climbed in himself and went back to the wheel on the starboard side, stepping over people's out-stretched legs, feet, and fins lying in the floor of the boat. The boat quietly backed out of its slip wafting exhaust fumes over the passengers until it pivoted and moved out around the short jetty protecting the dock from the main bay. June looked back and could see Malcolm hoping onto his own catamaran and with much uncoordinated effort between the tiller and working the sail, set out from the dock himself; the attendant standing on shore appeared to shout directions to Malcolm, still wearing his dark dress shoes and an added life vest, trying to hold his hat in place and operate the mechanics of the light boat. Eventually, the attendant dropped his head and appeared to just shake it slowly from side to side, knowing he needed to go back and get the keys for the other boat for a future rescue of Malcolm.

June looked the other direction, out to sea and around the edge of the bay, looking for the Russians. She saw nothing. There was nothing for Malcolm to chase. They had already made the turn and were probably halfway to Castries by the time he set in the water.

As the dive boat entered the main part of the bay, Swill lifted the eye-patch to check the instruments over the wheel just before he spoke. "Avast mates and mateys alike," One-Eyed Swill said, lowering the eye patch back into place before his voice drew attention to himself. "We'd be in the open waters of the Caribbean now on our way to who knows where. Gird yer loins, grab your lover—living or the one god gave ya, and stand by for flank speed to meet Davey Jones!" And with those words, One-Eyed Swill pushed the throttle forward and the boat sat up in the water and jumped across the small waves, causing everyone in the boat to find something to hold on to. Men with ball caps turned them around and women with hats planted a hand to hold them in place. The bow raked up and down, causing the cut sea to splash over the bow and spritz across the face of the customers. Sunglasses were sprayed useless with salt water.

The worried little girl from the dock spoke. "Mummy, why does the man keep saying those things?"

The little girl looked worried, as if she knew something no one else did. There was no response from her parents.

They were just trying not to empty their stomachs in front of the rest of the guests.

June looked back at the resort. On a boat, in Labrelotte Bay, was the only place a guest could see the whole resort site as one. Everywhere on land, you could only capture the resort in sections, through or around the trees and flowers. But here, in the bay, the resort went from the corner of one eye, to the far corner of the other. June's entire vision was filled with villas, hotel rooms, mansion rentals, and red tiled roofs. White stucco buildings climbed the side of the hill the resort claimed and each building was surrounded by dark green jungle. The red tile roofs on each were like a painter of canvas had highlighted each villa's existence, from the top of the green hill, clear to the water's edge.

The snorkeling trip was only an hour round trip between shoving off and the boat's return. One-Eyed Swill changed demeanor once on the dive site and was a gracious and fun host, helping everyone into the water and making sure they all had a good time. He took a special liking to the women and June in particular, June thought, because she was alone. He helped her over the side and down the ladder into the water.

"There you go senorita, easy does it. Might you be going to the dance tonight?" He asked as she worked on one of the fins after she got in to the crystal clear warm water of the cove they anchored in.

Floating on her back, June adjusted the mask "Probably so." Her answer was nasally because the swim mask was pinching her nose shut.

"Then, I'll see you there. Maybe we can dance a tango." He had a smile of a man who had done this before, delivered these lines, many times before, and June was sure, successfully "danced the tango" with others—before.

"Maybe, but make sure you have that patch on the correct eye. I don't want you stepping on my toes," she said pushing on her facemask for a tight seal and pushing away. Her last sight of him was his smile turning to one of surprise and thought, then quickly moving the patch to the other side.

All the resort guests on the dive boat spent about thirty minutes in the water before returning to the boat and then back to the dock. One-Eye was quiet on the way back. June noticed his patch was moved back. From the time she climbed in, he didn't look at her, June thought, because she knew his secret. He had moved himself to the front of the craft, helping others get out of their gear and checking the anchor line. June remembered that according to Malcolm, everyone knew his secret, except maybe One-Eye himself.

The Sergeant Major's wife was planted on the bench on the starboard side, next to the point of the bow. She was breathing hard as her husband plopped down next to her. They looked at each other and smiled. Detoxing from the night before by snorkeling in the sea was probably not a good thing to do, either of them thought. But someone needed to go with the children and they couldn't say mummy and daddy were hammered from too much drinking. They also couldn't put the burden on just one of them to take the children alone while the other rested in soft comfort of their suite, not good form. Besides, it was snorkeling in the Caribbean. It felt exhilarating once they were in the water and after thirty minutes, their headaches and nausea were gone.

On its return to the resort, as the boat pulled around the point, separating Labrelotte Bay from the cove they were snorkeling in, June scanned the water for sailboats, specifically, anything like a resort catamaran with a drowning black-shoed man. She saw only a container cargo ship heading in to the harbor at Castries. She was sure the Russians made the turn towards Castries before she and the rest of the divers had cleared the bay on the way to the dive site. She was almost equally as sure Malcolm was in the same channel when she returned, which would put him with the container ship and its large wake.

She smiled.

After the guests disembarked from the boat, June walked back up to her villa through the tropical beauty. Every plant just beyond the resort's lobby was wet, an apparent down pour was just missed. The air was heavy and moist, laying heavy on her skin. By the time she got there, sliding the key in to the heavy wooden door and pushing it with extra effort due to its swelling from humidity, she was ready for another nap. As she again curled up under the mosquito net, she debated whether or not to go to the events later that night. It was her last thought before she took a deep breath, letting it out slowly, and then slid into a deep sleep.

THE PARTY AND CAJUN-JERKED CHICKEN

England and America are two countries separated by a common language.

—George Bernard Shaw

The *'Manager's Night on the Beach'* party was a weekly event for the resort's guests. The local steel drum Calypso band again played and spiced rum flowed. Just the regular spiced rum, not the twigs and sticks spiced rum. June checked and the amber gallon jug was still under the counter behind the bar.

There was Cajun jerked chicken woven on large wooden kabob sticks, displayed on large wooden platters as well as fried plantains, fresh coconut, mangos, fried breadfruit, and pineapple, all of it harvested from the paths and walkways around the resort. All the guests seemed to be there or at least June thought so. She really wasn't keeping track. She just recognized some she had seen walking around the resort and figured they must own one of the timeshare villas. Nicholas was there in civilian clothes, wearing an open neck polo shirt and khaki slacks. He walked over to her and smiled.

She smiled. "You off or working?" she asked sipping on her drink, holding it with two hands.

"My boss thought I would make myself visible today to give our guests some exposure we are a participant in the task of finding Mr. Hollingsworth. His family is calling our government and there is pressure running downhill."

"And landing on you. Yes, we have the same gravity phenomena in the U.S." She took another sip. "Anything new?"

Nicholas looked around before he spoke. "He still isn't back?"

June frowned, then it dawned on her what Nicholas was talking about, thinking first it was Hollingsworth then realizing Nicholas was talking about Malcolm. "No, I don't know. I saw him setting off on the catamaran after the Russian couple and it was the last I saw of him, which was about eight hours ago. You knew about him heading out after them?"

"Yes, unfortunately, his people in the U.K. hadn't heard from him either for a few hours and were calling here. I found out what he did, going after them in a catamaran." Nicholas just shook his head. "We have no lab reports on the blood and won't for a long time. There was nothing else we were even testing. We dusted for prints but got only his and his wife's along with housekeeping. Mr. McCain, however, is reporting to his people there are numerous suspects who could be helping Mrs. Hollingsworth get rid of her husband. Those people are calling and saying we are not doing enough to find their relative's killer. My commander is asking what we are doing and I keep telling him we do not believe we even have a death let alone a murder. I am not sure how much longer I can hold them off." He looked at June before he spoke. "Do you think there is any truth to any of this?"

June smacked her lips and then took her thumb and wiped down the corner of her mouth. "I have seen murders on less evidence and non-murders on evidence much more than what you have here."

"That is not very helpful."

"I didn't think it would be."

They both turned when they heard the yapping. Mrs. Alabama was holding her dog and wearing a white sequined blouse scooped almost down to her belly button, black spandex slacks and black stiletto heels. The dog wore a similar sweater vest and from what June could see, hot pink nail polish. Mr. Alabama was in a pair of linen loose fitting slacks and a flowered shirt open half way. June wasn't sure either were wearing underwear. Both of them, June noticed, were three shades darker than they were the day before.

June frowned. "Can I borrow your pistol?"

"Why?"

"I want to murder that dog. Everyone here wants to murder that dog."

Nicholas smiled. "From what I hear, you would be a hero."

So, what do you think?" June asked.

"I think you are not allowed to shoot the dog."

"No, about the case."

"I think of nothing else. Unfortunately, my life has become this case. I think Mr. Hollingsworth is alive, although I can't explain why he would want to spend any time away from his wife."

"I'll tell you why," came the distinct voice from behind them.

"You're alive," June said. "I thought your catamaran ride would be the end of our suffering, the last time we would ever hear from or about you. Except for when a piece on the news saying a man in shorts and dress shoes washed up on shore of West Africa."

Malcolm laughed. "West Africa? That's a bit rogue, what? It'll take more than a ride in an open sailing ship, in choppy seas, almost getting run down by a cargo ship, and temporarily held for inquisition by the harbor patrol to keep old Mackey away or there ain't a bee in your bonnet, I say. "

June noticed not only was he missing eyebrows, the brown marker now fading, but one half of his face was redder than the other half. Like he only got half his face sunburned. "Were you able to track them?"

"No, the bastards must have known I was hot on their heels, beached themselves and fled through the forest on foot to their rendezvous."

"Rendezvous?" Nicholas asked.

"Yeah, Malcolm here saw the couple from the other night take off this morning on a catamaran. He figured they were going to meet someone and he followed them in his own boat. He lost them," June said pointing her thumb at Malcolm.

"I didn't lose them, dearie. You can't lose something you never had."

"But you 'had' them in sight. You lost sight of them, vis-à-vis you lost them. You said no one could out-sail a Brit except maybe two Russian underwear models." She looked at Nicholas and winked the eye farthest from Malcolm then looked back at him and sipped her drink. It was almost empty.

Malcolm smirked. "Potato, tomato. They had a quirky lead and I think the tide changed as I was setting off. The wind was like a chuckwalla in the trees." He stood sipping his own Guinness from a bottle and holding a skewer of jerked chicken. He turned to the detective. "So, you're in plain clothes. You must have a lead on someone. Let's go get the bugger." Malcolm's shaved eye brows raised and his voice went up three octaves, excited about a hunt.

"No, Mr. McCain, I'm not here for anyone. My Lieutenant just wanted me here."

"Aye, keep the natives peaceful, eh?"

June interrupted. "Malcolm," She could see Nicholas was close to a brain rupture whenever he talked to the man. He didn't need to be pushed too hard to have a full-on melt down. "I think I saw the Russians by the upper pool as I was coming down. If you can get close, I bet they have no idea you would be eavesdropping on them. I think I saw the Gardener up there too. In your professional opinion, could it be a connection?"

Malcolm's eyes lit up. "I'll be right back!" He spun, dropping the skewer in the trash can on his way off the patio.

"Thanks," Nicholas said. "Did you really see them up there?"

"Hell, no," she said with a look of distain on her face. "I didn't think we really needed a homicide to really investigate. You looked like you are about ready to shoot him yourself." June smiled. "Now, if you will excuse me, I need a refill." And with that, she made her way over to the bar for another rum punch.

The resort was expansive, but this time of year was only fifty percent full. The party was for everyone who owned on the property, but not everyone attended. Both British couples were there, so were the Russians, showing up right after Malcolm left. The Russians were matching black silk tops and he wore a pair of leather pants.

Fifteen minutes later, Malcolm returned shaking his head and dripping sweat from the climb to the upper pool half way up the hill, but seeing the quarry upon his return, he became revived. "Aye, they're here. I must have just missed them. Buggers must have cut through the hedgerow to avoid me. I bet they feel the noose tighten around their sinewy taunt neck lines," he said to June and Nicholas. He took up a position on the far side of the patio, away from the bar, in another of his flowered shirts and tan shorts. June noticed he had changed his shoes from the wingtips to brown shoes with tan calf-high socks.

At least, June thought, the socks matched the shorts. She shook her head and watched, sipping her rum punch. *I really like this drink,* she thought. She had a plate of the food, a drink, the weather was warm but there was a breeze, she had a nap, *I could get really used to this.*

After about a half hour, one of the timeshare owners' representatives in charge of the night, started a conga line—another conga line. She had to go around and pull people off their tables or in Malcolm's case, away from the post he was hugging, having to set his drink down on a neighboring table, taking two steps towards the dance floor, then going back to get the drink. June could tell he already needed the poll for more than just cosmetics. She figured he had at least one drink before she arrived.

She, however, jumped right in line. It surprised her how fast she joined, inhibitions having dried up, and building a tolerance to the rum. She was three people behind the Russian woman, who was wearing another black beach cover up around her see through spandex pants which didn't cover a whole lot, a red tube covered in a black shirt, and a pair of high heels, the uniform footwear for the stylish women here. Behind the Russian were the Alabamians. The dog had stopped yapping due to the swaying of the mother and the dog's head wedged tightly between the side of one breast and the arm. June had one hand on the shoulder of Mr. Alabama who was behind his wife. Both British couples were somewhere behind her.

Mrs. Alabama stayed with her leopard theme with a halter top covered by the white see-through blouse and a long skirt slit up to the hip where it was tied off, nothing appeared under it. Her hair was pulled up to the side of her head, held in place by a flowered and rhinestone hair clip. The stiletto heels, June had seen once used in a murder involving a husband and wife who worked as circus clowns, were worn without a single trip or stumble as she moved around the wooden deck. The husband had his hair perfectly placed and was dressed in a flowered shirt unbuttoned to the naval, linen pants which were a little too tight and a little too thin, a pair of sandals and questionable underwear or lack thereof. He was also responsible for his wife's drink as well as his own. He held their drinks, one in each hand and she carried the dog and shuffled in the conga line in front of him. The humidity caused the two to have a glow of sweat. June could feel a puddle under Mr. Alabama's shirt as she held on to his shoulder while balancing one drink in the other hand. It was like holding on to a wet dish towel. Mrs. Alabama, without a word, lifted her hair up off her neck, it was the signal for Mr. Alabama to blow air on her exposed skin. A difficult task since she was moving to the beat of the drums and he was trying to carry two drinks without spilling them. No one realized he was trying not to hyperventilate while trying to breathe cool air on his wife's sweaty body, as well as dragging June and the rest of the line, now about thirty people, behind him like a sea anchor.

June finally stepped out of line and set her drink down after first catching the eye of the bartender and signaling to him she wanted another, then stepping back in line farther back as it passed her. June was hooked that night and admitted to herself how she felt. She didn't care if she was alone. She was having more fun than she had ever had, maybe even while she was married. The thought somewhat sobered her—but not enough to make her get out of line. Even the possible homicide was exciting. Reading a magazine in the rain, naps, murder, all of it caused her to smile.

One-Eyed Swill showed up wearing a Detroit Tigers game shirt. "Aye, there be the wench of the boat today," the voice came from her right. He had on some clean shorts, his *fancy* patch, another one with all the rhinestones around the edge intact, no skull and crossbones, and a pair of well-worn flip flops.

"That is just what every girl wants to hear. To be called a '*wench*.'"

"Aye, I figured you did," One-Eye said. "The women from the Motherland and Canada love it. Makes 'em feel like they're livin' the danger," he said nodding his head and trying to find his drink.

"'Danger'? Like kidnapped and sent to sea in chains or 'danger' like one-hundred milligrams of penicillin kind of danger?"

"You got yourself some wit there. You 'Mericans have some wit. How about you and me castoff from here and see what the tide has for us?"

"Hi Captain Swill," came the southern tinted voice of Mrs. Alabama from halfway across the room. Swill and June looked up and saw the woman waving like she was saying goodbye from the dock to her family standing at the railing of a cruise ship.

June smiled. "One of your fans?"

"Aye, she likes the Capt'n—a lot." Then, he winked at June with his uncovered eye.

"Isn't that how you kinda got here? Noodling where one shouldn't, well—noodle? The woman is married to that man standing next to her. Worse than that, where ever she goes, that dog goes," June said.

"Aye, you heard about my little mishap in the south. Purely a misunderstanding of all concerned. I was set up to be made an example of. And as far as the dog is concerned, it won't be a problem."

"Yeah, well setting sail with the Mayor's underage daughter will do that to you."

One-Eye looked at her like she just gave up the greatest secret on the planet. His face changed, almost washing white, so did his voice, highlighted with a crack in the response. "How do you know about that?" The accent was gone and his voice went low.

"I thought it was common knowledge."

Turning to block his conversation from the rest of the crowd. "God, no lady," he said. June thought his voice changed to Spanish mixed with a little West Virginian.

Mrs. Alabama was still in line holding her dog, her husband, giving up trying to blow on her neck due to light-headedness from hyperventilation, but every time the line took a turn, her eyes were tracking the Captain, like ground based radar.

"If anyone finds out about the age thing, I could be done here," One-Eye said, his voice almost had a plea to it. "I think that country has extradition agreements with St. Lucia. If not, a long boat may pull up here some day with some of daddy's friends and throw a bag over my head and drag me off."

June frowned. "This, is not a secret. I think most of the island knows about your past. No one really cares. I think you can relax. Maybe the daughter found someone else, someone daddy might like."

"Do you think?" he asked with an edge of hope. He appeared to calm, sitting down in a nearby chair and sliding back into character with a smile.

"Just be careful with that one," June said pointing with her head towards Mrs. Alabama. "In our country, she wouldn't launch a thousand ships as much as sink them to scuttle their cargo just to redecorate her living room in rosy pastels and gilded high-back chairs."

He looked at the dancing woman, then back at June. "I hate that dog."

June nodded. "The world is coming to agree with you."

June shuffled more in the conga line then watched from the bar, finding a seat near the corner where here comfort level was at its best. Malcolm had become unhinged and was doing the gator off to the side during another conga line.

The two British couples were both somewhat subdued in their dancing, especially the Sergeant Major and his wife compared to the prior nights. The stay and late nights and liquor consumption was beginning to take its toll on the two of them. The father of the other British couple from the first day had a large bandage on his ear. The blister from the second degree sunburn popped.

There was laughing and fun, music, and a cooler breeze as the night got older. Even the manager, Eldin Cornwall, got in to the party mood, dancing to one of the songs and doing some pelvic thrust move which looked like it hurt, his arms over his head, swaying from side to side all the time still in his white shirt and knotted tie. People didn't know that day his bet in the third at Santa Anita came in, $134.76. It wasn't a lot but guaranteed he would be betting again, tomorrow, his plan apparently working.

It was a quarter to one in the morning, leaving the party still be in full swing when June felt her way into her dark villa, flopping across the bed, barely kicking her sandals free from her feet. She laid there, without moving. She woke about six in the morning and couldn't go back to sleep and didn't feel like trying. She sat on the edge of the couch, not at all startled it was the couch and not the bed, and thought it would be a good morning for a walk, maybe even an early breakfast. For her, anyone for that matter, with her last eight hour history, she had an overwhelming amount of energy. Even after the night she had, she felt remarkably rested. There was a bounce in her rise and steps to her closet in the other room. She threw on a pair of shorts, a tank top, picking up a bra first and then putting it back in the drawer, deciding to go commando for maybe the first time since she was a teenager, a pair of tennis shoes, and headed down to the *Dragonfly* restaurant for breakfast.

She was early. The restaurant didn't open for another half hour. She decided to take a walk down the beach.

Arriving at the edge of where the wooden deck ends and the sand begins near the restaurant and fitness center, she slipped off her shoes and stepped out into the raked sand, the first in the world to set foot here.

Rodolfo was just finishing raking the beach, another of his duties. He wore a pair of headphones and had a good sweat going, working his way back up toward the sidewalk where June watched him, erasing his footprints behind him. He looked up and saw her smiling at him. Taking his earphones out and smiling back.

June said. "I wondered who did this. You are a man of many tasks,"

"I am the *new* man," he said. "I am the man who gets the many tasks."

"This is beautiful," she said looking down the beach and gesturing with her hand. I don't want to walk on it." The entire beach had been raked from waterline to behind the stacked loungers.

"Oh, that is the best part," he said with a smile and then walked over to her and reached out his hand to take hers. "Here, let me show you." And with that, he directed her out on to the sand a few steps. "Now, look back."

June looked back at her own steps in the powder-soft sand.

"You're footprints are the first steps on this beach today, but the picture you see right now, they will be the first prints on this beach in your mind for the rest of your life. A new beach which has never been walked on. A beach that will never be walked on like this ever again by you or anyone else, you are the first." He held her hand for a second more and smiled. "Now, go, walk on my beach. I did it just for you today." His smile magnified the words he spoke.

She smiled at him. June had never thought of it that way, never thought of *anything* that way. She took a few steps, looking down at her feet as if she was learning to walk for the first time in her life. Each step was like she was a baby again and each step was chosen, by her, to be stepped and remembered. Then, she turned around and looked back at Rodolfo.

He stood watching her, leaning on his rake and smiling at her. He gestured to her with his hand as he swept it in a wide arc. "Go, walk on my beach and leave a part of yourself all the way down to its end."

June found herself smiling and looking down one direction on the beach and then up the other direction towards the sea wall, as the pre-dawn light with rich morning colors was filling the bay and the surrounding palm trees. The waves, touched her feet as she reached the waterline, but were not big enough to cover the top of her feet. She walked slowly and at first, watching her feet as each step touched the sand and left its impression.

She continued down the beach, farther towards the sea wall then looked back at her path. It was hers and hers alone marking the beach clear back to where she left the deck almost two hundred yards. Rodolfo saw her turn and look back and he stopped, resting both his hands on the rake and watched her. She could see him smile the white, toothy smile. It lit up his dark face. Then, he took his long arm and made a long, slow, sweeping arc of a wave towards her. She wasn't sure who was enjoying the walk more, her or Rodolfo watching her on 'his beach.'

When June got within fifty yards of the sea wall, she happened to look over at the small beach bar responsible for that end of the long beach. It was not much more than a couple of planks of wood over some bamboo woven timber and topped with a palm frond shaded canopy. In a lounger, under the canopy, next to the bar, lay Malcolm. "Oh god, not again."

He was snoring so loud he could be easily heard along the quiet and empty beach. He was wearing what June could only describe as a startlingly beautiful and elegant red chiffon gown, evening length dress with spaghetti-straps, a scooped neck and an old, well-worn, professionally made sash with the words *Miss. St. Lucia 1989* scribed on it in blue glitter. He still wore his dress shoes, but his socks were missing, however, the tiara was nicely adorning his head. He wasn't dead. The snoring answered that. She then saw his French-tip painted fingernails which caused her to look at her own. There was a folded towel on the bar and she opened it and draped him with it—again. She wasn't sure why she did it. He was obnoxious and deserved whatever or whoever found him. But still, she felt some compassion for him, wanting someone to do the same for her if she ever found herself passed out on a beach in the Caribbean wearing a dress like that. Hopefully, she would look better in it.

She looked again towards Rodolfo. Who nodded and shrugged. She continued her walk down to the sea wall and climbed up. Her life, her whole life was there in front of her, lapping up gently on the rocks. She figured out her compass directions and looked as far out on the horizon she could, knowing if she continued, somewhere on the other side of the Gulf of Mexico, was her home, her life.

Something allowed her to stand there and look back on her life and not be afraid of the emotion this week was bringing to the surface. Even with her husband's death, she was never able to look and really feel it, the deepness of the pain and later, the callousness of the wound, a hard cover over soft tissue that still existed. She never thought of it, at least not consciously, but the guilt, she knew she had to own. It caused her to shut the rest of her life and memories off because she knew she would wind up, wallowing in those memories and it was one place she didn't want to go—ever. What was the point? But here, on this wall, walking on this beach, sitting in these beach chairs, breathing the air, it seemed—safe. Here, she was able to connect with the dark time that lived just below the surface. In all the years, she had never dealt with the scars. The scars were right there, just below the skin. Mist from the small surf hitting the rocks splashed high enough to be caught by the wind and found her face. The salty sea water joined the salty tears on her cheeks.

THE ADORATION

No man deserves punishment for his thoughts.
—Anonymous

"Look, how else do you explain it? She had to have killed him," Malcolm said to Nicholas as he walked over towards the window of the Hollingsworth's villa. Nicholas had asked Mrs. Hollingsworth permission to come back and look around one more time, thinking they might have overlooked something. She opened the door and let the three in along with a uniformed officer. She looked tired, but June noted even though she looked like a person who had been worried and not gotten a lot of sleep, looking like she had been crying, she was still beautiful.

"Why? Why do you keep saying I had to of killed him? I *loved* him," Mrs. Hollingsworth said again exhaustively. She was getting tired of saying it.

"See? Right there!"

Malcolm and the worn out Nicholas were in to the investigation on day five. Nothing new had developed from day one when they found the blood. Nicholas had typed the blood but the report still hadn't returned from the crime lab in Jamaica. Nicholas had taken June's advice and sent another sample to the lab in Miami for typing and DNA. It would take a month to return. Even investigations ran on island time.

"See what?" Nicholas said with a furrowed brow. He was standing halfway across the room.

"Yeah, what?" June echoed. This was getting old, but she had to admit, if only to herself, it was getting strange the husband had been gone for almost five days.

"She said '*loved'* as in past-tense love," Malcolm said grinning, as if it was another smoking gun.

"Well, that is the appropriate form of the root word, *to love*," Nicholas said.

"Yeah, I agree. Although she should have said 'I love him' keeping it present-tense," June said. "*Love* is an action verb, although it could be a noun, depending. It would never take a helping verb like *did.* You wouldn't say 'I did love him'."

Nicholas shook his head. "I would respectfully disagree. I think you would use that version if you wanted to show it as an action, instead of a state of being. I would agree you would never use the past perfect form of *done* in this case. Unless, of course, you were from your state of West Virginia." Both June and Nicholas laughed, forgetting who else was in the room.

"That's a good one—*I done loved him,*" June said, resulting in more laughter.

"Oi," Malcolm said. "I'm trying to solve a homicide here."

"Why do you keep saying that? Why do you think I killed my baby?" Mrs. Hollingsworth said, almost in a panic.

"You have a baby too?" Malcolm said with an edge of surprise. 'There's another box of crackers we need to delve in to, probably when we get back to the motherland, probably some poor bastard who is your product of some more of your debaucherous ways. Your talons lured some milk-toasted sap to an alley somewhere and had your way before you ripped out his spine and made a trophy out of his hair."

Nicholas interrupted. "That will be enough, Mr. McCain."

June asked "Is 'debaucherous' even a word?" the officer with them. He simply shrugged his shoulders.

"No one killed your baby, my little Lump of Clay," a familiar voice came from the open front door, causing Frances to spin quickly. It was her husband, the apparent victim in this hammer and tongue sequester, Jonathan Hollingsworth III. He was dressed in Bermuda shorts, leather sandals, a braided belt, a very expensive silk island shirt, open at the neck, a Panama hat tilted to the right, and a rosewood cane complete with a brass duck head as a handle. June figured he must have walked up just as they arrived and followed them inside. He stood fully erect and squared his shoulders, with a solid silver goatee, filling the doorway almost touching each side. June's quick observation was Johnathan Hollingsworth was a robust man of apparent successful means.

"Aaghh," she screamed and ran towards him. "My little Umpa-Loompa," she said and smothered her husband in short bursts of kisses and hugs, ending in a kiss only seen in the movies—late at night—on an adult channel. He kissed her in return, standing on his tip toes so she didn't have to lean over so far. Although June noticed he was robust, he was about a half a head shorter than his new bride. He had girth, she had height.

Mrs. Hollingsworth surfaced for air. "Where have you been? I've been worried about you. I called the police and they have been looking for you for five days. They thought, well, that one right there," she said pointing at Malcolm with her red-lacquer nails, "He thought I killed you."

Mr. Hollingsworth said with a frown "My little Honeysuckle, I left you a note. I heard about this situation and came right back."

"What note?"

"On the white board in the kitchen. I told you I needed to have some time to myself for a few days."

Frances moved to the kitchen and looked at the board. "There is nothing here."

June remembered the day she was called in and Malcolm writing down an address on that particular white board after erasing it first. She thought about mentioning it but then changed her mind. She figured she didn't want to investigate a real homicide, committed by Nicholas who was looking over their shoulder at the empty white board. Malcolm didn't read it before he erased it. He now stood very quiet.

"Oh, my little bunny rabbit." He held her face and kissed it again. Their tongues and lips and eyelids and hands and arms were moving so fast around each other's bodies it made everyone in the room look away. Everyone except Malcolm who watched—without blinking.

Jonathan Hollingsworth turned in Malcolm's direction. "So, Malcolm McCain, we meet again."

"Mr. Hollingsworth," Malcolm said with a flex in his voice.

"I told you in England when you came and talked to me I was going to marry this woman and that I *loved* her."

June and Nicholas looked at each other and smiled, mouthing the words *past-tense* to each other.

Malcolm swallowed hard. "Mr. Hollingsworth, the family just doesn't believe—"

Mr. Hollingsworth, with one arm around his wife and the other hand gesturing with his duck-headed cane pointed it at Malcolm. "I couldn't give a monkey's ratchet what the family thinks. I love her and she loves me. Now, I understand you are getting paid handsomely by them to find out something about this. I will pay you thrice what they are paying, *plus* your expenses, to find us happily ever after," he said, holding his wife, his head at her shoulders, her taunt body propped up by five inch stiletto heels.

Malcolm smiled "Thrice, eh?" His felt-markered eyebrows going up.

"Thrice." Hollingsworth huffed.

Nicholas stepped in. "Mr. Hollingsworth. Just so I have something to tell my supervisor as to why we were looking for man who seems very healthy, may I ask where you were and why you were gone?"

Johnathan Hollingsworth the III sighed before he spoke. In his heart, he was not too happy for what he was about to say. "Well, I am not too proud of it, but—" he turned to Frances before he spoke.

Frances covered her mouth with her fingers "Oh, my little Love Doll, was it another woman? I feared this. I feared not being able to keep a man like you satisfied. You found an island woman, didn't you? It is all right, I fully understand. I am from here and know these island women can tempt even a man of your character and stature to seek pleasure elsewhere. I forgive you and will try to be like what you have found." She hesitated before she spoke again. "You know—things. Sweet, wonderful, delightful, things. If you come back, I promise I will try—"

Mr. Hollingsworth looked at his wife tenderly before he spoke. "Frances, please. As you might have guessed, I have not been very happy lately."

"But why?" Frances said. Her voice softening. "I said I would do—"

He took two fingers and placed them gently on her lips, to stop her from talking. "Well, ever since we've met, our relationship has been wonderful, absolutely wonderful, but—"

"But what my little Panda muffin?" Frances' voice was almost a pool of a soft, porous foam. "There is another woman. I knew I would mess this up. I've chased you away, into the arms of another woman. I was crazy to think I could corral a stallioned draft horse like you!"

He paused before he spoke. "Frances, my soft bundle of womanhood, we have been having sexual relations every day, morning, noon, and sometimes at night since we've met. Whenever I want to talk about something serious, one thing leads to another and I never get to finish my thought or discussion. Frankly, you keep making me lose my place in our discussions."

Everyone in the room, except the husband and wife, stood with their mouths open. The couple's eyes were locked on each other. Their hands, roving.

Frances looked at him coyly. "But I thought you liked it."

"Oh, my Little Love Monkey, I do. I really do. I like it—a lot." He glanced over at the officers. "And that's the rub. I started to think you just liked me for, you know, my body—and those 'things' you mentioned."

"I love your little monkey body! My big gorilla man," she said tenderly.

"I know. But there is more to me than just my prowess as a lover. I have a mind you know." He looked down sheepishly.

June thought he was looking at her cleavage. Later, Nicholas confirmed from his angle he *was* looking at her cleavage.

"Oh, Johnathan," she said as she pulled him close. There was a moment of concern the old man might suffocate, his face buried between the breasts into the deep cleavage and the medallion necklace the size of a half dollar his face was now buried in. She pulled his head back with both her hands and looked into his eyes. The audible sound of him sucking in air as his face was freed could be heard across the room. There was a red outline of the medallion in the middle of his forehead. "I love you and I want whatever you want. I would *love—*"

June and Nicholas looked at each other and nodded in agreement to the proper usage of the word again.

"To have a conversation with you about anything—*anything.* You know so much! I want to hear all you have to say. I must admit, I do not think I can keep up with you intellectually. Maybe it was part of why I did not let you wander too far into your thoughts. I am not the intellectual like you are. You know me intimately. I'm worried though?"

"What, my little jelly bowl?" his face looking up in to hers.

Frances hesitated for a moment. "If we have conversations like our love making, I am afraid I will not be able to keep up here as well. I'm afraid I will disappoint you. But I will try."

Her husband was gentle. "Oh, my butter love stick, you have never disappointed me, never! You see? I thought so! I knew I just had to have the stems and fruit to talk to you about it. I just wanted some time to think, about us, and to maybe heal a little, let things—rest. I don't even know what political party you are affiliated with, if you're a Tory or a Laborer."

She smiled. "I'm a member of the *British First.*"

He smiled. "I'm *England First.*" He reached up and kissed her and then she rested her forehead on the top of his head, pulling him in to her breasts again, threatening his respiration and poking out an eye with her medallion.

June leaned over to Malcolm. "Is that good, those two parties?"

"Apparently so," Malcolm said, again staring at the two as if it was late night cable.

Nicholas asked again. "Mr. Hollingsworth, where were you for all this time?"

"It had been so long, Lieutenant. I was in town. I rented a flat just above the market and listened to NPR and the BBC."

"This whole time?" June asked. "This whole time—you were in a room with a radio?"

He turned to his wife. "I needed to make sure I was connected still and hadn't lost my identity as a man of thought instead of some woman's *sex kitten.*" "Maybe tonight, over dinner, we could talk about the European Union and the bloody hell the Greeks are causing."

Frances threw her long jet black hair back and swirled it about her husband's bald head after tossing his hat across the room then pulled him into her bosom. "Only if we can also talk about the trade discrepancy with the non-G20 unionist groups who want solidarity in their list of demands."

"You have an opinion on it?" Came his muffled voice from her breasts.

"Oh, yes, yes!! Many opinions. I want to tell you all of them!"

"I'm outta here," June said as she headed for the door.

"Yes ma'am, me too. Have a good day Mr. Hollingsworth, sir," Nicholas said. "Come on Malcolm," Nicholas said as he tugged on the private investigator's shirt. He was stuck in place—watching.

"Oh, yeah. Right behind you," Malcolm said coming out of his trance.

Hollingsworth stopped Malcolm in his tracks. “Mr. McClain, do we have a deal?”

Malcolm stopped and turned. “Thrice?”

“Thrice, Mr. McClain.”

“Mr. McClain, you are the happiest man I have ever seen.” Malcolm finished with a smile and turned and followed the other two out the door.

THE MASSEUSE

Life is a long lesson in humility.

—James M. Barrie

It had been almost a week, a true week in June's life, at the end of which, on this second to the last day on the island, a feeling people get when there is dread in their life of leaving something like what June was living and going back to reality. The dread was going home the next day; back to her life, back to her way of living she had done for so long. She wanted to stay, be a part of the new community, away from the years and pain. The week here began a healing she knew wasn't over and she wanted to stay and absorb more of it. She wanted to live here in this life, in this feeling of care she had discovered and wanted to wrap it around her, like a warm blanket. If she went back, those things, those hidden items she never wanted out of the box, would be put back in the box and left there on a dark closet shelf in her mind, maybe forever. Never being aired and dealt with like moments here, tilted on the edge of healing. She found herself standing on the patio sipping a cup of coffee and nibbling a breakfast bar. She had scheduled her massage, changed it, and then changed it again until it was almost too late.

The appointment was at nine and it was eight thirty. She jumped in the shower and tried to blow dry her hair but the humidity made it a challenge not worth the fight. She walked down the path and just beyond the upper pool by her room, was the spa.

Her appointment was with Bernice. She was one of two massage therapists working that day. She had the morning shift and June was her first client. She looked like what June was expecting. June had never had a massage before so the idea of a masseuse was whatever she saw in brochures or movies. Bernice was at least as tall as June, maybe close to her age as well, with striking ebony skin and another white-perfect smile. She was wearing a white masseuse tunic with white slacks and had two of the four walls slid open to allow the air to participate. A cooling cross breeze filled the room with the fresh smell of jasmine and a large ceiling fan spread the scent of the flowers in the room.

Bernice, with a simple hand motion, directed her to a small room where she could change out of her clothes and climb up on the table, leaving June a towel to cover herself while Bernice left the room to allow her some privacy.

June returned, quickly moving to the table to lay face down covered only in the towel, looking out at the bay and the green canopy tops of the hillside below her.

Bernice spoke softly. "So, this has been a challenge to get you scheduled in here today?" Her voice was a perfect English/Cajun diction, each word enunciated and spoken clearly and precisely. It was soft and liquid her tone relaxing to the listener. June sensed Bernice moving around the room, turning on a stereo to some soft instrumental music then she moved to a cabinet, getting the oils and other warm towels she used to cover June's legs and to wrap her in as she worked on her body.

"Yeah, I guess it has."

"You're reputation proceeded you, unfortunately," Bernice said. "Not in a bad way. Oh dear, no. The staff have known you have been working on something and it has used up your holiday time. We all have been very sympathetic to your plight. I am just so glad you have finally made it in."

June felt the towel pulled back from her shoulders and Bernice's hands went to work on the muscles there. "Yes, unfortunately. It turned out all right, though."

Bernice found a spot between June's shoulder blades and began to work it loose. "Yes, I understand that as well. Oh, you have been tense, lots of tension here. So, tell me about yourself, where you are from, what do you do?"

June wasn't sure she felt like talking, but she started briefly with just her job title and her life so far. Her voice somewhat muffled by the round head pillow she was lying face down on.

"Ah, a police detective. Very interesting. That explains all the talk about you. What about a *Mr. Police Detective*? Do you have a man in your life?"

This was why June didn't want to talk. It always seemed to lead here. She took in a heavy load of air and let it out slowly. "No, he was killed years ago. He was a police officer too," she said. She could feel the hands on her back slow, then start again.

"Oh, I am sorry."

It was here where most people got uncomfortable and avoided the rest of the discussion. But the rhythm of the massage didn't stop. They all get *uncomfortable* when she tells people what happened to her husband, so she was surprised when Bernice spoke.

"It has been a long time. How come you have not remarried?"

June was stopped by the question. She had never had anyone ask her before, at least not so bluntly. She was sure people had thought of it, but they never asked, other than to try to be encouraging with 'oh, you'll find someone else again.' It just always seemed so absurd, so unthinking, like she was buying a new car. "I, ah—"

"You are a beautiful woman. You seem to be smart as well or you could not do the job you do."

"I guess I haven't found anyone."

Bernice was quiet.

June was waiting for a follow up question and when none came, she almost felt relieved.

"I think you have found many. You have just chosen to live elsewhere in your mind," Bernice said, moving her massage from one side of June's spine to the other.

"Oh, no, not too many men want to date, let alone marry, a homicide detective. On bad days, we can smell funny."

Bernice laughed a little. "You do not smell now. That is why they make soap. If you smell, you may bathe."

"I, ah, just haven't —"

"I, also, was like you. My husband died in a hurricane almost two decades ago."

"Hurricane?"

"Yes,—it was terrible. Many people died that day. My husband was one of them—along with our son."

Now it was June's turn to be quiet.

"There were many years I did not want to live, but did so anyway. I carried a lot of guilt. My husband was picking up our son from school. Something I was supposed to have done several hours before."

That sentence hit a note with June. She got a chill up her back as her face lay cradled in the massage chair. The night her husband died, came back, all of it, including the secret. The secret she had stolen away and put in a box in the corner of her memory. The box, with the secret, was now open in front of her, laying under the table, her face cradled in the open pillow looking at its open contents long since hidden away. She was staring at it, as if it had just happened. It didn't go away or fade—it was right there. Its contents were freshly laid out so she could see them in the daylight. The chill turned to a cold sweat.

June, herself, had switched shifts with her husband that afternoon so she could go shopping by herself. She remembered, she thought she needed some alone time, away from Maggie and life, even if it was just for a couple hours. She didn't realize how alone she would be or for how long. "So, what did you do?"

Bernice walked around the other side of the table and took June's left arm and began at the shoulder, applying pressure to the shoulder and the triceps at the same time. "Hmm, there is a knot of stress over here as well. I cried. I cried a lot. I began to drink—a lot. I worked all the time. I never wanted to be home. I didn't sleep and when I did, it was not well."

"How long did it go on?"

"Years—many, many years," Bernice said.

Minutes passed in silence.

June's face lay heavy in the pad. She closed her eyes and for those minutes, she traced her own years. "Yeah, everything but the drinking. They don't like their cops to be drinking and working murders." Minutes passed again. "So, how are you now? You're working. You don't look like you have a drinking issue anymore. How is life—now?" June asked. Then she heard a slight snicker.

"I will always have a drinking problem. But I have not touched liquor in years. Life is grand."

"'Grand?' You went from what you were describing to 'grand'?"

Bernice moved back to the other side and worked the other arm. "Well, it took time. Time is a great healer of things. It does not replace the scars, but instead is a balm for them. I also had to believe there was a reason for things, all things. My husband and my son, although I loved them both, had a reason to leave. They're time here on this earth was done."

Silence, with the exception of the occasional deep breath by June, filled the room. She was now vetted in the conversation. Her arm was being lifted like a butterfly behind her. June thought about what she was going to say. "Did you ever—want to go, too? I mean—"

"Suicide?" Bernice said.

"Well—"

"Of course. I told you, I was not one to stay here. I somehow got up in the morning and stepped out, but had no desire to do anything but follow them." She was quiet for a moment. "I used to go into each room and—"

"Just stand there," June finished.

"Oh, I would spend hours, sometimes just curled up in a corner, smelling my husband or my son's clothes. Sounds crazy, doesn't it?"

There was a pause. "Oh, not so bad." June closed her eyes again. She was back in her house hours after her husband's death. Curled up on her bed having removed one of his t-shirts from the hamper and was holding it to her face as she sobbed. She could see it. The shirt is still in her top dresser drawer, never having been washed. "How—when did you—"

"Climb out?" Bernice asked.

June's arms were like lead. Where ever Bernice laid it down on the table, it felt like one hundred pounds. "Yes."

Bernice worked on one of June's legs. "Never."

"Never? That's not very encouraging."

"What I mean is, the pain is gone. I first had to forgive myself—the secret, I had to forgive myself for what I thought I was responsible for. But if I stop and picture them, think about them—I still talk to them on occasion. What has made it livable, almost enjoyable is the idea they're time is over. My time is still, well, my time."

"You said that before, time is over, what—"

Bernice stopped the massage for a moment. June felt her hands rest on her leg as if she was thinking what to say before she spoke. "I mean for whatever purpose they were put here, that purpose is completed. They can now—go home. I still have purpose here, I still have something to do."

"Home? Like heaven? "

"That is up to you. You need to decide what *it* means. But I realized that one idea, brought with it many other questions, all of them leading to what it really means, what that place is—if it is for you. If there is a heaven, like we have been lead to read about in our lives or see on television, then the idea of who made it is also possible. You cannot have one without the other. If it is true—"

"Then home is a possibility."

"For me to believe, I found great healing in it. I also found my time here is not done. I have something, maybe many things, yet to do, but when I am done—"

"You will go home too."

"Yes, home."

June sensed Bernice was smiling. Her voice changed as she spoke while she rubbed June's legs.

"That simple idea has given me such peace and a feeling for life again. After I forgave myself, I began to live. So, tell me, what is your secret?"

June flushed again. "What secret?"

Bernice's hands stopped again for a moment before they continued working. "When I talked about my guilt, your body gave you up. Your body grew cold and clammy."

"I don't have—"

"You do not have to tell me. You just need to tell yourself. Then let it go. You must let it go in order to live. Like I did. There is nothing more freeing than to truly forgive, starting with yourself."

June paused in her thought. "Not sure it is something I really want to do. I think—I've grown use to it in my life."

"Oh, sweetness. Have you seen our beaches? Have you watched the sunsets? Do you have any children?"

"A daughter."

"Oh, precious one! Live to see what beauty she will create in this world because of you. You will have some wonderful times ahead. You just need to let your past be your past."

June could feel the tears again welling up in her eyes. She couldn't wipe them away, she couldn't reach them, not that she even wanted to. June had to ask. "So, is there a new Mr. Masseuse, in your life?"

There was a loud burst of laughter. "Oh, I have to admit, I might have found some life there, too."

June realized she was smiling and an image of a trail ride back home came to her mind. "So, who is he? What does he look like?"

"Which one?"

"Bernice!" Both women laughed now.

"Oh, Ms. June, nothing will take the place of my husband and son, but I am breathing again and I have a life worth living until I too, am finished. Maybe you will be my last client."

"I hope not. I think I want to come back next year."

Bernice worked on the other leg. "You think you might like to live life well enough to come back next year? I would like that." She paused for a moment. "It is funny."

"What?"

"In all these years, I have never told that story to anyone—ever. It is as if, when I spoke, I was supposed to.

Silence filled the room again. June closed her eyes as it lay in the head cradle and quietly wept. She was sure, Bernice knew she was crying, her hands kneaded her broken body while she hummed an unfamiliar tune. After a while, June fell asleep. She, for the first time in years, was clean.

LABRELOTTE BAY

PATRICK AND THE DOG

If you haven't forgiven yourself something, how can you forgive others?

—Dolores Huerta

By the time June was finished with the massage, the sun had crested the mountain and life at the resort was preparing to end one rotation of guests and start another week of new vacationers. Everyone was trying to stuff time into a sack, explore, and play, rest, one last time before their week in paradise was over. Mr. and Mrs. Alabama were taking their dog for a walk on the greens, smelling the jasmine mixed in the hibiscus and breadfruit and mango trees. Mangos grew so plentiful they fell and rotted on the ground. The Yorkie liked, when he was ever put down from his master's arms, to try to bite a chunk of the fruit.

Mrs. Alabama, when she caught him, reeled him back in to her arms and did a finger sweep of the dog's mouth. Mr. Alabama wanted to take a picture of his wife in front of the plants. "Just for a second, I want just you in the picture, Snuggle Bunny. Can you put Beauty down for just a moment?"

Mrs. Alabama put the dog down, still holding on to its leash, not wanting Beauty to run away, chasing falling mangos. She was wearing a white one piece bathing suit again held together in the middle with a large gold capital W, with white short-shorts. Her skin was one shade darker from the day before. She struck a model's pose which indicated at one time, she was a runner up for something, probably including a sash with her dad's car company name written upon it.

She didn't fill the tug at first and it was Mr. Alabama who heard the muffled yelp. He pulled the camera down to see Beauty draining bottom first into the mouth of the boa. It had been waiting for just such a moment for hours, under the beautiful hibiscus bush behind where Mrs. Alabama was standing. At first, she just saw her husband's mouth drop open as he began to point his finger and stutter. She looked down and with two large lungs full of air, let out a scream so loud, the gardeners came at a run from the hills they were tending to, thinking someone had been hit by a car and were trapped under a fiery wreckage.

The scream startled the heron from their nests in the large magnolias up on the side of the hill at the far end of the resort by the water tank, and heron's don't scare unless you're in the nest with them and then only because there isn't any room.

The lizards and geckos scrambled for cover, thinking something large and unknown was coming their way.

The guards at the main gate, ran out of their posts in the direction of the sound, calling on the radio to see if the guards on the beach heard what sounded like someone had punctured the swim slide again, letting the air out to squeal out a painful octave.

The guards on the beach were, at the same time, calling the guards at the main post about the sound of a fiery car accident they thought they heard.

The entire resort stopped, held its collective breath, and listened.

The Gardener was the first one to the chaotic scene, followed by three of the other gardeners who were working nearby. They came upon the couple from Alabama, she doing a panicked jog in place, pulling on the leash while Mr. Alabama, although making several attempts to grab the panicking dog, didn't quite have the fortitude to follow through, reeling back every time he reached for the two animals.

Mrs. Alabama screamed between steps. "Quick, quick my baby, that thing has my baby!" The four gardeners formed a circle around the snake, which did not appear to be bothered by the audience.

The Gardener stood for a moment before he spoke to the others. "We found it."

"It is bigger than we had first thought," the first gardener said.

"It is doing very well with that dog," a second chimed in.

"Is that the dog we keep—hearing?" the third one asked.

"I believe so," the Gardener said.

There was a pause. Lots of thinking was taking place. "We should save the dog," the third said, catching the look of the others. He shrugged his shoulders. "We really should."

"But the yapping—it will stop if we wait," the second said. All four of the men looked at each other and nodded. They were oblivious to the screams and nervous dancing by the American couple.

"Do we have to kill it?" the first ask.

"The dog?" The second gardener asked. "I do not think we should kill the dog. It has done nothing to the snake."

"No, the snake," the first clarified. "I think we should try to save the snake. It is just living its life."

There was another pause. "I think we should name it," the third said.

"I think the dog already has a name," the second said. "I do not think we should give it another. It will be confusing."

The dog was almost half swallowed.

"No, not the dog, the snake," the third clarified.

"What should we name it?" The first asked.

There was another pause.

"Patrick," the Gardner said. "As in St. Patrick."

The men nodded, appearing to be in agreement.

"Now, we can do this, *no problem*," the Gardener said and with hand signals, he had the others grab the body, and he the head, all three and a half meters, while he worked his hands in the snake's mouth and around the dog, holding open the jaws so the dog would not be any more torn on its way out. The Gardener pulled as gently as he could, holding the head and upper torso of the terrified dog in both hands while another held open the jaws of the reptile, extracting the dog causing a slurping-sucking sound.

"My baby!" the relieved woman said, taking the saliva soaked pet in her arms. He wasn't shaking nor was he yapping. He was just still, relieved to be out of the place he was just in.

The first gardener had some duct tape and taped Patrick's muzzle shut so they could release the head and concentrate in the rest of the body, which weighed almost as much as one of men. The Gardener shook Mr. Alabama's hand and got a kiss on the cheek from Mrs. Alabama along with her saying something to him in his ear, punctuated with a wink. He didn't hear all of it and what he did hear sounded like she owed him something and she wanted to pay him. It was something he did not want the payment for.

The Gardener and his colleagues picked up their machetes, pruners, plastic tarps and now Patrick, and walked off back up the hill where they had come.

For the rest of the day, June noticed she never heard the yapping dog from anywhere on the compound. She saw the Gardener driving a small truck, with his entire crew in it, up the hill into the back jungle area of the resort. June could see, in the back of the truck, rode a large gunnysack with the crew. The Gardener, simply adding another skill to his long resume—that of saving dogs from the jaws of large snakes named Patrick.

The last night, June had most of the lights to her villa off, with only a couple of candles lit in the living room and the small light in the bathroom. She decided to dress up. "Tonight is your last night with us Miss June?" Stefan asked as he brought the menu. June, for the last time, sat at her wobbly table overlooking the beach. The sun was just melting into the horizon and the last light of the day was trimming the near edge of the palm trees and buildings, giving off a golden hue of color. As it sank, the sky changed from yellows to orange, eventually to a deep purple.

June was distracted by what she saw and the thoughts were running through her mind of the past week. Stefan brought her back to the now. "Yes, I'm afraid so. Have to go back to work to save up enough money to come back." It was then she noticed Stefan was carrying a tray and there was a drink on it.

"Berman and I wanted to treat you to your favorite drink. As a reminder of this week. We have had the pleasure of serving you. You have become a friend of ours." He set the drink down on the table and smiled. It was the same smile she had seen all week, a sincere, honest smile of people who cared about each other and her.

She said nothing, but smiled. It wasn't the drink. It was the act that kept her quiet, an act of kindness at just the right time. Stefan left the menu and went to another table. He had no idea what he did, then again, maybe he did.

She sat and watched the end of the sunset and when Stefan came back, she ordered and then sat back in her chair. She had a tinge of loneliness, something she hadn't felt in a long time, year's maybe. She had guarded herself from relationships, actually thinking she could be responsible for their deaths like she did the first. It had taken this trip to fix that thought. The time on Bernice's massage table was key to that realization to her. It was an odd place to come to the reality of one's life.

The restaurant soon had all the players from the week. The young couple from England, the Sergeant Major's family, Mr. and Mrs., Alabama, and about a half dozen others were at the bar or at tables, quietly eating and drinking their dinner. There was relaxed laughter and a casualness was at this place's core. After dinner, she said goodbye to Stefan and Berman, waived to the others whom she came across during the week, then walked down the three tiers of deck to the beach.

She started at one end by the dock, walking out on it and stood at its end point, looking at the water; then, she walked back up the way she came all the way to the other end of the bay and stood on the sea wall looking out at the Caribbean Sea. She would stop every few yards and turn to look at the lights along the water or up the hill, trying to see if she could see her villa from there. She had been trying all week and still, on this last night, couldn't sort hers through the darkness of the trees. But she could see Castries, a cargo ship was leaving and she stood and watched it pull out of the channel into deep water. A week prior, she was dragging her feet to come here. Now, she was trying to figure out how to stay.

She turned and walked up into the jungle and by the tennis courts, up the hill towards the villas and the roads wound their way up and down the hills. She tried to hit them all as she slowly found her way back to her own place.

She spent time packing and organizing her things for travel the next day. Then, for the first time all week, she turned on the television. She had just realized she hadn't had it on at all. It was a Caribbean news channel. She left it on while she packed, the voices giving her comfort of not being alone. When she was done, she walked out on her patio and sat in one of the deck chairs and watched the trees move. A simple thing she hadn't done before, just watching the world turn, causing its own breeze.

She sat there for an hour or so, before she came back inside, brushed her teeth and crawled into the cool sheets under the mosquito netting for the last time.

She awakened early and got up, turning the coffee pot on. While the coffee brewed, she quickly threw on some shorts and tennis shoes, grabbed a cup and left for a walk on the resort's hills again, up and down each, finding herself in the beauty of the trails, surrounded by flowers and tropical plants. The smell of the cool pre-dawn air, mixing with the sea breeze was hypnotic, even after a week of experiencing it. June realized her parents, aunt, even Maggie, were right. She needed this place to finally let go, not only of her husband and the life they had started to build so long ago, but the guilt she carried for his death. What ever happened, whatever it was that caused the sequence of events leading to the outcome, she was able to release it, here in this tiny spot in the Caribbean.

By the time she had walked every path, the sun was cresting the hill behind her and she was soaked with perspiration. Her driver, Garlen, would be picking her up in an hour for the drive to the other end of the island. Her trip was now just the reverse, St. Lucia to Miami and Miami home. There was a part of her excited to get back to Maggie and her life. She was actually excited to return to work, her parents, and her life. She wanted to sit down and actually talk to them about it, share what she saw and experienced. She was happy, to her core, she was happy for the first time in years.

There was also a part of her that knew she wouldn't share all of it, keeping a part locked away in her mind and heart, the healing part, the closure, which was hers and hers alone. There was also a large part of her wanting to stay, to hold fast to the comfort and protection she found here. During the walk, she actually thought through what she could do to stay, to make this place her home, but she knew she couldn't. Then, a smile crept in. She knew she could come back, she would come back. She might have to bring her aunt, since it was *her* timeshare.

Back at her room, she showered and dressed, giving up on her hair again. She had gone days without makeup and decided she would make it one more day. She looked in the mirror and liked what she saw—who she saw. She looked down at her wedding ring. It was time, she knew it. She licked the ring to lubricate it and then slid it off her finger, holding it for a moment and smiled. She was able to do it now. She reached over on the counter and pulled out two tissues from the dispenser and rolled the ring up and tucked it into the side compartment of her bag, placing it inside the vase she liked from the Hollingsworth villa that somehow found its way into her luggage.

June went over to the phone and called for a shuttle, then finished with her shoes and one last look around. She grabbed her bag and rolled it out to the front stoop, looking back one last time before she shut the front door.

June smiled as Andy rounded the turn, coming up the drive. He had his flight helmet on. "Good morning Ms. June," he said as he jumped out of his driver's seat and ran around to open her door before taking her bag and placing it in the back of the van.

"Good morning, Andy."

"Today is the day you are to go. I'm sad you're leaving us," he said as he ran back and hopped in.

June settled in to the front passenger seat. Andy, put the van in reverse and backed up into a corner and turned around, heading back down the way he came up.

June said with a smile. "I really like that flight helmet."

"I knew you would like it. I wore it just for you today. I am not sure I will wear it again around here. I do not think there are many guests who would understand, like you. You must come back."

"Only if you promise to wear the damn helmet."

Andy laughed. 'Ms. June!"

"I will come down next year."

"I'll wear it. You can count on it, Ms. June. You will be missed. Some of the staff, they have talked about you and want you to come back soon."

June looked out her window as the shuttle found its way down the hill. She wanted to go home, she needed to go home, but to hear what Andy said, her desire to find her way back to the island, would occupy her time. She found the love of the island and the people now found and occupied a spot in her heart empty a week before. Now, she began to tear up at the idea of being cared for as she was for this week. She turned and smiled at her driver. "Then we better make this a good mission." She smiled and her eyebrows rose. "We shoot anything that moves, you just have to call it."

Andy smiled a bright smile and turned his head as if on a swivel. June made the first call with two guests walking down the hill in the same direction. 'Light 'em up, my friend." And with that, both Andy and June opened up on the unsuspecting tourists, with their machine gun noises, filling guests with hot pretend lead.

The shuttle pulled in to the lobby bay, filled with other travelers leaving and some arriving. It was transition day for week owners. The arriving guests were met with the same silver tray and warm towel and a glass of a familiar pink beverage. Andy slid his helmet off his head and then jumped out and ran around to June's door, then went to the back of the van and removed her suitcase and put it on the side near an empty bench. On the far side of the parking bay, she saw Garlen. He waved and was ready to take her when she was ready. Andy, after placing the bag down, turned and offered his hand to June to shake. Instead, she hugged him. "I will miss you."

"We all will miss you, Miss." He turned to the main breezeway and looked over, causing June to look as well. There, standing in the opening were Stefan and Bernice. They waved to her with Bernice blowing a kiss.

June lifted her hand to her mouth and smiled. Her eyes filled.

From behind, Morgan and Nicholas made their way through the crowded parking area filled with guests over to where June was standing. Within the last twenty-four hours, Morgan had achieved his dream. He was now the resort manager, at least the acting resort manager, having taken Eldin's place. Eldin had bet on the ponies using a credit card with the name 'Shankton Fillingbarb', a name he had made up and applied for credit and somehow he got from a bank out of Canada. He overlooked the fact he hadn't ever made a payment as well as the fact he used his own mailing address on the island. Morgan was asked by corporate to take over on such short notice while Eldin was escorted off the property by a couple of Nicholas' peers in plain clothes. The police needed to talk to him—alone.

"Congratulations on your promotion," June said. Morgan said nothing and simply hugged her.

"I will owe it to you," he said.

June frowned. "Why do you owe me anything?"

Morgan just smiled, never answering. "Do you have everything? Was your stay a pleasant one?" he said, changing the subject.

"Yes, I think so. Garlen is taking me to the airport. As far as the stay—words can't describe it."

"You will be back?"

June smiled. "As quickly as I can." She then turned to Nicholas who was standing next to Morgan, holding his cap in his hands. She reached out and hugged Nicholas as well.

Nicholas said. "Thank you for your assistance this week."

"Frankly," June started. "I thought on the first day with you asking, it was going to be, well—"

"Like a booger in a bucket?" The voice came from behind the men. The three turned to see Malcolm walking up. He had the two surgeons, one on each arm.

"Dear Baby Jesus," June snickered. "Like a what?"

"A booger in a bucket. You Americans call it being 'bored'. You thought when we first asked it would bore you, didn't it?" Malcolm said as the two women held on.

June just shook her head, then looked at the two women who each were partially clad in buxom building ironware with bright flowers in the fabric. "Malcolm, I am pretty sure anything dealing with you will never—ever be boring." She reached out and shook his hand. She then turned to the two women, looking each in the eye and smiling. "You two have a great man here, or my uncle wouldn't be named Bob."

"Dearie, that's not how you say it."

"Say what?"

"Bob's your uncle."

"I don't have an Uncle Bob."

"Mumbley-peg to you too, dearie," Malcom said with a wink.

She turned back to the women. "You two have been specially chosen by this man. Be prepared for Mr. Toad's Wild Ride."

The two women looked at her and then each other with a look of non-comprehension. The older one spoke for both of them. "We have come to know Malcolm over these last few hours and have found him to be such a honey lamb chop, what was it you called yourself? Oh, I remember, a 'sophisticant'. Charming, absolutely charming."

June smiled. "Malcolm, I never thought you were attracted to the brainy kind."

Malcolm shrugged and had a giggle of a four year old. "I know, right? Surgeons, no less. They can *operate* on me—anytime!"

The two women giggled. June wasn't sure what med school they went to but was sure she didn't want either operating on her—for anything.

Malcolm looked at June. His grin, went from ear to ear. "But these two, they *know*-things!"

June turned back to Nicholas. "I've been trying to figure out how to live down here. If ever you need a consultant who will work for spiced rum, let me know."

Nicholas smiled. "Every time you come down, I will save my best cases for you."

"Deal," she said. For three heart beats no one said anything. June simply smiled and turned to her suitcase, taking the handle and walked towards Garlen and his car. She walked past the couple from Alabama, who were loading their bags into another taxi going to the Castries Airport. Beauty was cradled in the woman's arms, snug against her zebra striped low-cut blouse, the dog's rear legs and half its head bandaged. June frowned, not knowing what had happened but knowing not to ask.

"All set to go, Miss?" Garlen asked as he took her bag.

"No, but I guess it's time."

"You will be back. And I will be here to pick you up."

June smiled at the first man she had met on this island nation. She would be back and maybe next time, with Maggie or her aunt—maybe not her aunt.

She got into the front seat this time, wanting to be a part of the drive and converse with another of her new friends. Garlen drove the car carefully through the covered bay, around the driveway and up the hill.

"Mr. Morgan," the Gardener said quietly in Morgan's ear, coming up behind him as Morgan and the others waved goodbye to their friend.

"Yes?" Morgan said over his shoulder. He was going to miss that woman.

"Our issue we have been talking about and we moved? We found another. This time it is about two and one half meters long. He must have had a wife."

Morgan, simply closed his eyes and sighed.

HAPPY TRAILS

Most folks are about as happy as they make up their minds to be.

—Abraham Lincoln

She woke in the morning to the smell of coffee and bacon cooking. This time, she smiled as she stretched in the bed she always slept in when she and Maggie spent the night at her parents' home. She laid there and smiled for a moment, rolling to her back and staring at the ceiling. There was a difference from before, she felt it. It was like a weight had been removed from her chest. A weight that had been there for so long she had gotten use to carrying it. The time on the island, the time with Bernice, simply laying there on the beach, listening to the sounds of the island and its people, made this moment so much better in its own way. She had decided to give herself permission to live again, whatever that was going to look like.

She had been living a life for years and for all explanations, it was a good life. She knew nothing else. There was no other model for her to follow other than how she felt before the island and then, on the island. She knew she wanted the feelings, the core change to keep living in her. She actually wanted to go to work, to listen to Maggie, to be with other people, even men. She wanted to see the life she had shut the windows and drew the blinds to. The life her own guilt had convicted and sentenced her to abandon. The people on the island, the island itself, gave her something to look at her own life through.

She rolled out of bed with a spring in her step, *if one could have a spring at my age,* she thought. She slid her feet into her slippers and grabbed her bathrobe lying at the end of the bed. She walked down the hall while tying her robe towards the kitchen and the smell of coffee.

"Good morning Junebug," her dad said.

"Good morning Daddy," she said, and walked behind him and stole a piece of bacon from the plate then went over and poured herself a cup of coffee. She glanced at the paper, as always, laid open on the kitchen table where her father was reading, probably since the sun came up. She could hear her mother showering and knew they would be heading for the barn and ready for their ride within the hour, right after breakfast.

Her father grabbed a piece of bacon he just cooked. "Better shake a leg if we want to go," he said, just like always.

And just like always, she responded. "Dad, it isn't noon. We still have some time," finishing with giving him a hug while he finished moving the bacon to the plate. "Okay, I'm going to shower and be back in ten minutes," taking her coffee with her down the hall to the bathroom. She came alone this weekend. Maggie stayed to study for an exam.

June came back into the kitchen after she showered and dressed and carrying her empty cup in one hand and her riding boots in the other, setting them down at her seat at the breakfast table. Mother had made it to the table as well. The three talked and ate and there was some laughter.

"Good morning everyone," Aunt Eleanor said, exploding into the silence of the kitchen through the back door, just like every other time. "Everyone but me is going for a ride today, eh? Well I will be right here reading your paper and drinking your coffee when you get back." She slid into one of the chairs around the kitchen table and opened a section of the paper after first placing her designer purse the size of a small suitcase, down on the corner of the table. "I didn't get a call from the police while you were gone so you must not have had any fun while you were down on the island," she said while looking over the paper. "When you come back, I want to hear every dark little secret," she told her niece, looking over the top of the paper, winking.

June's father had already walked down and gotten Mitch and brought him back to their barn to saddle. The three left after eating and saddled their horses in silence, with the exception of June, who was talking to Mitch while scratching him under his chin. Her mother and father stealing glances at each other. Something was different with their daughter.

The morning was cool. The smell of the high desert, holding the hint of creosote and moisture filled the air. She loved this time of day, just her and a horse in the desert. They were missing Beryl. She wondered if he was going to join them at the Y, like he usually did. She wanted him to. She had thought a lot of him on her return trip. She thought as part of her life being released, he might be a good, safe place to start.

As they approached the trail intersection where they usually met, she called to her parents riding in front of her. "Hey."

"Yes, dear," her mother said over her shoulder.

"Is Beryl coming?"

"He said he would try. He had some things to do this morning and he might be busy today," her father added.

"Oh, okay." She was disappointed, truly disappointed as they walked passed the trail intersection

Beryl would have come riding down to meet them whenever they went out. She looked down towards his house and didn't see him. She didn't see her mother and father look at each other and smile. "Maybe next time," she said still looking.

Her father said "Yeah, Junebug, maybe next time," as he took the lead and spurred Jackie into a canter. June was too far back to see or hear her father on his phone as he pulled ahead of his wife and daughter. The other two following, June distracted by the empty trail from Beryl's home.

Its okay, she thought. She would follow up and maybe even call. She didn't care who made the first contact. After all, she thought, he actually did make the first move when he asked her out for coffee. She was just too stupid to see it for what it was, coffee. She just figured it would be nice if he was along for the ride. She could understand his thoughts and feelings about her. She didn't give him much indication she was interested in him let alone willing to go out with him, even if it was just for coffee.

She lost herself for a minute in the world around her. She had forgotten how much she truly loved to ride, being out on her horse and free, the low mountains around her, the wildlife, all of it seemed especially enjoyable that morning, like it was in place just for her. The air was fresh and clean, as if all her senses were able to take it in and enjoy it, all at the same time. She didn't notice the first whistle until her father pulled up and stopped. "What?" she asked, looking at her dad, her mother was in front of her as well and turned around and looked back. Her father pointed back down the trail they had just come up.

The Y was now about two-hundred yards back. They could see the rider make the turn and head towards them at a full gallop. He was whistling as he did. It was Beryl riding to catch up to them, seeing them stop, he slowed to a cantor and then a trot. June noticed, he rode well, really well.

"Thought I missed you people," he said as he pulled up and the four began to walk again. He tipped his Resistol to June and her mother. "Ladies."

"Almost did," Father said. "Finished what you needed to finish?"

"Well, almost. I decided I needed a ride instead. How was your trip, June? You look— tan." He walked next to her and her mother and father rode in front.

"It was interesting. Very—interesting."

"Well, I'd like to hear about it sometime," Beryl said as a side note.

"How about today or tomorrow?"

Mother and father glanced at each other.

"Excuse me?" Beryl said. He caught himself almost choking on the two words.

"How about that cup of coffee? You asked me out for a cup of coffee. How about today or tomorrow?"

"There's a piece from a few years ago. I think that pot is a little tarry by now."

"Well, a girl doesn't like to rush into things."

He smiled at her and she smiled back. Father just shook his head. "No, no, I guess a girl doesn't like to rush in to having a cup of coffee. I can't today, but how about tomorrow—early. I have appointments all day today."

She smiled. "That's good. I have an autopsy to witness in the late morning. I should drink and eat before."

He smiled. “Sounds like my day. I have to geld a horse about the same time.”

There was a pause before she spoke again. “And just so you know, I don’t have anything in mason jars next to my cereal boxes.”

Beryl gave a wary smile. He had no idea what she meant.

The four broke into a canter. The smell of the creosote bushes, just after the rain the night before, filled the air—sweet, cleansing, soothing rain and a slight, refreshing breeze, wafted by the slow back and forth movement of an unseen gentle hand.

Other works by
Mark Williams

Emancipating Elias

Holy Ground

Looking for Indianola

Father's Day

Made in the USA
Charleston, SC
22 February 2016